JANE DOE IS MY MOTHER

MEGAN LEE HEWELL

For Jensen, Freddie and Georgie with love

Trademark & Copyright Acknowledgements

Crazy Eights

Pollyanna by Eleanor H. Porter

Tim Hortons

Jimi Hendrix

Rolling Stones

Winnipeg Blue Bombers

BC Lions

The Grey Cup

Note From the Author

I graduated from university in 2017 with a BA in Criminology and a vague intention of perhaps applying to law school. I had ambiguous plans for the gap year I planned to take, including writing the LSAT and trying to find an internship with one of the many law firms in Vancouver to gain experience in the field.

That I might find inspiration and write a novel over the course of that year didn't occur to me, at all. During my undergrad career I had taken several creative writing classes for what I considered "easy" credit, and they were easily some of my favorites. It was from these classes that the idea for *Jane Doe* came about in its earliest form. Under the tutelage of my professor in a third-year Crime and Literature class, I began drafting what I imagined to be a monologue performed by an actress on a stage. The character didn't have a name, but her voice outlined a tragic backstory. This was the character who would, at a later time, become Jane Doe. This attempt was a fun (albeit amateur) attempt, and at the end of the semester, the draft went into a box of university notebooks. Then a new semester began, and in the flurry of writing academic papers and quantifying statistics for my degree, Jane Doe's voice was promptly forgotten.

A year later, I was working at a firm in downtown Vancouver, learning about various court processes and legal procedures in efforts to determine if law school truly was what I wanted to pursue. My partner and I had recently relocated to the suburbs outside of the city, and it was during our unpacking that I happened to find the boxes of textbooks and notepads. The chores of organizing and cleaning were set aside for a trip down memory lane. I found that long-abandoned draft of the character I'd created, and the pieces slowly began to fall into place. It was only too easy to weave the narrative of the young woman running to escape the trauma of her past and the tragic consequences of her actions. As her journey took shape in my mind, I began to imagine telling the story of tracing her path, and this led to the creation of Nora Devrey, a character trying to trace the mother she had never known.

It must have been providence that the following day at work I drafted several court documents concerning a plaintiff known only as Jane Doe. The name leapt off the page at me, like the obvious solution to a math equation. I had the stories of Nora Devrey and her biological mother Jane Doe, though I hadn't yet found Jane Doe's real name. The narrative tying the two women together took longer to puzzle out, and the project didn't come to fruition exactly as planned. Along the way, I met characters I hadn't expected, and saw relationships evolve in ways I hadn't imagined. I was able to borrow some elements of Nora's experience from my own life, such as her cozy world in Vancouver and her trips to small towns.

I was aided greatly by my many excursions to the interior of the province of British Columbia. BC has an incredible landscape encompassing almost every terrain–mountains, forests, deserts–and amazing opportunities for hiking both in the provincial parks and in the backcountry. During the summer of 2018 we took every opportunity to escape the city. Several times that summer, we followed the Canyon Route—Highway 97—alongside the Thompson River, sandwiched between looming faces of rock that formed the mountains towering above us. This is the same journey that Malcolm and Nora later follow, and the details are very much unchanged, from the many waterfalls mere meters from their car to the abandoned cemeteries carved into niches of rock.

It is to my partner Jensen, my Malcolm, that the first thanks need to be given. You are a constant positive presence in my life. Your incredible support and unyielding optimism have been invaluable to me during our many years together. I am fortunate to have you and so grateful for you. Thank you for challenging and inspiring me to be the best possible version of myself.

I would also like to thank my sisters Georgie and Freddie, my fellow mischief makers and oldest friends. You have both been so encouraging at every step of the way, and I am lucky that you are my sisters.

To my best friends, Mandy and Breanna, whose presence have made such an incredible difference in my life. You are both so very much appreciated!

As well, to Carolynn, the reason that this journey has been possible. You gave me the courage to dare to dream, and when I faltered, you are the reason I kept trying. Thank you for being my biggest fan and loudest cheerleader, and for shaping this novel into what it became.

And finally, to the staff at Scarsdale who gave me an opportunity and guided me on this amazing and unbelievable journey–Sharona, Kimberly, Stephanie, and Rain. I owe you the deepest debt of gratitude.

I would like to provide the following note: much of what follows reflects real people, places, and events. I have changed names and locations to protect both privacy and reputation. I have also taken liberties with certain facts, turning them into fiction, for the same purpose. Any mistakes are my own, whether through deliberate misinterpretation or accidental omission. I do hope the residents will forgive my lapses.

I would like to dedicate this book to survivors everywhere. We each are faced with obstacles that must be overcome, whether our struggles are well-known or hidden. I honor your struggle and wish you every success in your own journey.

Megan Lee Hewell
Vancouver, British Columbia
November 2020

<h1 style="text-align:center">Preface</h1>

Two major cities dominate the province of British Columbia, Canada: Prince George in the north and Vancouver in the south. Highway 97 connects the two, snaking through hundreds of kilometres of forested mountain range, flat prairieland, low-lying desert, and past the banks of lakes and rivers. This highway provides a lifeline to the small, isolated towns that dot the region.

Jane Doe's story began in one such small town. Lachlan, BC, lies due east of Prince George and directly north of Cold Lake in the Williams Lake Region. A single narrow, dirt-packed road, Chesamore Way, links Lachlan to Highway 97 and to civilization. Lachlan is bordered on three sides by vast stretches of wilderness. It seemed to me, on my first and only visit to the town, that the town sat with its back to a forested wall, observing all who came and went with suspicion.

Before February 2010, I had never heard of Lachlan. Or of Tome, BC. Tome is slightly larger than Lachlan. It sits directly on Hwy 97 and on the banks of Cold Lake. Tome residents trace their ancestry all the way back to the settlers of the Gold Rush, prior to Confederation, and some back even farther still, to a time when the area was inhabited by the Aboriginal and Metis peoples.

Most people who are born in Tome are raised in Tome. They reach adulthood and marry young and start families, and the cycle that began with their parents and grandparents and great-grandparents continues into the new generations. There is little in the town to attract skilled workers or tempt young families to relocate and settle down there. Most who arrive are simply passing through on their way to other destinations. There are few vacationers and even fewer tourists, though the residents of the township will escape on the weekends and travel to Cold Lake for camping, hunting, and fishing.

In short, Tome is an insignificant town that simply exists. Yet for me, it looms large, for this small, tight-knit community is where my story began. Tome is where I was born, abandoned, and found.

Tome is also the town closest to where Jane Doe was found. The clearing where she lay buried for so many years, unknown and entirely forgotten, is several kilometers southwest of the highway, deep in the backwoods of Cold Lake Provincial Park, a hike of two or three hours off a rarely used utility path.

It's safe to say that nothing of great significance ever happened in Tome. Yet in July 2005, the town seemed to be holding its breath.

Prologue

Scott Duggan wanted to escape from Tome, if only for a weekend. His wife, Tina, was pregnant again, and as the first trimester turned into the second, Scott found her to be even more of an unbearable cow. He needed time away from her and his two little brats. So, he convinced his brother Terry to camp out in Cold Lake Provincial Park.

Now Terry wished he'd refused. He gritted his teeth in impatience as he watched Scott try (and fail) to set up the tent. Already, the canvas flap had a large, jagged hole. Scott's foot had gone through it in frustration when he lost his temper with the poles.

It was Terry's tent. It was also Terry's gear, truck, rifle, ammunition, beer, and dog. Scott hadn't really wanted Terry's company, just his stuff. Scott's driver's license had been suspended again—not that the suspension would have stopped him from driving—but his truck was out of gas, and he wouldn't be able to fill it up until next payday unless he siphoned from someone in town.

As Scott was currently unemployed, or "between opportunities," as he liked to say, Terry couldn't be sure when the next payday would come. Scott had already pawned his rifle, and what money had come from that had likely already been squandered. That was why Scott needed Terry's rifle and ammo and beer, and that was why he had wheedled Terry until Terry had agreed. And now, Scott was setting up Terry's tent and using Terry's gear and drinking Terry's beer.

Of course, Scott couldn't borrow all these things without asking Terry to come along.

Terry swigged the lukewarm beverage from the can in his hand. Then he hollered to his dog, Joad, who sniffed about on the far side of the clearing. Joad was barely visible in the shadows of the large cedar trees.

Terry wondered why they weren't setting up the tent in the shade and clenched his jaw even harder. He hollered at the dog again. Joad was snuffing at mole holes and fallen branches and dried grass.

This trip was a last-minute decision. Most likely, Scott stormed out of the house after Tina nagged him about his drinking or his spending habits or his lack of a job. That's why they hadn't made a reservation for a campsite at Cold Lake Provincial Park, and why they had loaded the entire cooler's worth of beer into their backpacks—instead of water, Terry reminded himself—and trekked down the utility path for an hour or two before plunging into the unmapped underbrush during the heat of the day. They hiked for hours around the northern edge of the lake until they were grumpy and sweaty and hungry and tired. Scott's confident assurances that he knew exactly where he was going had turned to grunting and cursing, neither of which did anything to improve Terry's mood, and when they finally collapsed into the clearing at the edge of the lake—an area rife with mosquitoes, no doubt—Terry threw the tent at Scott and snapped that he could put it up himself.

Terry hollered at his dog again. Joad was digging at something in the shade under the cedar trees. The last thing they needed was a disturbed racoon or skunk or some other nocturnal animal to increase the misery of their afternoon.

Already, he was regretting telling Scott to put the tent up himself. Scott was now four beers in, and the alcohol did nothing to improve Scott's proficiency in erecting the tent. Terry winced when the canvas ripped again.

"Stupid fucking poles," Scott growled, and then added with an ugly snarl, "Get your fuckin' dog before he finds a coyote." He pronounced the word "kye-ot," like he'd heard in all the western movies.

"It was your idea to bring him," Terry snapped back, but drained the last of his beer, threw the can into the brush, and stomped across the clearing to where the dog nosed a pile of leaf rot.

At least, it looked like leaf rot from a distance. When Terry got closer, he realized the dog wasn't digging at organic material. He'd found a bit of plastic or rubber, something that didn't break down in the elements. The material might have been blue once, though exposure had weathered it to a dingy gray. Joad mouthed a scrap no larger than Terry's fist, and Terry noticed that another piece lay a few feet away. Whatever it was had been slashed and torn, probably by a wild animal.

"Joad, git!" He swiped at the dog, but Joad continued to paw at whatever he had unearthed.

The gray material was a jacket of some sort, Terry realized, or had been, at some point. It might have once been a windbreaker or a raincoat. Maybe previous campers had left the garment behind in their haste to leave.

Terry slapped at a mosquito. He wanted to go home.

The dog moved to nose a large, smooth rock that lay nearby, bleached white by its exposure to the sun.

"Joad!" He raised his voice and smacked the dog on the side of the head with his open hand.

Joad gave a startled yelp and whined, hopping about, but he didn't scamper away.

Terry wondered at the dog's odd behavior. Then he wondered how the rock had been bleached by the sun and weathered by the elements when it lay protected by the overarching tree. He reached down and turned over the rock, curious, and jerked his hand away when he saw it for what it was...a human skull.

Part One

THE BEGINNING

Chapter One

I REMEMBER CLEARLY THE DAY MY PARENTS TOLD ME I WAS adopted. I was eight years old, and I punched Jake Mulligan in the face at recess. I hadn't intended to hit him, and it hadn't really been a fight. Jake was my best friend; we played together practically every day. His house was right behind mine, and our parents were friends. Thus, we were destined to spend a great deal of time together, and rather than fight the inevitable, we formed an easy friendship. On most days after school, he came home with me because his parents worked late. We spent long afternoons playing in the backyard until the streetlights came on and his parents came home.

I don't remember what we fought about that day. Perhaps Jake wanted to play Spies and Bad Guys, and I wanted to play Cops and Robbers (they are, of course, the exact same game, but try explaining that to an eight year old). Or perhaps we agreed on which game to play, and Jake insisted on being the good guy, as he always did, and I was tired of being arrested and spending most of recess locked in the "jail" behind the big tube slide while Jake gloated and then ran off to play football with the other boys.

Whatever it was that caused our fight, the squabbling escalated when Jake shoved me and called me a girl, which was an unforgiveable insult for a tomboy like me. When I regained my footing, I rolled up my sleeve, balled my fist, and deliberately hit him in the nose, which started bleeding immediately. I hollered that I wasn't a girl while Jake doubled over, yelling, hands covering his face. He didn't cry–crying was for girls, after all, and he was tough—but he attracted the attention of the playground attendant who marched us to the office.

I squirmed while our principal, Mrs. Van Buren, called Jake's parents and then mine. My dad was a journalist. Most evenings, he got home in time for dinner. My mom was a librarian whose hours were the same as the school day. So, neither of my parents was home when the call went out.

Mrs. Van Buren gave me "The Look" as she left a message on our answering machine detailing my transgressions.

When Jake's nose stopped bleeding, Mrs. Van Buren made me apologize to him, and we walked back to class together in silence. Then Jake told me a joke at the classroom door, which was his way of apologizing for calling me a girl. When he stuck out his tongue, he was telling me he forgave me for punching him.

I still had to stay inside at second recess under the supervision of a teacher, burning in shame and humiliation, while my classmates ran past the window, screaming and shouting and having all the fun denied me. I hated the looks of smug, superior pity they threw me. Already, I was fidgeting at the thought of what my parents would say and how much trouble I would be in. If I were a real spy, not just playing one with Jake, I'd figure a way out. That was when a plan started to form in my mind.

My mom picked me up from school every afternoon. She always waited until we turned into the driveway to hit the garage door remote. Then we sat in the car while the door opened.

What if I dashed out and opened the front door with my own key–I was old enough to have my own house keys–then rushed to the answering machine and erased the message before Mom pulled into the garage?

With this plan in mind, I climbed confidently into the backseat of my mom's car that afternoon and greeted her rather smugly. Jake didn't come home with us because he had a guitar lesson with our music teacher. So I didn't have to worry about him telling on me.

For this reason, I was feeling invincible, with the confidence of a card player who has called "Crazy Eights!" and holds an eight card in their hand.

My mom started the car and asked, "How was school?" her voice pitched higher than usual. As she waited to pull out of the parking lot, she kept glancing at me in the rearview mirror and drumming her fingers on the steering wheel. When an opening in the traffic appeared, she pressed more heavily on the accelerator than was her usual, cautious way of driving. The sudden speed surprised me because, as my dad loved to quip, Mom and the brake pedal were great friends, but she'd never been introduced to the accelerator.

As we neared home, Mom mentioned that we would get pizza and root beer for dinner as a treat.

I'd been choreographing the next few minutes carefully, already discreetly removing my housekeys from my backpack, but her words made me feel slightly guilty considering what I had already done and what I planned to do to cover up my crime.

But I was determined. When Mom stopped in our driveway and reached for the remote, I launched from the backseat and raced up the front steps.

I think my mom shouted something in surprise. The garage door opened, and the car rolled forward slowly as I threw open the front door and bolted into the living room.

The answering machine on the end table next to the couch flashed red three times in rapid succession. I didn't have time to listen to the messages, I just hit "delete" when I heard the car door slam.

Success!

I sauntered into the kitchen as my mom entered from the garage. She commented on my behavior, and I responded breezily, something to the effect of winning the race into the house. Then, all peaches and cream, I offered to finish my homework quickly so that we could have pizza as soon as Dad got home.

In the years since, I've often wondered about the two other

messages I deleted. Neither of my parents ever mentioned them, but were there people somewhere still waiting for return calls twenty years later?

Dad arrived home shortly after I finished my math quiz sheets with two steaming boxes of pizza from Pete's and a two-litre bottle of root beer. I emptied my first glass of pop before Dad handed me two slices of extra cheese, his eyebrows raised in amusement.

I happily stuffed my mouth with burning hot cheese, my eyes watering, but as I chewed, I noticed neither of them filled their plates or glasses. *Uh oh*, I thought, my heart sinking. *They know.*

My mom spoke first, nervously, breathlessly. "Now, Nora, Dad and I want to have a very grown-up conversation with you, alright? Because we think you are very mature and will be able to handle what we want to tell you."

My dad chimed in when my mom glanced at him as if at a loss on how to continue. "We want to reassure you, honey, Mom and I love you very much, no matter what. And we are very proud of you, okay? We have some news we need to tell you that might come as a little bit of a shock, but we will always love you and support you."

"We're here for you, sweetheart," Mom added. "Whatever you need from us. Okay?"

My initial dread that they might know about my fight with Jake turned to relief, and then confusion, and then to fear. I had classmates whose parents were divorced, and that was the news I worried they had to tell me. I was relieved when Mom started to explain the differences between biological and adopted parents.

Whereas most children go through the phase of wondering where they came from and learning what mommies and daddies do to make babies, I already knew. Jake and I were five years old when his little sister was born, but in my conceit, I never gave the matter a second thought. I hadn't wondered why I didn't have brothers or sisters, and I hadn't wanted any.

"You remember how I told you that moms and dads make babies together," Mom said delicately.

I nodded, wondering what in the world that had to do with anything.

The look on my face must have been funny because Dad started chuckling.

"Dad and I didn't make you, sweetheart," Mom said. "We found you."

"Well, other people found you." Dad corrected. "At a church in a small town in the Interior. It's a long ways from here."

"And when we found out about you," Mom said, "we drove through the night and most of the next morning to get you. We have a friend from school who is a doctor, and he was taking care of you, in a city called Prince George."

"He knew we would love to have a pretty little baby girl," Dad said, "and we were so happy to see you."

As they told this story, I wondered vaguely who had made me. I thought it was strange that a place could just be called "the Interior," and I wondered who Prince George was and why he was so important that he had a whole city named after him. Then Dad's voice broke through my mental ramblings, and I tuned back into the tale.

"We started driving to the hospital because no airplanes were leaving that night, and we drove right to the hospital where you were. Dr. Bradley and Mom and I took care of you in the hospital for several weeks because you were so small you couldn't go on an airplane or in a car yet. But then Dr. Bradley said you could come home, and Mom stayed with you so you wouldn't be lonely while I came home and made sure you had toys and clothes. And on Christmas Eve, Mom and I brought you home."

I listened silently, nibbling my pizza down to the crusts. All the while, heavy guilt settled in my stomach over the schoolyard fight, and for having gone to such lengths to deceive my parents. So when Dad stopped to draw a breath, I blurted, "I punched Jake in the face today at recess and made his nose bleed, and I got in trouble, and Mrs. Van Buren called to tell you, but you weren't home, so she left a message, but I erased it cuz I didn't want to get into trouble."

Dad started chuckling, and then he was laughing so hard, tears filled his eyes. Mom couldn't help chuckling herself, though anxiety never left her eyes.

I wriggled in my seat, laughing nervously, relieved, but not entirely sure that I was out of trouble.

"Well, let's come back to that, Naughty May." Dad's eyes sparkled down at me.

Mom quietly asked, "Do you understood what they were telling you?"

I nodded and asked for another slice of pizza.

Mom then asked, "Do you have any questions?"

Even at that young age, I sensed that she needed to talk about this. She needed me to ask questions, to make sure I was all right.

I frowned in confusion. I had a beautiful house, loving parents, and a gaggle of friends at school. Mom and Dad's story might have been someone else's entirely. In fact, I had recently read the book *Pollyanna*, and I thought how cool it was that she and I had something in common. It made me feel unique, a feeling I rather liked.

I also appreciated that I had gone to parents instead of to an aunt. "But you're nicer than Aunt Polly was! She was mean. I don't like her."

Dad laughed again.

Mom asked, "Do you have any questions about your adoption?"

"So, I have a different mom and dad somewhere," I said.

After a beat, Dad said, "Yes."

I was silent for a long moment, digesting what he said. Then I asked, "Do you know who they are?"

"No, we don't," Mom rushed to answer.

"Do you know where they are?"

Dad shook his head while Mom said, "No, we never found them."

"So," I said slowly, "They aren't looking for me."

They didn't seem to have been prepared for this question, and they exchanged a glance before Mom said, "We don't know, honey. We don't think so."

"So, they aren't gonna come and take me home with them?"

Even before I finished asking, Dad was shaking his head, and Mom almost interrupted me with a firm, "No." She seemed to brace herself as if worried I might burst into hysterical tears.

"So nothing's going to change?" I asked.

"No," Dad said. "Not unless you want them to change." A smile played at the corner of his mouth, as if he were amused by my indifference to the life-changing news.

I didn't know how things possibly could change, unless my parents raised my allowance or let me stay home from school the next day. Even then, I knew such requests would be pushing my luck. So, I shrugged and asked, "Can I have more root beer?"

Habitually, Mom prompted, "Please."

"Can I have more root beer, please?" I repeated.

She shook her head, hiding a smile. "No, you may not have more root beer."

That was the end of the serious conversation. My dad was amused by my antics and the tension eased from Mom's face.

"So, you punched Jake in the face," Dad said casually a few minutes later, causing me to groan and sink down in my seat. I hoped he'd forgotten my confession.

I was too old for a spanking, so they grounded me for the weekend, and I had to apologize to Jake again in front of our parents, in spite of my protests that Mrs. Van Buren had already made me apologize. So, I pouted and apologized to Jake, and he magnanimously accepted my apology, and our parents made us shake hands and promise not to fight anymore. Then we went outside and played basketball in Jake's driveway while our parents visited.

I didn't need to worry about Jake telling on me, and I still had an ace up my sleeve for any future fights. Only I knew that he had climbed onto Mrs. Sander's gardening shed the summer before and broken the skylight. As I helped Jake off the shed and scrambled with him through the hedge and over the fence that afternoon, I promised I would never tell. The parents in the neighborhood never figured out which kid had done it.

Our easy friendship survived later fights, high school, and university. He was Man of Honor at my wedding, and I donned a tuxedo and broke tradition to stand on the groom's side when he married a year later. Even though he and his wife moved to Ontario, I still saw him several times a year.

. . .

MY FULL NAME IS NORA JANE MARGARET QUINN. FOR A BRIEF time during my undergrad years, I tried going by "Jane" instead of "Nora," but I slid back into the comfort of my given name shortly after I met my future husband. In choosing what to name me, my parents honored everyone by including the names of both grandmothers as well as a deceased aunt, none of whom I've ever met.

My Aunt Nora passed away when she and my dad were young. My grandmother Jane died when I was a baby. Mom's mother, Margaret, lives in England. They speak twice a year by phone and often exchange letters, though they haven't seen each other since the late 1960s when Mom moved to Vancouver to attend university. Neither of them seems motivated enough to make the trip for a visit.

For such an Irish-sounding name, I have rather dark features, and it isn't difficult to tell that my parents didn't conceive me. Dad has light brown hair and light blue eyes; Mom's hair is golden, and her eyes are green. My hair is black and thick, my eyes are dark brown, and I have highly pronounced cheek bones, a mouth slightly too large, and a dimple in my right cheek amid a smattering of freckles.

For a few short weeks as an angsty teenager, I became moody and brooded on the lot I'd been dealt, trying to create drama in my life. My dad challenged me to name a single way in which my life could possibly be better. When I couldn't come up with a response, he firmly told me to get over myself.

I graduated from high school with honors and was accepted to the local university. I lived at home with my parents, who agreed to pay for my education provided I get a part-time job and begin saving for my future while maintaining my grade-point average. I readily agreed.

With my love of history, I intended to pursue a teaching certificate and become a high school history teacher. Until I met an impressive young professor whose job gave him the freedom to focus on topics that interested him. Knowing I could choose what I wanted to study if I became a professor, I changed my mind about teaching high school. I pursued a PhD, and my parents resigned themselves to helping me pay for more years of education.

While taking a beginner-level statistics course in January, I met Malcolm, a marketing student whose first-year statistics requirement hadn't counted toward his degree. He needed this last credit to graduate that semester, and I heard all about his frustration during our first stats lab, when he was assigned to my study group.

A few weeks later, he came home with me to study for our midterms and meet my parents. Not long afterward, I went to his parents' home to meet his family.

After spring graduation, Malcolm was hired by a prestigious advertising agency. He made every effort to see me on the weekends and after classes and any other time our schedules allowed. In May of 2001, at the end of my third year, Malcolm proposed, and I accepted.

Three months later, my parents threw an engagement party for us in their backyard. We greeted our closest friends and family as the day drew to a close. Shortly before sunset, Malcolm and I stole away with our co-conspirators to change clothes. The commissioner arrived while we were upstairs and announced our imminent vows to the yard full of guests.

This was how we successfully threw a surprise wedding in the backyard of my childhood home. On our marriage certificate, I changed my name slightly. I kept Nora Jane but dropped Margaret. I was several months shy of twenty-one and my husband had just turned twenty-five. After sunset photographs, Malcolm toasted the stats class he had once cursed. My parents welcomed their new son to the family, and in Malcolm's parents' speeches, they mentioned the grandchildren they expected post-haste. The caterers served salmon and chicken and later, we cut the cake. We spent the next day moving into a basement suite and stayed there until we saved enough for a deposit on our condo.

Nine years passed. We didn't have children and weren't sure we wanted to. We were happily married and satisfied with our careers, though both sets of grandparents were eager for little ones. I had casually mentioned to Malcolm in our first year of dating that I was adopted, and he accepted this. Perhaps my adoption had something to do with our lack of interest in children, but neither of us examined this too closely.

I never knew why my parents chose that specific day when I was eight years old to tell me of my true parentage, and it never occurred to me to wonder or ask. For years afterward, the subject simply never came up. But all that changed shortly after my twenty-ninth birthday, when a student showed me a newspaper article with an accompanying police sketch.

Chapter Two

I DON'T RECALL THE NAME OF THE STUDENT WHO GAVE ME the newspaper article that changed my life. I know I met with him in February 2010, on a Thursday morning, during my normal office hours.

The entire campus was alive with excitement over the upcoming Winter Olympics. The 2010 Games were being held in Vancouver, and the administration promised to live-stream the opening ceremonies and all sporting events in the central atrium for those students in between (or skipping) classes. Every day on campus felt like a giant party. Students and faculty alike were proud of their nation and their athletes. Red and white colors were displayed everywhere, and maple leaves adorned cheeks, toques, scarves, and backpacks.

The Olympics would open the following evening, Friday, February 12th. In anticipation of this, and to celebrate the upcoming week off, the student union had scheduled our very own "Awful Olympics," a parody of the Games. Students in wheelchairs raced across the courtyard, and the cafeteria became a make-shift indoor hockey rink complete with plungers and rolls of toilet paper in place of hockey sticks and puck.

A game of toilet-paper hockey commenced while our class was in session, and in the spirit of the festivities, I let my first-year students out early. I paused briefly in the cafeteria and watched the antics for a few minutes before going upstairs to keep my scheduled office hours.

Only one student waited in the hallway outside my office. I expected the student to have questions pertaining to the research paper I'd assigned, especially as we were approaching the deadline for submissions. Many first years had emailed inquiries about the suitability of topics and sought recommendations on how to get started. Most students wound up in the library looking into archived newspapers, as I had intended. I gently corrected those who approached the assignment in a decidedly more abstract manner.

The student who waited for me had proposed an interesting analysis comparing the themes in propaganda between Axis and Soviet powers. I was helping him limit the scope, so he didn't end up overwhelmed by the sheer volume of research available.

He handed me a newspaper before he even sat in the chair on the opposite side of my desk.

The article's banner caught my attention. Its bold font declared, "Police Appeal to Public for Help in Identifying Jane Doe." Beneath this headline was a police artist's sketch of a woman, and a short paragraph, which I read disinterestedly.

Police in British Columbia are asking members of the public for assistance in identifying a woman whose remains were found in Cold Lake Provincial Park in July of 2005. Jane Doe was between seventeen and twenty-one years of age at the time of her death, estimated to be between 1980 and 1985. Jane Doe was five-foot-two inches with dark hair and eyes and wearing denim jeans and a blue windbreaker. Police have not released her cause of death but have instead asked anyone with information to call authorities in 100 Mile House.

A long-distance number followed.

The student sitting across the desk from me was watching me closely. After skimming the paragraph again, I wondered why he had brought this particular article to me, as it fell outside the scope of his research topic. I looked up at him, hoping he would launch into an explanation without my having to prompt him.

At his eager expression, I glanced down at the newspaper again.

What in the world did a Canadian cold case from thirty years ago have to do with propaganda in the Third Reich and the Soviet Union? I wondered if I was the butt of some joke that I had missed, and felt a little impatient that he seemed to be wasting my time.

Then I looked at the picture. *Really* looked at it. And was seized by overwhelming incredulity. Though the sketch was skillfully done, it wasn't the quality of the artist's work that stunned me into silence. My own face stared up at me from the sketch, as surely as if the artist had received a photograph of me and recreated my face in pencil strokes.

The eyes held my gaze. They were exactly the same shape and color as mine. So too were the low hairline, the eyebrows, the space between the eyes, the pinched curve of my nose, the protruding cheekbones, and the slightly too-large lips.

I might be looking into a mirror. That was how much this woman looked like me. But she didn't just look *like* me. She *was* me.

I have never been as stunned as I was in that moment. I forgot that a student sat in front of me.

For the first time ever, I began to wonder where I came from and what happened to my biological mother and father. Could the resemblance really be coincidental?

I vaguely recalled the conversation with my parents all those years ago over cheese pizza and root beer. Hadn't they mentioned that I'd been found in a small town somewhere in BC? Could it have been the same town mentioned in the article, 100 Mile House?

Without thinking, I started to reach for my pocket to withdraw my cell phone. I would call Mom and ask her about this, ask her the name of that town. Then the student opposite me cleared his throat.

I blinked in surprise. I forced the muscles in my face to quickly form a gracious smile. I thanked him for bringing the newspaper article to my attention and agreed that the similarity was remarkable. Then I asked him about his thesis.

We chatted for half an hour or so. I can't remember a word he said or how I responded. He seemed satisfied with what we discussed, and at last he rose to leave. I glanced at the newspaper I had pushed back across the desk toward him, and when he reached to gather it up, I impulsively asked if I could keep it. He nodded and left, closing the door behind him.

I slid the newspaper closer and studied the woman's picture for several minutes before shifting my gaze to the small article. I read it aloud, then pulled my laptop from my shoulder bag and logged onto the university's wireless network. I began searching for everything I could find about the Jane Doe discovered in Cold Lake Provincial Park in the summer of 2005.

The first results pulled up short newspaper articles published by small towns in the Interior. The articles mentioned that the remains of a woman had been found outside of Tome, near the lake, by two local residents. The discovery of human remains seemingly warranted barely any notice.

The day after the story broke, one newspaper placed the story on the front page with the headline "The First Homicide Victim in Cold Lake for Decades," along with a photograph of the local hikers who found the body, posed in the clearing where she'd been discovered.

By the third day of coverage, news reports included the names of the two brothers, Terry and Scott Duggan, who found Jane Doe, as well as the efforts of police to recover evidence from the scene. One article ominously warned that foul play was suspected, as evidenced by the remoteness of the burial site, and promised salacious details in subsequent editions.

TV and radio stations in Vancouver and as far north as Prince George picked up the story. A news crew complete with photographer and cameraman were dispatched to interview both hikers. A police spokesman and a provincial park official provided quotes, and each of those interviews, as well as more pictures of the park, the clearing, and the nearby lake, were available online.

Earbuds in place, I listened eagerly as the reporters asked the questions that flashed through my mind. I began memorizing the details of the stories. Terry described pulling his dog away from what he thought was a mound of grass, dirt, and leaf debris. When his dog scampered off, he saw a sun-bleached rock in the shade of the cedar trees, and when he turned it over, he realized it was a human skull. He described the weathered jacket that seemed to have been torn by animals and faded by exposure: "They looked like they belonged to a kid. The jacket, or what was left of it, was so small, and so was"—he choked, apparently deeply shaken—"and so was the skull. I thought we found a kid. I'm so sorry for the family who lost their child."

The park official offered his condolences to the unknown family, but had very little of substance to add to the official reports. His contribution mainly outlined the history of the park and the peak seasons. He speculated that it would have been very hard to have left Jane Doe there during the height of summer as they had so many visitors during those months. He concluded that she must have been left in that clearing in late spring soon after the snow melted or early fall, before the new snow came.

Within that same broadcast, a spokesman for the local police described the efforts of his colleagues to preserve the woman's remains and afford dignity to the deceased. He detailed their efforts, from analyzing layers of soil underneath her remains for biological tissue or other matter, to examining the topsoil for hundreds of meters in all directions. Using fine mesh sieves, forensic analysts sifted for hours, searching for traces of personal effects, cigarette butts, clothing, and anything else brought into the area that didn't break down when exposed to the elements. He described the lengths to which they would go to identify the body and bring comfort and closure to her family. He remained tight-lipped when asked to speculate on a cause of death, however, or how long ago the victim had died.

As I listened, I scribbled on a notepad, and added questions I would have asked if I'd been in the interviewer's position. Next to my questions, I wrote down the names of those interviewed, certain that the names would be important. I had to remind myself that these interviews took place mere days after Jane Doe's discovery, before any substantial information would have been available.

I searched for every article I could find pertaining to Jane Doe. When

I finished reading one, I sent it to the printer and opened the next one. As each article printed, I paper clipped it and added it to the growing stack on my desk.

Finally, I ran out of articles to read and interviews to watch. The printer fell silent. I counted twenty-seven paper-clipped documents in addition to the newspaper propped up, open to the woman's face. Her sketch appeared in multiple articles, each with the sad eyes staring up at me. Had the artist deliberately added the slight shading to the face that turned her features melancholic?

Glancing at the clock, I was startled to see it was now late afternoon. I had spent hours obsessed, researching Jane Doe.

What next?

I decided that the resemblance between Jane Doe's picture and my own features was coincidental, and that it wasn't possible we were related. After all, I knew only that I had been found somewhere in the Interior region of BC as a newborn, the woman named Jane Doe was found in the Interior of BC, and that in the police sketch, she looked exactly like me. This evidence was flimsy, at best. Any number of plausible explanations existed, and I couldn't waste time and effort looking into Jane Doe's past, or my own. Of course, this woman wasn't connected to me.

I imagined Malcolm's smile as he chided me for letting my imagination run away with me. I shook my head, knowing his rebuke would be justified.

Malcolm was away on a work trip, scheduled to return Sunday evening. I would forget about this whole thing until he returned, and then mention it to him briefly, and together we would laugh at my foolishness. Rather than be affronted by his teasing, I would find comfort and reassurance in it. After all, if the idea seemed ridiculous to Malcolm (as I knew it would) then it couldn't possibly be true.

The coincidence had momentarily distracted me, but I wouldn't waste more time on it. I closed my laptop and put it away. But when I picked up the printouts of the internet articles and held them over the recycling bin, I couldn't let them go. Instead, I put the documents in my laptop bag. As for the original newspaper piece, I took a pair of scissors from my desk and clipped out the article, including the photograph, the headline, and the author's name. I folded the clipping carefully and put it in my jacket pocket.

IT IS A HALF-HOUR DRIVE FROM THE CAMPUS WHERE I TEACH to the condo Malcolm and I share, the one we had saved for and bought around our first wedding anniversary. Four times on that half-hour drive home, I pulled the car over to the side of the road, removed the clipping from my pocket, and read it, then stared at the sketch.

Twice while stopped, I punched in the number for the hotline on my cell phone. The first time, I cancelled the call before lifting the phone to my ear. The second time, the line rang once before I shook my head, hung up, and put my phone back in my pocket. I wasn't one to be rash or reckless, so having my instincts dictate my actions was a little off-putting.

Besides, what would I say if I did make the call and someone picked up? It was ridiculous to waste more time and energy on a coincidence.

Wasn't it?

This circular argument raged in my head for the entire commute home and continued unabated as I pulled into the underground parking garage and climbed the stairs to our third-floor unit.

My plan for the evening had been to pour a glass of wine and spend a few hours watching old sitcom reruns while marking research proposals for the second-year class I taught on Wednesday afternoons. I did pour the wine and warm some leftover pasta, but the research proposals stayed in my shoulder bag next to my laptop. Instead, I pulled out the stack of newspaper articles and, highlighter in hand, dissected them for any details I missed during my first perusal. I felt crazed, filled with a hunger for knowledge I had never experienced before.

In the past, I hadn't cared to know the names and faces of the people who gave me life. Growing up, my parents had given me security, stability, support, love. My life couldn't have been enriched in any way, so I never felt anger or disillusionment that I had been raised by two people who hadn't sired me.

Then again, deep down, maybe I was afraid to ask questions or express curiosity. Better to keep those gates closed than to get answers I didn't want. But those floodgates were open now, the questions and obsessions washing over me. Jane Doe's face appeared to me every time I caught a glimpse of myself in the mirror, and the words from the original article played through my mind in a haunting tone as I fell into bed that night.

I couldn't turn off my brain long enough to fall asleep. After tossing and turning, I finally gave up. I made mental lists and flow charts in attempts to quantify and make sense of the situation, to find meaning, to determine some course of action that I could reasonably take.

When logic failed me, I surrendered to the questions that nibbled at the edge of my mind. Who was Jane Doe? What was her name? Her age? Where had she come from? What were her family members and loved ones thinking right now? For surely, she would have had a family, but their certain presence posed a chilling question—why hadn't they noticed that their daughter, their sister, their cousin, had disappeared?

My search was beginning backward, I realized. Children trying to find their birth parents typically had names but no people attached to them. I had a person but no name. To know if she was related to me, I needed to find out her identity.

But she isn't my birth mother, I reminded myself.

A smaller voice in the back of my mind asked how I could be sure.

Then, inexplicably, I began wondering what my life would have been like if my birth mother had kept me. I would be someone else entirely. Who would that person be? What might my name be? What would my childhood have been like if I'd been raised by my biological family? Had she been married? What was my father's name? Where was he now? Had he known about me? What happened to Jane Doe? Why was she in that clearing? Was she my mother?

Numerous implausible scenarios filled my mind. Perhaps I had been kidnapped away from loving parents, and the kidnapper surrendered to their conscience and left me to be found and reunited with my desperate family. Perhaps my mother escaped an abusive relationship and had to leave me behind. Perhaps she intended to claim me later but never got the chance. Perhaps my mother was young, too young, when she got pregnant. She kept her pregnancy hidden from her family and gave birth to me in secret. Perhaps she grew up, married, and raised more children, my brothers and sisters.

There were problems with each of those theories, problems I didn't want to confront. I wanted the story to be neat and tidy and uncomplicated, the truth idyllic and easy to explain. But this didn't seem possible. After all, the article stated that Jane Doe was estimated to have been killed between twenty-five and thirty years ago, somewhere between 1980 and 1985. I would have been, at most, five years old when she died. I hadn't known about my adoption then.

The same article mentioned that Jane Doe was between seventeen and twenty-one years of age when she died. Doing the math, the earliest Jane Doe could have been born was in 1959. If Jane Doe was my birth mother, she was a young mother. Perhaps that was why she left me behind.

Again, I was working under the premise that this woman was my mother. Perhaps she was simply related to one of my birth parents—a sibling, or a cousin. Her connection to me could be quite distant or even nonexistent, though it was unnerving that our appearances were identical.

I wondered how forensic scientists had perfected the techniques of facial reconstruction, how they had narrowed down Jane Doe's age and year of death from so little evidence, and wondered how accurate their estimations were. Surmising what had happened to Jane Doe after the passage of so many years seemed insurmountable—as impossible as identifying who she had been. The pit of despair that had started in my stomach hours earlier finally overtook me. The numbers and facts lost all sense and meaning. I hovered in restlessness, watching the digits on my clock count down until my alarm rang at 5:30 a.m.

I acted on autopilot that morning, dressing and driving to campus, and gathering my notes from my office.

I had only one class that morning. Instead of lively discussion and banter, the mood was subdued as I droned through the significance of the rule of Tsar Alexander III. We finished with twenty minutes to spare. After answering some questions pertaining to the upcoming midterm, I dismissed my seminar class early and drifted to my office to hide.

Being a Friday before a week off and just before the start of the Winter Olympics, the campus was largely deserted. No students waited for office hours that day. I was grateful for the alone time. I had sixty research proposals from my second years to mark. I had emails to review from my first years regarding their ongoing research papers. I had a midterm exam to finish writing that concerned the Romanov Dynasty from 1709 to 1801, which I would administer to my third years two weeks from today.

I did not do any of this. Leaving the assembled piles of papers where they sat on my desk, I pulled the newspaper clipping from my pocket and let my finger trace the sketched features of Jane Doe.

With effort, I pushed away the new questions that arose. I was driving myself crazy. I needed to find a way to let go of my obsession.

I threw all the class materials into my bag, put the newspaper clipping back into my jacket pocket, turned off the lights, and locked the door to my office. I needed to talk to someone. Malcolm was out of town until Sunday evening, but my parents always welcomed me for dinner. I could reach their house in less than an hour. Mom and I could sip tea and talk while we waited for Dad to arrive home from work. Perhaps we could finally have the conversation she'd been eager to have with me twenty years ago, when they told me I'd been adopted.

One way or another, Mom could be the decisive factor. She might know whether I had been found in 100 Mile House. If the answer was a simple "no," that would solve the riddle and I could let go of my obsession with Jane Doe. I could return to not wanting to know about my birth parents.

Of course, if the answer wasn't simple, if I had come from the same small town—then what?

I didn't try to answer that question. Instead, I walked to my car while rehearsing how I might bring up the subject of my adoption. It wasn't that I was worried about hurting Mom's feelings—she'd wanted to talk about my past—I just didn't know how to explain why, all of a sudden, I was seized with a manic focus.

I reversed out of my faculty parking spot and was on the highway a few minutes later, heading toward answers that would put the Jane Doe mystery to bed. Or so I hoped.

Chapter Three

I called Mom from the highway to let her know I was rudely dropping by, just to make sure she was indeed home and didn't have plans. Mom had retired from the library several years before and now had fun being bored. She raised swans in the backyard, attended book clubs, and took art classes to learn how to paint with acrylics. Her landscapes done in bold, abstract colors lined the upstairs office-turned-studio.

My dad could have retired too, but he swore he would just have to return to work to keep from going crazy.

I pulled into their driveway in the middle of the afternoon and reached for my laptop bag. I hesitated, wondering if I was *really* going to have this conversation with my mom, and whether I was brave enough to show her the newspaper clipping that had awakened my sudden interest in my past. I'd imagined several scenarios during the long drive, but I still had no idea how to approach the subject.

I decided to carry my bag inside but leave it near the front door and see how the conversation progressed. Perhaps I would casually ask about the small town where I'd been found. I might not even introduce the topic of Jane Doe.

Mom was staring through the front window as I left the car. Her face lit up. I was barely through the door before she pulled me into a hug and offered to take my coat. "Come in! Come in! Shoes off, honey. I'm glad you came over. How are you? How's Malcom? How are his parents?"

"One at a time, Mom!" I laughed. I suspected she was full of gossip about family friends and distant relations.

"Are you enjoying the subjects you're teaching? How are your students?"

I followed her into the kitchen, where the tea kettle was whistling. "I'm teaching three different classes this semester. The classes are fairly predictable so far, but everyone's excited and distracted by the Olympics. Did I tell you about the games the student council hosted?" I described the contests for building the largest snow structures in the atrium, and skating races on the iced-over fountains behind the science building. Then I asked, "How are Othello and Desdemona?" Mom had chosen those names for her swans because of her love of Shakespearian literature.

Mom beamed. "Oh, they're doing wonderfully. They wintered quite well, and I expect hatchlings later this spring. And just this morning, I finished recreating Mount Baker in acrylics. I like painting landscapes, but I think I want to start working with watercolors, or perhaps challenging myself by working on portraits."

"I'd love to see your new paintings later," I offered.

Her smile widened. "Oh, and once the weather turns, I'll be playing tennis with Trudy twice a week. Did you hear that Jake and Denise are visiting in a few weeks? We can finally meet the baby! We should have a party, just a little get-together. Nothing too fancy."

This was a pleasant surprise. I hadn't known that Jake and his wife would be coming back so soon after their holiday visit a little over a month ago. Denise had been heavily pregnant, and gave birth to their second baby, a little girl, three weeks after Christmas.

I eagerly accepted Mom's invitation to the party and agreed that Malcolm and I would make the appetizers.

Mom studied me closely as she joined me at the table and poured our tea. "What's on your mind, honey? Is Melinda after you about grandchildren again?"

Malcolm's mother had been vocal about grandchildren during our first years of marriage, and her disappointment grew more palpable as the years passed. Mom's question made me chuckle, which eased my tension. "You know me so well," I joked. "No, Melinda's been sweet as always. A little heavy-handed with the hints, but she means well." I took a deep breath. "I have to be honest, I don't know how to begin or what to say."

She waited patiently until I finally stammered, "I-I need to ask about the day you and Dad brought me home."

Mom spooned sugar into my tea and poured in milk. Only when my tea was properly prepared did she say, "Of course, honey. What brought this up?"

I mutely pulled the newspaper clipping from my pocket, smoothed it out, and placed it on the table facing her.

As soon as her eyes fell on the photograph, she sucked in a sharp breath and lifted her gaze to mine. "My goodness!" She set her teacup on the table and pulled the clipping closer so she could read every word.

"What a shock this must have been," she said a few moments later. She stared into my eyes.

I nodded. "I want this resemblance to be a coincidence, but I'm scared. I've never been curious before, but now, it's like a switch has flipped somewhere in my brain and I can't stop thinking about Jane Doe." I gripped the handle of my teacup. "Even if not Jane Doe, my birth mother is out there, and I can't stop wondering who she is and where she might be. I want so badly to go back to my happy indifference, but I don't think I can."

Mom nodded while I spoke, as if she understood.

I hastened to explain that I was not seeking to replace her and Dad in my life. I had no interest in contacting or building a relationship with the family that gave me up decades ago. As a historian, I was interested in the facts. I was curious about names, birthdates, locations, dates of death. I didn't want to tangle with the emotions that came with justifications and explanations. I only wanted the cold comfort that comes from logical statistics that can be quantified for discernible meaning.

"Of course, sweetheart. What do you want to know?"

"Can you tell me the whole story? All the details you know?"

She nodded and took a fortifying sip of tea. "As you know, your father and I met in university in 1968, and we married slightly more than a year later. We started trying to have children right away. We so badly wanted a family. But months passed, and then years, and it was heartbreaking for us. We finally found a doctor in 1974 who confirmed what we feared. After an illness I had as a young teenager, I wouldn't be able to have children," Mom's voice trembled slightly.

I placed a hand on hers and squeezed gently.

As if recalled to the present, Mom blinked several times and shook her head slightly, returning my hand squeeze. "We were devastated. For a time, we thought we would simply give up. But we both wanted a child so badly, we agreed to look into adoption. The process to apply for and be approved as adoptive parents took years, but we were finally accepted in 1978. Then we waited.

"That last week in November, Vancouver didn't get the heavy rains that usually come with winter. Your father and I were wrapping presents that evening when the call came from Rob—Dr. Bradley.

"I took the call." Mom paused. "Rob said the hospital had a baby girl in stable but serious condition and asked if we would come right away. Your father was throwing clothes into the suitcase before I finished the call." She laughed. "In his haste, he packed only jeans for himself and no shirts, and we never finished wrapping those presents. We called the airport, but the next flight to Prince George was cancelled due to weather. The one after that didn't leave until the following morning, fourteen or fifteen hours later. We decided to drive ten hours through the night.

"Rob met us at the ER entrance and took us straight upstairs. We met with a social worker and signed the papers that made us your temporary guardians. Then we had to put on gowns, gloves, and masks before they took us to you." Her voice caught. "You were in some sort of incubator, under a heating lamp, a tiny tube inserted in your nostril, and a bracelet around your ankle that simply said 'Baby Girl.'

"A nurse said that we could give you a name if we wanted to. We didn't even have to think about it. We had decided that if we ever had a little girl, we would name her for Dad's sister. We weren't allowed to hold you, not yet, but that same nurse gave me a marker and let me scratch out 'Baby Girl' and write your name instead. My hands shook so badly, I don't think my printing was legible. Then they let us touch you. You had a few black curls on top of your head. You gripped my finger and I was amazed at how tightly you held on. We told you stories and sang you songs.

"At some point, the RCMP came. They talked to Sherry—the social worker, I can't remember her last name—and then us, and I don't think we stopped asking questions. We wanted to know everything—where you came from and how you were found. All they could tell us was that constables from their detachment were canvassing the area in the heavy snow looking for any trace of a young woman who might have recently given birth, and there was little information available. They promised to keep us informed about the search for your family."

She smiled. "Later in the morning, people started arriving, maybe a dozen or so, all from the same church, and they brought their priest with them. They told us they were from the town where you'd been found, and they braved the aftermath of the snowstorm to come keep vigil and pray with us. Every single one of them brought something for you—diapers, clothes, hand-me-downs. The whole time you were in the hospital, you had visitors."

"How long was I there?" I asked.

"Almost three weeks." Mom took a sip of tea. "We slept in chairs and cots next to your incubator. Dad drove the car back alone that first weekend and made arrangements with the office before flying back with fresh clothes and supplies for both of us. We were finally allowed to hold you, and the nurses brought in a rocking chair so we could cradle you while you slept. It quickly became apparent you were a fighter. You cried when you weren't being held. You gained weight, and the entire ward erupted in cheers when you were taken off the feeding tube. I sobbed with joy when I gave you your first bottle.

"After two weeks, in the absence of any family to claim you, we were given legal custody of you and brought you home the day before Christmas—the most amazing gift we could have asked for." The tears that had been threatening spilled onto her cheeks and she squeezed my hand.

I tried to remain detached, as if this story described someone else's birth, but early in the story I developed a lump in my throat and struggled to work past it. I pressed my lips together, swallowed over my emotions, and turned a watery smile to my mom. She seemed to understood the love in the gesture as the only thanks I was capable of at that moment.

Finally, I cleared my throat. "Have my birth parents ever come forward?"

Mom shook her head. "Not that we ever heard. Early on, Dad and I talked about hiring a private investigator, but the need seemed to fade as time passed. Shortly after your second birthday, we legally adopted you. We agreed that we would tell you when the time was right, that we would wait until you were old enough to understand. We also agreed that we would put aside funds for a private investigator in case one day you may want to look."

"Why did you choose that Wednesday in the middle of the school year to tell me I was adopted?"

Mom chuckled sheepishly. "We'd been planning to tell you soon anyway. That was why we bought you the book *Pollyanna* at the beginning of the school year. Remember that?"

I did, and grinned.

"We were trying to prepare you. But a day or two before that Wednesday, we'd been talking with Rich and Trudy about your adoption and Jake happened to overhear. He started asking questions. Rather than run the risk of Jake blurting out the truth, we decided to tell you ourselves." Mom shrugged.

I took a deep breath, smoothed out the newspaper clipping, and tapped one of the names in the article. "Is this town, 100 Mile House, where I was discovered?"

To my surprise, Mom shook her head. A mix of relief and disappointment passed over me.

"We drove through 100 Mile House and Cold Lake to reach Prince George." She bit her bottom lip. She looked at the clipping on the table.

When she looked up again, her eyes were moist. "You were found at the Parish of St. Raymond Ignatius in the town of Tome." She inhaled deeply. "Tome lies twenty kilometers north of the town of Cold Lake, on the northern edge of the lake, on the border of the provincial park. Tome would be the closest town to where this woman was found."

With a deep sense of foreboding, struggling to breathe, I murmured, "So…this means Jane Doe could be related to me. Jane Doe could be my mother."

"Let me refill your cup." Mom reached for my cup and we both stood. She brewed another pot of tea and I fetched my computer bag from the front hallway. After the kettle boiled, I suggested we talk in the living room. I settled on the floor next to the coffee table and arranged stacks of articles into piles around me.

Mom watched me.

I hastily explained, "This is everything I found in the media about Jane Doe's discovery."

"What a coincidence," Mom said. "I have my own collection to share with you." She went upstairs and returned a few minutes later with a dust-covered shoebox, its corners worn and colors faded. "This box is as old as you are." She passed the box from her lap to mine and accepted a stack of papers I offered in return.

Inside the box was a stack of newspaper clippings. Mom explained that Dr. Bradley had saved everything he could find about their new baby, from articles describing my discovery to the search efforts for my family. For years after they brought me home, he sent anything that mentioned me, though never was I identified by name. The most recent clipping was an obituary dated 1999 for Thomas Lloyd Chance. Chance had served the town of Tome as an emergency volunteer for close to forty years before passing away peacefully. His obituary was included in this box because he was the one who, along with another, unnamed man, drove through the snowstorm of 1980 to take the foundling baby girl to the hospital. The article mentioned this proudly, as if he were a returning war hero who should have received a decoration.

I thought he should have received a medal for his role in my past. He would always be a hero to me. I was only sad I'd never had a chance to meet him before he died.

Underneath this obituary was a second one, dated 1986, for Father Patrick Francis, the parish priest at St. Raymond Ignatius in Tome. His death also resulted from natural causes, and again I was mentioned in connection with his history and service. This death, too, caused me sadness, as if learning that a distant friend I hadn't seen in years but loved fondly and esteemed greatly had passed.

I pulled out clipping after clipping, exhilarated by the discovery. I was curious why Mom hadn't shown it to me when I was younger, but perhaps it was my own seeming indifference on the subject that had deterred her.

We spent the afternoon sipping tea and reading and occasionally bringing something to the other's attention. We were remarkably relaxed considering the topic of contemplation, and this was how my dad discovered us when he arrived home in the early evening.

He greeted me with delight, then smiled in puzzlement over our setup on the floor of the living room. I could understand his confusion. The normally spotless space was covered in paper, newsprint, dust bunnies, and various pens and paper clips that had spilled from my laptop bag. I hurriedly tidied up while Mom started preparing dinner, and after a few minutes, I joined them in the kitchen.

We prepared dinner together, laughing and joking and sharing tidbits from the day. Eventually, Dad asked, "So what were all those papers you two used to redecorate the living room?"

Mom looked at me, seeming to ask how I wanted to respond.

I began by saying, "I had some questions about how you came to adopt me. Mom showed me all the articles she kept over the years."

His eyebrows rose slightly. "I see."

I could see his mind working through the implications.

"So, you're looking for your biological family."

"Not exactly," I said. "I found someone who might be related to me. It's a bit of a long story." My hands were full of the lettuce I was shredding and dropping into the salad spinner, so I couldn't retrieve the Jane

Doe clipping. "Basically, there was an article a few days ago about a homicide victim in the town of Tome."

His eyes widened and his gaze darted to Mom.

"They're calling her Jane Doe. And the sketch the police released looks incredibly similar to me."

"Identical," Mom chimed in.

Dad said, "And you wonder if there's a connection."

"Yeah. There's a RCMP hotline for tips."

"You could call to see if any more information is available."

"Not yet. I want to know…I guess I wanted to see…." I wrinkled my nose, wondering how to put my reluctance into words. "I guess I was hoping that after talking with you and Mom, I'd learn something that would make a connection impossible, or at least unlikely."

"The opposite seems to have happened though," Mom said. "If anything, the connection seems even more plausible now."

"I can show you the research I've done," I offered.

Dad shook his head. "That's okay."

As we sat down to eat, Dad began telling anecdotes and reminiscing about family memories. I laughed and shared memories of my own, temporarily forgetting about Jane Doe and my birth mother.

When I thought about our conversation later, I realized how unsettled my dad was, and how, by finding comfort in our memories together, he had been dealing with his emotions. Perhaps he had concluded long ago that I would never be interested in searching for my biological family. If so, I can understand he must have felt rather blindsided.

We laughed and joked for some time after emptying our plates. Only when Mom stood up to clear the table did I notice Dad watching me with concern.

"Nothing's gonna change, Dad," I hastened to assure him. "It's simply an itch that I need to scratch."

He chuckled.

"I'm not interested in building relationships with anyone who might share my DNA. You're my family. Our life is comfortable and predictable, and that's what I want it to be."

Dad nodded once.

"What does interest me is the possibility that I can find names and dates and locations. I want cold, hard, logical facts that can't possibly cause drama or complications of my life. Not the people attached to them. You know what that feels like. You love history as much as I do."

"So"—Dad leaned forward, elbows on the table—"what do you want to do with the information you learn? What would you like to see happen moving forward?"

Characteristically, when Dad confronted an issue, he narrowed down the main problem, then analyzed each possible solution and the potential repercussions of each possibility. Then, with all information considered, he made an informed decision and didn't second-guess. I had learned my analytical approach from his tutelage.

"It's not that easy." I frowned. "The solution to this isn't in my control. It's in the hands of other people I haven't met yet and may never be able to find. I guess the approach depends on what I want the eventual outcome to be, and that's why I can't answer that. I don't know what I want. I know what I don't want. But I'm experiencing an obsession where there wasn't one before. I can't go back to neither knowing nor caring. I need to find a satisfactory answer that makes sense and fits into place, and without that answer, I don't know how to move forward."

Dad nodded slowly as I spoke. "Did your mom tell you about the money we put aside if you wanted to hire an investigator?"

"She did, and thank you both so much. But until absolutely necessary, I'm content to search on my own."

"You sure?"

"I know I'm only an amateur, but I can't accept answers from someone else. It's a contradiction, I know. I need answers as quickly as possible to move forward, but I need to find them for myself."

Mom returned to the dining room and resumed her seat, just in time to hear my dad suggest, "Perhaps you should start by calling the hotline listed for the RCMP."

"That makes the most sense to me, too," I agreed. "I was tempted to earlier today, but I wanted to talk to you both first. You have a way of putting things into perspective."

"Then perhaps we should take the night to sleep on it," Mom suggested. "Things often make more sense after a decent night's sleep."

It could have been my imagination, but she seemed to peer at me as she said this. Likely, she suspected I hadn't slept well the previous night.

I couldn't deny the wisdom of her words and agreed that we could revisit Jane Doe in the morning.

We took decaf coffee and cookies into the living room to watch the opening ceremonies of the Vancouver Olympics. Dad settled on the left side of the couch, Mom nestled into him, and I sat on the floor at their feet, head resting against Mom's knee, just as we'd sat for as long as I could remember.

The effect of having unburdened myself to my parents was soporific. That night, I slept uninterrupted, my mind clear of questions or concerns. When I awoke Saturday morning, I lay in my childhood bed for almost an hour before rousing myself and treading downstairs.

Mom greeted me in the kitchen where she nibbled on fruit and sipped coffee. "Morning, sweetheart! Coffee's fresh." She gestured to the coffeemaker on the counter. "I thought about making pancakes for brunch, if you're hungry."

"Pancakes sound amazing. I'm starving!"

As she cracked eggs and whisked mashed banana into the batter, Mom said, "Dad's gone for an early round of golf with Rich Mulligan, but he'll be back early afternoon. I thought maybe you and I could go shopping for a few hours."

I suspected her suggestion had more to do with keeping me distracted than actually purchasing anything, but I was only too happy to accept.

That afternoon, we gathered in the living room. I laid my cell phone on the coffee table, turned on the speakerphone function, and dialed the number for the RCMP.

As I waited for the call to connect, my pulse pounded in my ears. A faint click caused my heart rate to jump. A computerized voice asked me to be patient. I swallowed several times, trying to moisten my tongue, and glanced at my parents from under the screen of my lashes.

Then a woman came on the line. In a professional voice, she rushed through a greeting and informed me that I had reached the hotline for the Royal Canadian Mounted Police detachment in 100 Mile House.

I cleared my throat, glanced at my parents, stammered out my name, and said I was calling from Vancouver. Then I told her that I might have information about Jane Doe, but I wasn't really sure.

"Go on." She seemed only slightly interested.

I explained that I had been adopted as a baby, and that my parents confirmed I had been found not far from the town of Cold Lake. Then I realized that, out of context, this information had no meaning to someone unfamiliar with the events of the previous thirty-six hours. I apologized and began again with an explanation of who I was and how I had come to read the newspaper article. I finished by saying the accompanying sketch looked exactly like me.

After a brief silence, the woman said, "I see...." in a lingering tone that told me she was humoring me.

Afraid she wasn't taking me seriously, I explained that I wasn't trying to waste her time. I only knew for sure that Jane Doe didn't just look like me—she *was* me. I then explained that I had been born in early December of 1980 and that I'd been left on the steps of the Parish of St. Raymond Ignatius in Tome around that time. I knew nothing about my birth family. Then I shared my theory that Jane Doe might be connected to me.

The woman thanked me for calling and asked for my name and contact details. She assured me that she would pass my tip to the proper individuals investigating the matter, and that if anything further was needed from me, an investigator would be in touch. As I recited my name and phone number, I realized they wouldn't call.

The woman bid me goodbye and hung up, leaving me feeling rather stupid.

My parents sat side by side, tightly clasping hands. Their tension eased visibly as I put my phone back in my pocket, next to the newspaper clipping.

I smiled with what I hoped looked like nonchalance. "Well, that's that," I said. "Things should be back to normal in a few days."

I joined them for dinner but declined their invitation to stay over a second night. As I drove home that Saturday evening, I cringed at how I had handled things. Was I allowing my imagination to run away with me? Had I convinced myself that it was possible I was related to Jane Doe because I wanted it to be true? I had never allowed myself to be curious before, but was it really because I simply hadn't cared? Or had I convinced myself that I wasn't curious in order to protect myself from whatever painful truths I might discover?

I didn't want to think about Jane Doe anymore. I was emotionally overwhelmed and wanted to spend a few hours doing something fun and relaxing. My possible connection to Jane Doe had consumed too much time in the previous few days. Malcolm would certainly enjoy teasing me when I told him.

Before I crawled into bed that night, I pulled the crinkled clipping from my jacket pocket, smoothed it out, and stared at the face. Her face. My face.

My dreams that night were filled with hikes past a lake and through underbrush to a clearing where this nameless woman stood. Her face was hazy around the edges, as if glimpsed through an unfocused camera lens. She called to me, but I couldn't hear her voice over the rushing of the wind through the large cedar trees that cast her in deep shadow.

She had a name. I was determined to find it.

Chapter Four

As much as I desperately needed Malcolm's perspective and advice on the matter, he would be tired after the long weekend and hungry after the flight. A creature of habit, he would want a shower and a quick bite before relaxing, and he'd be dozing on the couch by 8:30. So I made up my mind not to inundate him on his first evening home.

His flight came in from Calgary late that afternoon. I placed dinner in the slow cooker, then drove to the Vancouver airport. Malcolm kissed me at the terminal and handed me a beautifully wrapped gift box, which I opened immediately. I squealed when I recognized my favourite chocolates. We ate several pieces while waiting to collect his bag. He shared the highlights of his trip during the drive home. Over dinner, I gave him his Valentine's Day gift, a bottle of his favorite scotch, and told him about my visit to my parents. I passed on their well-wishes, and we chatted about the coming week.

After dinner, Malcolm poured a glass of scotch and headed to the den. I hurriedly put the supper dishes in the dishwasher, then settled on the couch next to him and tried to lose myself in the television show he watched.

I squirmed, shifted, kicked my feet up, and lowered them to the floor.

Malcolm gave me a sideways glance. "Is something on your mind?"

I took a deep breath and faced him. "There was an article. In the newspaper. Hang on, I'll show you." I tripped over my feet as I rose to retrieve the clipping from my bedside table.

Malcolm read the article and studied the picture. When he finished, he looked at me. "So, you think this woman is related to you because she looks like you?"

The idea did sound ridiculous. "I can't get it out of my head. I'm obsessed with researching everything I can find about the discovery of Jane Doe."

"And your students will never get their marks back," he joked.

I knew he would tease me; I welcomed the familiar reaction. "I know my interest in this case doesn't make sense. I'm basing everything on feelings, which is completely unlike me." I explained that my parents had confirmed that I was found in the same area where Jane Doe's body was discovered. I told him everything Mom knew about how I came to be left at the Parish, which admittedly, wasn't much. "So, yes, I think Jane Doe could be related to me. She might even be my mother. Which is why I called the hotline."

"Well then, that's that. You've done everything you can, and they'll get in touch if there's any reason to think the idea is credible." After a brief pause, he added, "I remember reading something for a forensics class once, about how medical examiners could determine if a woman had been pregnant or given birth based on the position of her pelvic bones. I don't know much about the process or the science behind it, but there's something about the way a woman's abdomen expands that leaves marks on her bones. So, forensics would be able to tell if Jane Doe was pregnant or gave birth. If we don't hear back from the RCMP, we can assume they've ruled out the possibility that you are somehow connected."

I was relieved to hear his use of the word "we." I'd always appreciated how supportive Malcolm was—of my schooling, of my career, and now of this rather improbable discovery. I knew he had a point about me having done all I could, but I felt restless as I realized I couldn't just wait.

Malcolm nudged my shoulder, pulling me out of my contemplation. "Can I ask why now? Why are you so intrigued by your biological family? I mean, you've never shown any interest before."

I shrugged, not sure how to put my obsession into words.

He reached for my hand and brought it to his lips. "Let me know what I can do to help."

That was the end of the conversation that night, but not the end of my obsession.

THE NEXT MORNING, MALCOLM LEFT FOR WORK AND I SLEPT in, then made a cup of tea. As the tea cooled enough to drink, I located a red pen and began reading the first few lines of the student proposal in front of me. After a few minutes, I shoved the stack of proposals to the far side of the kitchen table and opened my laptop. I had read every article about Jane Doe multiple times. I had listened to the media interviews. I had even pulled up a photograph of myself at the age of twenty-one and studied it side-by-side with the Jane Doe sketch. My efforts at denial didn't work.

I opened the box that Mom sent home with me and sorted through the clippings, placing them in chronological order as I read through them again. Then I opened each of the interview files and listened to them over and over, unable to disengage. The interviewers' questions and the responses began to burn into my memory. I memorized the inflection of every question and the facial expressions that accompanied each answer. I reread the articles. I subscribed to publications in Vancouver, Cold Lake, and Prince George, and lost myself in the archives of each, looking for details my mom and I might have missed.

This new search didn't uncover anything I didn't already know, but I saved and printed every article and attacked each with a highlighter as soon as it came off the printer. I grabbed a legal pad from Malcolm's desk and began making flow charts and brain maps and lists. I took scissors to certain articles and clipped out the important bits and organized them into categories. Then I took the printouts, the clippings, the legal pad, my notebook, and Mom's box of articles, and went into Malcolm's office to redraw my lists and flowcharts on his white board.

That was how Malcolm found me when he came home that afternoon. He cast a curious look over the fruits of my labor. "How many papers did you get through marking today?"

I stuck my tongue out at him.

I spent Tuesday drafting more of the same notes and charts. When Malcolm came home that afternoon, I stood at the stove stirring a pot of soup and listening for the umpteenth time to the interview of one of the campers who discovered Jane Doe. I vaguely heard Malcom call out a question while I lip synched questions along with the reporter.

When the video ended a few minutes later, I closed my laptop.

Malcolm came into the kitchen and asked, "What if this woman isn't related to you?"

"Listen, I know I'm not myself right now," I admitted. "I don't know what to make of all this. It's new, and scary to me, as well. But I can't get this girl out of my head."

"If you find out that Jane Doe isn't related to you, could you be happy going back to not knowing about your biological family? Or would you want to find out as much as you can about them, regardless?"

His question laid the issue out in black and white terms in a way I had been struggling to crystallize. I couldn't sort through and get past my emotions to focus on the actual problem. And this meant I couldn't start to sort out and calculate probable solutions. At some points, I leaned toward Jane Doe and my mother being one and the same, and at others, I convinced myself they were two different people.

"Putting aside the question of whether or not Jane Doe was my mother," I began, "there are two very distinct possibilities concerning my biological family. The first is that there are people out there who know about me and wonder what became of me. My grandparents, aunts, uncles, cousins, and siblings, who might greet me eagerly. It's also possible that my sudden appearance will cause awkward questions and hurt feelings. But either way, if Jane Doe is connected to me, the possibility is more likely that we come from a family that either doesn't know or doesn't care about either of us. How else do you explain the fact that no one came looking for her after she disappeared?"

Malcolm listened with a somber expression and nodded encouragingly when I hesitated.

"What if I find something I don't want to know? What if I don't want to know what is back there? I know this doesn't answer your question about whether I can go back to not knowing. I guess because I don't know what's back there, I don't know if I want to know. That's contradictory and doesn't make sense but I can't help it. I won't know if I want to know until the information is in front of me. I can't pick and choose what I want the truth to be, and it's impossible to unlearn something once I've learned it." I threw an angry glance at the whiteboard in the next room. "I hate this. I really do. I was never curious before. I never wondered, I never wanted to know. But now I'm determined to learn everything I can about this woman, and I can't let this go. I can't be happy going back to not knowing."

"You can't change the things that happened that led you here," Malcolm reasoned. "But the past is not who you are. You're not here because of who your biological parents were, or who your adopted parents are. Not fully, anyway. You got yourself where you are because of the choices you made. And you still get choices moving forward, whether you decide to start looking or not, and depending on what you find."

After dinner, we delved into the research I'd been conducting for the past week. He questioned me and noted every minor detail. He listened intently as I told the story of how I'd been found and brought home. I showed him the articles my mother had given me, and the compilation list I'd made of all pertinent details. Then I showed him the second stack of newspaper articles about Jane Doe's discovery. I recited everything I had read and researched. Finally, I pulled out my laptop and played for him the interviews with the two hikers and the police spokesman.

When the last interview ended and I closed my laptop, Malcolm asked, "Are you all right?"

I nodded slowly.

"I know it's a lot," he said. "We'll just take this process one step at a time. Someone might come forward with information to help the police identify this woman. Maybe knowing her identity will lead to clues about your biological family that help you decide whether or not to keep looking."

I had no idea how to even start looking, and Malcolm seemed to sense that I needed to take a mental break. He shared an anecdote about a mutual friend that made me laugh and eased my tension.

We said no more of Jane Doe that night.

I spent a third day brain mapping and flow charting and feverishly scribbling nearly illegible notes. Malcolm was concerned enough about my obsessive behavior to ask, "Have you heard back from anyone at the hotline?"

I shook my head.

After a moment's contemplation, he asked what time my first class began on Tuesday morning.

"Eleven thirty, why?"

Malcolm pulled out his laptop and began tapping at the keys. "You'll see." A few minutes later, he announced, "We're going away this weekend. I used personal days for tomorrow and Friday, and you have Monday off for Family Day. I rented an SUV to make the drive north since neither of us have winter tires or snow chains. I also booked a hotel in Tome. We can leave tomorrow after breakfast."

I was stunned by his gesture and anxious at the thought that the search was really beginning. When I turned a questioning gaze to him, Malcolm shrugged. "I haven't seen you this focused since defending your PhD thesis. This is important to you, so it's important to me."

The journey might prove entirely fruitless, but I had done everything I could from Vancouver. A trip to Tome seemed the logical next step since I'd be able to begin the search for my biological family and for Jane Doe. Malcolm suggested we visit the Parish where I was found, as well as speak to the police about anything more that might have been uncovered about Jane Doe. The worst that might happen was we'd be sent away without learning anything new.

The only thing left to do, then, was pack for our trip.

I hardly slept that night. The challenge I faced involved personal connections and emotional ties. I thought I would much prefer defending my thesis all over again. I knew that had ended successfully. I didn't know what waited for me at the end of this road.

Malcolm stirred each time I tossed, though I tried to keep from disturbing him. I gave up in the early hours of the morning and crept out to the living room couch, knowing I wouldn't sleep, but figuring that one of us should have a decent rest. Around four a.m., Malcolm got up and made tea. We sat together on the couch sipping warm drinks and saying nothing. As the gray light of morning lifted, Malcolm turned on the TV to catch an early news broadcast and I went for a hot shower to relax my weary muscles. I returned a short time later to see he'd grabbed the cooler from our closet of camping supplies and had already stocked it with bottled water and prepackaged snacks. I grabbed the ice packs from the freezer as he sliced veggies on the cutting board. While he placed the dishes he'd used into the dishwasher, I fried some eggs in a skillet while bread toasted.

We finished breakfast and cleaned the kitchen before tramping downstairs to make an early start. The rental agency opened at nine. By ten, we were on the road, heading east toward the Interior.

Creeping through the valley on Highway 97, which followed the Thompson River, we gazed through light snow at the mountains that rose on either side of the two-lane road. Beyond a concrete barrier, ice crusted the edges of the river mere meters from the car. We crawled through tunnels, arced around bends, and passed long-haul trucks and RVs. We saw small towns, isolated houses and farms, deserted buildings, and cemeteries full of crumbling headstones and overgrown with weeds.

Just outside of 70 Mile House, we stopped for a late lunch of veggies with dip and a bag of chips washed down with bottled water. After lunch, we continued north, gawking at the evidence of forest fires that had taken place years prior. Blackened tree stumps rose like the uneven teeth of a comb, stretching for kilometers.

The town names were unfamiliar to me. Lytton. Cache Creek. Lone

Butte. I followed our progress on a map unfolded on my lap, placing checks beside the dots that marked their locations.

As we drew closer to our destination, our light conversation dwindled and ceased almost entirely. Then we reached the outskirts of the community of Cold Lake, and I practically pressed my nose to the window, staring hungrily at the passing town. The streets were deserted, the inhabitants probably huddled inside the homes, protected from the elements, giving the town a lonely feeling.

Highway 97 formed the main north/south road through the community that shared its name with both the nearby lake and the provincial park, and the speed limit dropped to fifty kilometers per hour for those few blocks. Then the town of Cold Lake faded behind us, and signs announcing our approach to Tome appeared every few kilometers. Twenty minutes after leaving Cold Lake and six hours after leaving Vancouver, we crossed into Tome, and the anxiety I'd attempted to control exploded. Tears streamed down my face.

Thirty years after I left Tome, I had returned.

Chapter Five

As part of my frenzied obsession of the past few days, I had looked at countless maps of Tome and the surrounding area, including the Cold Lake Provincial Park. I also browsed the town on the internet. Because of this, I had a decent idea of what to expect. But as Highway 97's posted speed limit dropped, pictures from my laptop materialized in front of me. I found it difficult to breath.

Tome butted up against the northern shoreline of Cold Lake. A row of dilapidated storefronts faced the lake and announced their goods and services on tired-looking signs. I imagined this to be a popular stretch with local residents during the summer months.

Though old and seemingly broken down, the town had a certain quaintness that I hadn't really expected. What surprised me most was the almost complete absence of snow. Only a light dusting remained, most of the flakes having been scattered by the wind blowing past our rented SUV. The sun streaming through the windows created a sense of false spring, and this added to the impression of idyllic peace.

Malcolm turned onto a side street and pulled up to a hotel. The building looked like a converted warehouse. The décor was a little outdated, but the hotel itself was neat and clean.

The clerk asked several questions that I considered to be probing and somewhat rude before he handed us our room key.

"Where can I get a map of the area?" I asked.

"I have one right here." He reached under the counter and handed me a folded map. "Are you visiting family?"

Malcolm grinned wryly and answered, "In a roundabout way." Later, I discovered that the clerk's curiosity was the way of small towns.

After a cursory glance around our room to ensure its acceptability, Malcolm dumped our bags on the bed then began reading the welcome binder next to the phone, absently removing and placing a map and list of nearby restaurants on the pillow. He found contact information for the nearest RCMP detachment in 100 Mile House, punched in the digits, and asked to speak to the officer in charge of the Jane Doe investigation.

I fiddled with the catches on my bag while I listened to Malcolm's side of the conversation and scanned the room's offerings—a queen-size bed, two bedside tables, alarm clock, reading lamp, dresser with TV, desk, phone, and coffee pot.

Malcolm's forehead furrowed as he listened to what was being said.

"All right, could you tell me the investigator's name? Chilton? When is Chilton expected to be in the office next? All right, thank you. Bye now."

Malcolm spread the map on the bed and circled three locations: the church where I was found, the clearing where Jane Doe was discovered, and the RCMP detachment handling the Jane Doe case. He jotted the name of each on a legal pad and then added a fourth, the local high school.

"Why the high school?" I asked.

"I figure that even in remote areas, schools probably take group pictures of their student bodies every year. If Jane Doe is from around here and attended a local high school, her photo might be in a yearbook. Find a photo of a girl who looks like you and we'll have a possible lead on her identity."

I had to admit, this made sense.

"We have three days and three different places we want to visit," he went on. "Why not dedicate a day to each location? We'll start with the police. Tome falls into the jurisdiction of the detachment in 100 Mile House. The lead investigator is Inspector Doug Chilton, and he'll be in tomorrow morning." He paused and looked at me. When I nodded, he went on. "Saturday, we'll visit the Parish of St. Raymond Ignatius. The church won't be as busy on Saturday as on Sunday, and this gives us the freedom to spend as much or as little time as you want. And then Sunday, we can make the hike to the field near Cold Lake. I've already checked the weather for Sunday: overcast but dry. How's that for starters?"

I nodded again.

"Obviously, it's a skeletal plan, but we'll adapt as things arise."

Malcolm wanted a quick shower after so long a road trip. I called down to the desk clerk to inquire about nearby restaurants for dinner. Then I dialed my parents. We chatted for several minutes about our trip and our plans for the next few days. They wished us luck, unable to fully hide their concern, and Mom begged us to check in to let them know how we were doing. Finally, I made my excuses and said good night.

When Malcolm emerged, toweling his short hair dry, I told him, "Mom and Dad say hi. And the desk clerk gave me a few options for dinner."

We donned heavy jackets before leaving the room. The sun had disappeared while we were settling and planning.

Across the parking lot was a burger joint. We hurried to it, motivated more by our desire to escape the biting February temperature than by any craving for burgers and fries.

We ordered and then found a booth, and Malcolm began chatting inconsequentially about this and that. Midway through our meal, I admitted that I hadn't heard a word he'd said. I remained in something of a daze since arriving in Tome. This might have been the town in which my mother and father grew up. Is this what Tome had looked like when they lived here? Was this where I might find my family? Had they walked these streets, played in that park? Had she come to this burger joint as a teenager?

I didn't protest when Malcom suggested that we have an early night.

The temperature was too cold and the evening too dark to attempt a walk around the block. We returned to our room, changed into pajamas, and turned on the television to watch the Canada versus Switzerland preliminary round of men's ice hockey. I lost myself in the enthusiasm of the next hour and a half, particularly as the Canadian team won 3-2 in overtime. Through the thin walls of the room, I heard other Canadians celebrating the win.

We changed the channel, and as the opening credits to an old movie started playing, Malcolm began dozing. I stayed awake, staring at the TV but not taking in the plot, the jokes, or the actors. Instead, I focused on the picture of my biological family taking shape in my mind. The narrative wasn't based on any factual evidence, just pure creation borne of wishful thinking. With a sense of foreboding, I finally turned off the TV and curled close to my sleeping husband, suspecting that whatever the truth might be, it wouldn't be as idyllic or perfect as any of the scenarios that had occurred to me.

That thought kept me awake. Around midnight, I gave up on sleep, sat in a chair, perused my notes, and scribbled on a legal pad. Malcolm woke and asked if he could watch TV. I nodded, climbed back in bed next to him, and we spent a second sleepless night together.

FRIDAY MORNING DAWNED OVERCAST, THE SKY HEAVY WITH dark clouds that threatened rain. We breakfasted on cereal bars and yogurt. I took a long, hot shower in an attempt to relax the tension from my neck and shoulders. Finally, I dressed and dried my hair. We left the hotel room shortly after nine.

The drive to 100 Mile House took slightly more than half an hour. Groggy and almost silent, we clutched at lukewarm, acrid, and slightly burnt take-away coffee from the gas station. I sipped at it gratefully, appreciating having something warm to cling to.

We retraced our route from the previous afternoon, following the directions of the GPS to the RCMP detachment in 100 Mile House.

I couldn't stop shaking as we entered the building, but my shivering had nothing to do with the sleet that had pelted my face.

Malcolm squeezed my hand, and politely asked the man behind the reception desk if we needed an appointment to see Inspector Doug Chilton.

The man squinted at us, grunted, and said, "Chilton's busy."

With his friendliest smile, Malcolm asked, "Can you check to see if he'd be willing to see us? It's about a cold case. We don't mind waiting."

The receptionist waved us toward a row of stiff, metal chairs lining the wall before leaving through the door behind his desk.

I fidgeted, my gaze darting about the room, and flinched each time the double doors opened and slammed shut.

Malcolm asked if I had anything specific in mind for dinner.

I shook my head.

"If you feel like a little treat, I saw a sushi place not far from our hotel. We'd have to check to see what time they open. We haven't had sushi for awhile." Then he shrugged. "Or we can see how we feel later tonight."

"Sounds good," I said, not really processing his suggestion.

His slight grin told me he realized this. "It's gonna be fine," he said. "It's not like you're the murderer they're looking for."

He'd broken through my anxiety. I smiled in spite of myself and stuck out my tongue.

He playfully tousled my hair.

Half an hour passed before a door opened and expelled a harried-looking gentleman.

We jumped to our feet, knowing instinctively that this was Inspector Chilton. Malcolm offered his hand and introduced us. As the investigator shook Malcolm's hand, his gaze flicked to me. His eyes widened. He did a double take.

I cringed under the intensity of his scrutiny. I could see his incredulity.

I managed an awkward smile and an affirmative nod to his unspoken question. *Yes, I have the same face as the victim of the cold-case homicide you are investigating. That's why we're here.*

He ushered us into an interview room and closed the door behind us. "I'm sorry I'm not able to offer you coffee," he apologized. "The machine is broken and the instant coffee we keep on hand leaves a lot to be desire." He gave a wry chuckle.

Malcolm sat next to me and took my hand.

I appreciated the steadying calm of his grip.

"So, what can I do for you?" The inspector looked at me expectantly.

I took a deep breath. "I was adopted as a baby and raised in North Vancouver. I'm a professor of Eastern European and Russian history at a university in the Lower Mainland, and last week, during office hours, one of my students brought this to my attention." I pulled the clipping from my coat pocket and placed it on the table between us, open and smoothed over, so he could see what I had seen that sparked this crazy adventure. I added, "It was printed in a newspaper here in the Interior."

Inspector Chilton leaned forward to examine my offering. His nod told me that he was familiar with the article. He listened with a frown as I told him about the subsequent conversation with my parents. When I reached the portion of the story about being found at the Catholic Parish in Tome, his eyes lit up and a smile crossed his face. "It's you," he said, eyebrows arched. "You're the baby."

My confusion must have been evident.

Chilton grinned. "Everyone from Prince George to 70 Mile knows the story of the baby girl found in the snowstorm of December 1980."

I didn't realize I had achieved such a level of notoriety.

Malcolm jumped in. "We're interested in discovering as much as possible about the woman who left Nora behind."

"So," I concluded, off-balance and very aware of how ridiculous I sounded, "my supportive husband booked us a visit in Tome. To come here and see about my past, and hopefully to see what connection I might have to this." I gestured to the article on the table. "To Jane Doe. We're hoping you can help us make sense of it all."

Inspector Chilton had been scratching notes on a legal pad, the paper angled in such a way that I couldn't read what he was writing. Now he leaned back in his chair, elbows propped on the armrests, fingertips pressed together thoughtfully. He seemed to be mulling over my request.

I leaned forward. "Can I ask…. Jane Doe was discovered five years ago. Why did you make the investigation public now? Is this simply a matter of trying to close a cold case?"

"Yes and no." Chilton shrugged. "The investigation went cold pretty quickly, and it was only recently that our experts were able to form a realistic composite of what Jane Doe would have looked like. Unfortunately, the sketch hasn't generated any new leads. Only dead ends, I'm afraid."

"I don't know if you're allowed to tell us, but is there nothing in medical records or dental records that could help identify her?" I asked.

"Technically I'm not, but there's no harm in me telling you that efforts to identify her through official channels—including medical and dental records—have been unsuccessful."

"Which means"—I let the implication wash over me—"if she doesn't have any records here in BC—"

"Or anywhere in Canada," Chilton added.

"Then she isn't from here?" I was puzzled. "She immigrated to Canada? Is there another explanation?"

Chilton shrugged. "The only thing it tells us definitively is that she did not visit a doctor or a dentist in the country. Multiple conclusions can be drawn, but guesswork doesn't help us in this case."

I couldn't process how this detail might fit into the puzzle and made a mental note to revisit the question later.

Malcolm asked, "Have you been able to tell if Jane Doe ever had a baby? Or if she'd been pregnant?"

Chilton frowned. "I'm afraid that, as the investigation is ongoing, I can't discuss specific facts pertaining to the case." He looked at me. "I sympathize, I really do. And I do appreciate that you've come so far to see me. I'm grateful for the information."

Unabashed by the rebuff, Malcolm asked, "Can you tell us about any tips that have come in from the hotline?"

Inspector Chilton shook his head.

"Can you tell us anything at all?" I asked softly, hoping my voice didn't contain a trace of the desperation I felt at having run into a dead end.

Inspector Chilton studied my face and shook his head.

I understood his amazement; I hadn't believed my similarity to Jane Doe, either.

"You might have simply called the hotline." His voice held no trace of irritation or mockery.

My cheeks heated. "I left a message but didn't receive a call back."

The investigator grunted. "The lack of information available to the public is simply because there's an overall lack of information pertaining to the case. There's so little to go on, and after thirty years, there's very little that might be uncovered."

I nodded slowly. "I figured that might be the case when we came. The information I have doesn't really help in any way, and really, my possible connection presents more questions than answers. My resemblence"—I gestured to my face--"doesn't offer any clues as to who she was or what happened to her."

"Having a definitive DNA connection might give us a lead," Inspector Chilton mused. He scribbled something at the bottom of his legal pad, tore it off, and handed it to me. "That's the phone number and address for the medical examiner's office and the file number for the case. Call and make an appointment for a DNA test. The results will give you an answer one way or the other."

His intervention was more than I'd hoped for, and I thanked him profusely as he jotted down my contact information.

"Just one more thing," I said, staring at the slip of paper. "Will I have to call to find out the results of the test, or will you call me? Or if I hear nothing, I should assume the test was negative?"

"We'll call you in either case," he promised.

I thanked him again and took Malcolm's hand.

We had started out the door when Malcolm suddenly paused and turned back. "Excuse me, Inspector," he called over my head. "Does the local school publish year books?"

"They do, yes."

"How large is the school?"

"It's K through twelve. I'd say maybe a little over one hundred students. Kids are bused in from as far north as 130 Mile House."

"From Tome, too?" I asked.

He nodded.

Malcolm asked, "Would we be able to view the yearbooks? At the school, maybe, or the local library?"

Chilton considered. "The school has plaques of each year's graduate class hanging in the main hallway. I suppose they might have the yearbooks. If not, I would check the library here in 100 Mile."

Malcolm thanked him again and gave a friendly wave as we walked out. I scarcely noticed. I found myself wondering whether the investigator had ever considered examining the yearbooks as part of his investigation—and if not, why.

Anxious hope filled me that I might soon be staring at a school photograph of Jane Doe; in all likelihood, taken shortly before she died.

Chapter Six

ON THE WAY BACK TO THE CAR, MALCOLM SUGGESTED THAT I call the medical examiner's office to schedule the DNA appointment. Discovering if I was genetically connected to the woman was a big part of our trip's purpose, after all.

I hesitated. I was scared. The search for my birth mother—indeed, this whole trip—had seemed like such a good idea. I knew the DNA test was the only way to get definitive answers to my questions, but once it was submitted, the situation was out of my hands. Once I knew the truth, I couldn't unknow it. What might that knowledge do to me?

Malcolm smiled warmly. "We don't have to do this, babe. We can turn around and go home."

"I want to, but I don't want to. Does that make sense?"

It didn't, of course, but he nodded good-naturedly and reiterated that he wouldn't do anything without my say-so.

We reached the car and he opened the door for me. As he headed to the driver's door, I pulled my cell phone from my pocket and punched in the number.

My call was answered before I had time to prepare what I would say. I stammered through an incoherent introduction of who I was and why I was calling. The woman asked me to come the following morning—

Saturday. I blinked, a little taken aback by how quickly events were moving forward, then agreed and hung up.

Malcolm glanced at the clock on the dashboard. It was late morning. "What would you like to do next?"

I considered for a moment. "It makes sense, since we're here, to check the local school and the public library for yearbooks dating back to the early 1970s. I know we don't know for sure that Jane Doe was from around here, but it seems likely."

We reached the school's parking lot ten minutes later. The parking lot was full of cars and trucks, most of the vehicles decades old and splattered with mud. I was surprised at how small the building was, considering that it housed the town's entire student population. A playground stood to the left, a baseball diamond and bleachers to the right of it, with a basketball court sandwiched in the middle. Directly ahead of us, broad cement stairs ascended to double doors underneath arched gold lettering that announced the name of the school.

As I climbed the stairs beside Malcolm, I thought back to the schools I had attended. Each had been immaculate, with the latest equipment and technological advances to facilitate learning. Those schools stood in stark contrast to this building. What must it have been like to be a student here? And even more importantly, had my mother attended this school?

I entered the building imagining a young girl with a similar gap-toothed smile and pigtails walking this same route. I wondered what her childhood had been like—and why I was so curious, so determined to find out about her past.

The main entry was deserted except for an older woman seated behind a reception area's glass partition. Eyeing us like a hawk over her gold-framed eyeglasses, she slid the window open. "Can I help you?" Her tone left no doubt that she found our presence odd and that she held the power to deny us entry.

When I explained the reason for our visit, she pursed her thin lips. "You were hoping to look at our yearbooks," she repeated, her frown deepening.

"If it isn't too much trouble," I confirmed. I had a feeling this woman was going to deny our request but hoped that showing respect for her authority might gain her favor.

She shook her head. "Visitors are not allowed into the school while classes are in session. And even if we did, we don't keep yearbooks dated that far back in our library."

"You don't have *any* yearbooks in your library here?" I asked.

"We keep the volumes that include our current student body. This year's graduating class would have been in kindergarten in 1997, so that is the earliest yearbook we have. You'd have to look at the public library in town for years prior to that."

Malcolm stepped forward and turned on the charm. "That's incredibly helpful, thank you."

She seemed to melt.

"We were speaking with an RCMP officer this morning who mentioned that the school keeps graduation plaques with pictures of previous classes. Would they be hanging in this hallway here?" He gestured to our right.

She nodded.

"Could we take a look?"

This was permissible, apparently, so long as she accompanied us.

The graduation plaques hung on the wall at eye level, their bronze surfaces broken by neatly lined photographs of smiling teenagers. The first dated back to 1932 and held a single black and white photograph of a dozen young men and women posed on the steps in front of a different building than the one in which we stood, each dressed in the styles of that day, in the finest attire they owned. The students' first initials and last names corresponded with their positions in the photograph.

To the left of this plaque was another with a photograph of the following year's graduating class, holding a banner that proudly proclaimed "1933." Dozens more followed, down the length of the long hallway to the double doors and back on the opposite wall.

We walked slowly past classrooms and small, adjoining hallways, studying each photograph. The images reflected decades of history and change. Red poppies, Canadian flags, and men in uniform appeared during the war years. Black and white gave way to color. The current school building replaced the original one. In 1952, graduates were displayed in single headshots rather than group photographs.

I was impatient to reach the 1970's but tried not to let my eagerness show. By my calculation, my mother must have been at least fourteen or fifteen years old when I was born, which meant that the latest year she could have graduated high school was 1985. This assumed that she had graduated high school, and that she had done so from this school. Of course, she could have been much older than my estimate, which is why I stepped close to the plaque marked "1970" and scrutinized every image, looking for any face that leapt out at me.

There were three girls out of eleven graduates in 1970. I imagined each face amalgamating into mine, but I had to admit, grudgingly, that this was simply wishful thinking. None of the girls looked like me. I moved on, studying the girls in 1971, 1972, and 1973. Different girls. Same result.

I approached the latter half of the decade with growing apprehension, aware that as the years grew later, the age my mother might have been grew younger and younger. I already hated that she most likely had been a young mother, and now the likelihood of my finding a match dwindled with each passing year.

The year of my birth passed with no sign of anyone who bore a resemblance to me, who could have been Jane Doe or my mother. Then we were looking at 1981 and 1982, and I found myself wondering what my mother would have been doing during these years, when I had been learning to walk and talk. How old was she? Had she grown up and married well and begun a new family, entirely happy to forget an indiscretion from her youth? She must have been just a baby herself in 1980.

At last—1985. I scanned the faces eagerly, willing one of them to stop me in my tracks.

None did. Seven girls graduated in 1985. Three were very clearly triplets, the same face seemingly carbon-copied above three identical surnames. The fourth and fifth girls were clearly of Aboriginal descent. Girl number six was a blonde. The seventh girl's hair was red and her eyes, the wrong shape.

"She's not here," I said in dismay. I quickly perused the plaques up to the year 1990, just in case. Then with mounting dread, I rechecked the previous two decades before plunging back into the 1960s to see if I missed something. I hadn't.

"She isn't here," I said a second time, stunned.

The receptionist had been watching me with head cocked, though she politely refrained from comment. Now, she cleared her throat. "Is it possible that the girl you're looking for left high school before graduating?"

Malcolm asked, "Does that happen often?"

"It's not uncommon," she said. "Usually one every year or two, depending on what might be happening outside of school. A student might have to start working full-time to support their family, or help out with the family business, or on the farm. Or sometimes a girl gets pregnant."

I flinched, knowing that it was very possible that my mother had been one of those young women.

The receptionist either didn't notice my wince or respectfully chose to ignore it. "Some students run away to cities," she continued, "bored with small-town life. We couldn't keep teenagers in town during the 1970s. But most often, due to weather or other complications, students missed so much school by their grade eleven and twelve years that they couldn't keep up with their studies and preferred to drop out than flunk out."

So, my mother might not have graduated for any number of reasons.

Our search here had come to nothing. I thanked her for the information and for her time and started toward the main door as Malcolm asked for directions to the public library.

I knew we might not find Jane Doe at this school, but I had gotten my hopes up anyway. I couldn't pretend I wasn't disappointed or that our next stop wouldn't be another dead end, but I wasn't ready to give up. Jane Doe had a name, and I was determined to find it.

Chapter Seven

THE COLD HIT ME IN THE FACE AS I STEPPED OUTSIDE THE school. Shoulders hunched, I hurried with Malcolm across the parking lot and into the car. We sat there in silence for a few minutes while the engine warmed. Then I said, "So, she didn't graduate high school."

"She didn't graduate from high school *here*," Malcolm corrected, and added, "She might have moved away. She might have transferred to a different high school in another city. She might have dropped out to take a job or help at home."

Or she lost her life before she finished high school, the thought crossed my mind. Doubtless, the possibility had occurred to my husband.

We stopped for another round of burgers and fries on our way to the library. The cook left the pickles on mine, and I picked them out and playfully threw them at Malcolm, who stole my fries in retaliation. Shortly after noon, we arrived at the public library.

Like the school, the library was small. Originally, I thought the most striking part of 100 Mile House was the absence of big city noises, but as I stared at the library, I realized we hadn't seen a building taller than three stories since we left Vancouver.

The epitome of small-town quaintness, the library was a single-story rancher nestled alongside a grocery store, gas station, and strip mall.

Creaky wooden stairs led to a weathered wraparound porch where an old rocking chair housed a sleeping cat figurine curled up on a stack of books. Large bay windows flanked the front door.

Door chimes sounded above us as we entered. Readers scattered among standing shelves of battered books glanced up before bowing low again over their selections. The library resembled an old bookstore, or perhaps an older relative's attic, or even an antique store. Old posters of movie stars, shows, and celebrities dating back several decades hung on the walls, their colors faded by the sun. Shelves dangling from the ceiling held prototypes of toys, lunchboxes, and baseball cards from the 1940s and 50s. Another shelf displayed antique radios and cameras. A 1960s TV served as a shelf for several reading lamps from that same time period. In a far corner, a violin was displayed atop a piano that had several keys missing, both instruments covered in a layer of dust. In an alcove by a bay window stood a circulation desk holding an ancient computer.

When we entered, an older gentleman with a winning smile approached and asked if we needed help.

With a friendly smile of his own, Malcolm asked if he would mind pointing us to the collection of school yearbooks.

The man's facial expression became one of puzzled interest, but he didn't pry. "Certainly can. This is my place, and the house's been in my family for generations." With a wink, he pointed to the baseball cards and tricycle sitting on the shelf above us. "Those were mine. The others belonged to my brothers and sisters. I have an avid interest in history. Heck, I *am* history!" He spread his arms broadly and laughed.

"Very nice place you have," I said, not needing to feign enthusiasm. I would love to have a collection exactly like this, with artifacts from decades past. I could easily spend an afternoon perusing the history of each piece present.

He led us toward a nook located near the back of the house, in what must once have been the kitchen. "You are welcome to look at the yearbooks to your heart's content, but do not remove them." He stopped smiling to impress upon us the seriousness of this rule. "They are not to leave this building." The smile reappeared and he asked if he could help us find something or someone specific.

"No, thank you," Malcolm said politely.

The older man gave a slight nod and swept away to dazzle another patron.

The yearbooks were arranged in chronological order from earliest to latest, on a coffee table that looked as if it belonged in a 1950s living room. The books, spanning several decades, certainly reflected the changing years. The oldest volumes, those with the shabbiest and most worn bindings, were of plain coloring with black and white lettering and photos to match. No need to start back that far. The books became more colorful and less shoddy as the years progressed and modernity improved production.

I suggested we work backward this time, beginning with the most recent volumes. Malcolm took the odd years and I took the evens to cover more ground in less time.

Since the latest my mother reasonably could have graduated would have been 1985, and since she had been absent from that graduating class, it was easy to conclude she had left high school in 1984 or earlier. I picked up the volume for 1984 and flipped through the pages until I landed on a page displaying the grade eleven class.

I recognized some of the faces and names from the school graduation photograph. But I did not see anyone who looked like me. I flipped to the grade ten class and then the grade nine. The faces grew younger and younger, and still I didn't see anyone who looked as I had when I was a child.

Going backward through the years—1983, 1982, 1981— became something of a game to ease our tension. We watched faces slowly reverse in time, as if aging backward. We smiled at adorable kids and sympathized with missing teeth, acne, and bad haircuts. Malcolm told a funny anecdote about the year he'd decided to grow out his hair, in grade nine. I'd heard the story multiple times, the first time being from his mother, and I still thoroughly enjoyed it.

I pushed 1978 back onto the table. Beside me, Malcolm selected the 1977 volume and flipped through the grades more slowly than I had. In each book, he started on the page that showed the grade 6 class from that year, working on the premise that my mother might have conceived me very young, and that this was why she had given me up. He flipped page after page.

Then suddenly, he stopped. I heard his sharp intake of breath.

The hair on my arms stood on end. "Babe?"

Malcolm angled the volume toward me. His finger touched a photo, second row from the top, second from the right in a row of four.

In grade ten, I got braces to correct a slight overbite that, I thought, made me look a bit like a pug. I was self-conscious of my smile, so for that year's school photograph, I kept my lips closed and ducked my head slightly in embarrassment. My hair was parted to the left and hung loose, the front strands tucked behind both ears.

This photograph could have been mine. Her overbite was slightly more pronounced, and her smile fainter. No dimple in her cheek. But her cheekbones were as highly pronounced as mine, her hairline just as low, parted to the left and tucked behind her ears. Her eyes, the same shape and color as mine, stared into the middle distance.

I couldn't speak. I simply ran a finger over the face.

I had been afraid that the similarities I'd see if I finally found her would be so slight that I couldn't possibly be sure. But looking at the picture in front of me, I was certain. Maybe this woman wasn't Jane Doe, but she was related to me.

I glanced up in shock at Malcolm, who smiled, found my hand on the page, and squeezed. Wordlessly, my finger trailed to the edge of the page, where the students' names were listed. I located the third one and mouthed her name.

Marcia Garvey.

The face now had a name. Could this be my mother's name, or that of an aunt? I almost couldn't breathe, the connection felt so real, so tangible. My eyes burned with unshed tears as I scanned the page for other clues.

The top of the page announced that this was the Grade 10 Class of 1977. She was fifteen or sixteen years old.

I quickly calculated back—Marcia Garvey would have started kindergarten in 1966 or 1967, depending on when her birthday fell. I seized the corresponding ten years' worth of volumes from the table and stumbled to sit at a little desk.

Malcolm took the bottom half of the stack and began searching the kindergarten class in 1966. I opened 1976 to the grade nine class and saw Marcia Garvey's face again, albeit a year younger, staring up at me with the same shy smile.

"She's not in this one," Malcolm said, putting aside 1966.

He continued working forward and I worked backward, flipping to the grade eight class of 1975. Her picture was absent from this one, as well, and we found the same results in every other year we searched. It seemed that Marcia Garvey appeared suddenly in grade nine in 1976 in 100 Mile's school, but there was no trace of her before 1976 and no evidence of her beyond 1977.

Already, possibilities formed in my mind as I closed the final book. "She moved into the area around 1976," I guessed.

"Maybe. She could have attended other years, and maybe she just missed photo day. Got sick, maybe, or bad weather," Malcolm pointed out.

"She's not listed in any of the 'student absent' lists." I had seen multiple pages across all volumes that contained a list of students who had been absent, marked with a note of "not pictured" in parenthesis next to their name. Her name hadn't appeared in any of those lists. Marcia Garvey's first appearance had been in the grade nine class of 1976, her last as a grade ten in 1977.

"She went to another school then," Malcolm said. "Maybe in 150 Mile House, if she lived farther north in their catchment. It's the only other major town between here and Prince George."

"Or she was home schooled," I said, pulling out my notebook of research. I had three different lists on the first page. The first recorded facts we had confirmed, the second contained possibilities, and the third were unanswered questions.

"Do you want to go to 150 Mile House to see if we can find traces of her in the school there?" Malcolm asked, glancing at his watch.

"I think so."

"Probably best to go today then. The school will be closed over the weekend, and Monday is a holiday."

A quick perusal of the school district website told us that 150 Mile House had only two schools—an elementary school and a private Christian school. Malcolm pointed out that she very well could have gone to elementary school in 150 Mile, and it was worth looking into.

He had the grade ten page of 1977 open and was copying down the names of Marcia's twelve classmates from that year. He flipped to this same class in the previous year and compared the two. "The class more or less remained the same since 1966," he said.

I glanced over his shoulder and read the twelve names—Chad, Kenny, Tammy, Shelly, Kacie, Mary, Joe, Albert, Reggie, Leslie, Jackie, and Will. Any one of these people might be able to answer questions about who Marcia Garvey was, where she'd been before arriving at this school, and why she had been absent from the grade eleven and grade twelve classes. I tucked Malcolm's list into my notebook and used my phone to snap pictures of the pages, including several close-up shots of Marcia Garvey's photograph in both volumes, and the names and photographs of her classmates.

We had all the information we could get from the yearbooks. I reluctantly gathered the volumes to return them to their places on the table, feeling a strange attachment to each of them but especially to the two with Marcia Garvey's pictures. I knew I was jumping to conclusions, relying on sentiment and wishful thinking. I was letting myself grow attached to this woman without knowing for sure that she was connected to me in any way, simply because she looked so much like me and because we now had a name. There was a possibility, however slim, that Marcia Garvey was a red herring. While her connection to me fit so neatly, it would take quite a bit to prove a relationship between the two of us, and who knew what we might discover when we dug deeper.

I shook away my wistfulness and nostalgia, reminding myself not to get my hopes up.

The volumes went back onto their coffee table. I knew where they were if I wanted to return.

• • •

THE DRIVE TO 150 MILE HOUSE TOOK JUST UNDER AN HOUR. We followed Highway 97's winding curves around Cold Lake, past several small towns, including Tome, and even smaller communities that contained not much more than a few houses, a gas station, and a dilapidated fruit stand. We also drove by a seemingly abandoned cemetery inside a wrought iron fence. Its small plot held a dozen or so weathered wooden crosses that might once have been painted white. I wondered if Marcia Garvey—if that was who Jane Doe was—might eventually be buried in a cemetery like that one, once she had been properly identified.

I finally asked the question that had bothered me since I first saw the newspaper article more than a week before. "Why wouldn't her family have known she was missing?"

Malcolm started when my voice broke the silence and looked at me questioningly.

"Think about it," I said. "If either you or I went missing, our families would raise the alarm immediately. They'd be out searching for us themselves. They'd call out a hue and cry. They wouldn't rest until we were found. But her family hasn't come forward. The only one who might be searching for Jane Doe is me, the biological child she might have given up. No one else has gotten in touch to say their daughter went missing around this time."

"That we know of," Malcolm corrected. "Inspector Chilton might have located someone who is able to give him more information. Maybe he's identified her by this point."

"If that's true, then why hasn't he updated us?"

Malcolm gave me a sidelong glance. "Why haven't you called to tell him what we found out today?" he challenged.

I had no reply. I was teetering on the balance between wanting to shed light on my past and feeling safer staying in the dark. I needed more time before I plunged into the truth. Sharing Marcia Garvey's name with Inspector Chilton and the RCMP would force me to jump before I was ready.

Instead of answering Malcolm's question, I asked, "If they know who Jane Doe is, why send me for a DNA test?"

"Covering all their bases?"

I took a few minutes to wrap my head around this before going back to my original line of questioning. "But let's assume no one else has come forward. Why wouldn't they have?" I had been mulling this over, considering and discarding multiple reasons that this might be the case, and settled upon three possibilities. None were particularly pleasant.

"Maybe there just isn't anyone left to come forward," he said. "She died thirty years ago. If Jane Doe was an only child, and her parents are gone now, no one in her immediate family would be left."

He'd guessed one of the three. It depressed me to think of parents going to their graves never knowing what happened to their daughter. The loss would have been a lonely, gnawing wound that hadn't healed. My own parents came to mind, and I forced myself not to think of them.

"Surely the authorities would have begun their investigation by looking into missing persons reports from around the time Jane Doe is estimated to have died."

"True. And presumably, if her parents loved her enough to report her missing...." He broke off before saying, "You think she wasn't reported missing."

I shook my head. "The receptionist at the school mentioned that it's common for dropouts to want to escape the small town. If Jane Doe ran away to Prince George or Vancouver, her parents might not have known that she was missing." This was the second possibility I hadn't been able to discard.

"Or"—Malcolm shot me a look full of apology—"maybe they simply didn't care."

This, I felt, was the most likely reason her family hadn't come forward.

"There must have been someone who cared," I said quietly. "If not her parents, then a friend or other relative."

"Maybe not," Malcolm said gently. "If she wasn't wanted in the first place, or if there were a lot of children in the family, or if the family was poor and couldn't afford to keep her, maybe they turned her out to find her own way in the world. Maybe the family was involved in illegal activity and didn't want to contact the police. Or maybe she was raised by a single parent, and that parent died, and the siblings scattered. The possibilities are endless until we find the truth."

What happened to Jane Doe? We knew what her fate was, but what led her to end up buried in a clearing, unknown and forgotten, for thirty years? Was her family simply gone, or did they not know she was missing? Or had they simply not cared?

The kilometer markers on the green signs decreased as we went. We reached the outskirts of 150 Mile House, a town slightly larger than 100 Mile House. Billboards dotted the highway as we turned onto the off-ramp and found the main road that led to the elementary school.

At the school, we were sternly rebuffed by the woman in the front office who informed us that they did not have graduation photo plaques or keep student yearbooks in their library. Even if they did, the yearbooks wouldn't go as far back as we wanted. Furthermore, they did not release information about students who might have attended school in decades past. She also told us that 150 Mile House did not have a public library. Theirs was a distribution system linked with the public library in 100 Mile House. All physical books were kept there, and she recommended we might have luck searching their high school yearbooks.

With nothing more to learn, we thanked her and left.

At the Christian elementary school on the other side of town, the response to our inquiries was much the same. They did not keep yearbooks of the current student body, and as they were a private institution, their yearbooks would not be included in the distribution system linked with 100 Mile House. Unless we could contact someone who attended the school around the time we were interested in, we wouldn't be able to access their yearbooks.

We'd hit a dead end with this line of inquiry, and we left 150 Mile House shortly after we arrived.

Malcolm suggested we call it a day, and I was exhausted enough to agree. It was late afternoon when we left 150 Mile House, and it seemed practical to relax for a few hours in the hotel and review tomorrow's plans.

As we retraced our route to Tome, I pulled my notebook from my pocket and flipped to the page containing the names from Marcia

Garvey's grade nine and grade ten classes. "Do you think any of these people might be in the phone book?" I mused.

"It's worth a shot," Malcolm said.

As we trekked through the lobby of our hotel, I stopped at the desk and asked the clerk if he had a phone book we could borrow. He produced a yellowed book from a drawer underneath the desk and told us that we could keep it, as the hotel had several.

The phone book was the most recent edition, and covered the region along Highway 97 from 70 Mile House to 130 Mile House, spanning perhaps a width of fifty kilometers on either side. Its cover displayed names like Lone Butte, Cold Lake, Interlakes, Tome, Horse Lake, and Forest Grove. Even covering such vast territory, the book was only slightly more than an inch thick.

A thought occurred to me. Turning back to the clerk, I asked if they had any previous editions. After a few minutes of rifling through boxes behind his desk, he withdrew a water-stained and crumpled volume from 1982.

I thanked him again and followed Malcolm to the stairwell up to our room on the second floor. Malcolm collapsed onto the bed and stretched out. A few minutes later, he suggested we send out for a pizza and relax while catching up on the highlights of the day's Olympic events.

Later than night, unable to sleep, I placed the list of classmates from the high school yearbooks on the room's table, then began flipping through the older phone book. If the students' names didn't appear in this edition, they probably wouldn't be listed decades later.

I found several in the older phone book. Elated though I was at my luck, I reminded myself that they weren't necessarily the same people, and those people I reached might not answer my inquiries. Turning to the newer edition, I wrote down all the corresponding addresses I could find and was rewarded when I saw that only one address had changed in the intervening years. Once I exhausted my list, on a whim, I flipped to the Gs and scanned the phone books until I found "Garvey." I located a single entry in the older phone book: Todd and Louise Garvey. I wrote down their address, as well, ignoring my excitement that this couple could be my grandparents or an aunt and uncle.

I needed to relax, but was too restless to sleep. For lack of anything more productive to do, I turned to a blank notebook page and began drafting a letter to everyone on my list. I started by introducing myself and explaining who I was. Then I faltered.

When it came to explaining why I was contacting them and how I'd learned their names, I was at a loss. I was also very conscious that I didn't have all the facts, and that I was prying into the lives and pasts of total strangers, none of whom were obligated to respond to me. After all, they might not know anything about Marcia, or if they did, might prefer to keep that knowledge to themselves, especially if it cast them or Marcia in a bad light. I set aside my pen and notebook. Then I pulled out my laptop and researched what I could find about the hospital I would be attending the next day, along with the RCMP detachment in 100 Mile House and the Parish of St. Raymond Ignatius in Tome.

Although I was exuberant at our productivity, I recognized that these tasks were distracting me from facing the long-buried secrets and tragedy of my past. I couldn't bear the thought of another sleepless night chasing the same macabre thoughts, and hoped I was exhausted enough to fall into a dreamless sleep.

Tomorrow, we had the DNA test scheduled in 100 Mile House, and then planned to visit the Parish of St. Raymond Ignatius in Tome.

Chapter Eight

The next morning, Malcolm drove us to 100 Mile House while clutching a coffee. Halfway there, I pulled out my notebook and reviewed everything we had learned the previous day, though I had mulled over the new information all through the sleepless night. I also memorized the file number given to us by Inspector Chilton, and only stopped repeating the digits when we pulled into the parking lot of 100 Mile House's hospital.

From the night's research, I learned that the hospital was built in the 1970s after the previous medical complex was torn down. The stark white, four-story building bore maroon and sea-green accents typical of 1970s architecture. We exited the car and followed signs to the main entrance.

Inside, we took an elevator to the basement office where I filled out the necessary paperwork, then we followed a lab assistant into an examination room. She handed me two fresh cotton swabs and demonstrated how to collect the samples from inside my cheek. "We always take two," she explained. "Just in case."

I did as instructed, and dropped the damp swabs into plastic vials labeled with my name, date of birth, and file number. She twisted the lids securely shut and said, "That's it. We'll contact you with the results in seven to ten weeks."

After so much nervous anticipation, the process was over with quickly. I blinked several times. "Will you contact me even if the results are negative?"

She seemed surprised by my question, but nodded, then held open the door.

That was our cue to be on our way. I hastily thanked her before walking with Malcolm back out the glass doors and down the hall toward the elevator.

There. It was done. The next steps were completely out of my hands. This prospect both relieved me and made me anxious.

Back inside the car, Malcolm gave me a reassuring smile. "Ready?"

I nodded. We had everything we could get from 100 Mile House.

Malcolm pulled out of the parking space and headed toward Tome.

It was almost noon when we arrived in Tome. I wondered if anyone would be at the Parish at this hour.

The Parish of St. Raymond Ignatius was a white, one-story building with green trim and a long ramp leading up to its main entrance. Its weathered siding was clean, just as the lawn was neat and trimmed, but showed several bald spots. The faithful no doubt loved this place.

I wondered what it was about this church that made a mother—my mother—decide to leave her infant daughter here, certain she would be found quickly and cared for. Had there been lights shining through the window, visible through the winter storm?

Malcolm parked and turned off the engine. "Are you ready?"

I smiled wryly. "This is all a bit dramatic, isn't it?"

"It doesn't have to be if you don't want it to be." He looked at the church. "It's a start, being here. Just don't be too disappointed if it isn't what you expect."

On those words, I summoned my courage and stepped out of the car, inhaling the chill deep into my lungs to steady myself.

We stood at the bottom of the long, sloping ramp, staring up at the doors. The wind rattled tree branches, lifted my hair, and bit my neck, while I tried to put myself into the place of the woman who had brought me here thirty years ago. Had that young mother been Marcia Garvey? What had been her hopes, her fears, as she'd stood in this same place almost thirty years before?

I imagined her dark figure in front of us, stealing closer and closer to the stoop through the blowing snow while casting furtive glances left and right. Did she scoop snow off the threshold before placing her baby there? Was I crying, or was I sleeping in the warmth of the blankets I had been wrapped in?

Perhaps it wasn't my mother who left me here. Maybe my father did, or one of my grandparents, or perhaps a close friend who had helped and supported my mother through a secret pregnancy and birth.

I started up the ramp. Ten steps from the door. Now five. Now three. Malcolm followed a step behind me.

When I was close enough to touch the doors, I stopped and turned to look back down the ramp, imagining a crying infant at my feet and marveling at what the unknown woman must have thought and felt as she walked away.

This is where I had been left and found. I stood in the same spot where I had lain, snow falling around me. Awkward and vulnerable, I fought an urge to make a joke to cover my unease. I looked at Malcom with uncertainty.

He reached my side and gripped my arm." Are you all right?" he asked.

I shrugged. "I'm not sure."

I didn't know what I had been hoping or expecting. I certainly hadn't expected this detachment. I could only stare down the ramp and into the distance, wondering where she, he, or they had gone after leaving me here. How long had I laid on this stoop before someone found me? What did the person who left me think as they walked away?

In that moment, I wished I had never seen the article. I wished to be back home in Vancouver, enjoying the reading break, wearing pajamas, sipping tea, and marking assignments while the TV broadcast the Olympics in the background. What had possessed me to come?

Malcolm shifted beside me as if sensing the change in my mood. "We don't have to stay," he murmured. "We can get in the car and go back home."

I shook my head. We had come this far. It seemed silly to not complete the task now that we were here. I turned, reached for the handle, and pulled open the heavy metal door.

We entered a narrow, deserted hallway that encompassed a reception desk and several closed doors. A handful of chairs lined the wall. A sign on the far wall pointed the way to the sanctuary. A distant murmur of voices indicated the presence of others.

We crossed to the sanctuary. Inside, a handful of people sat scattered throughout the pews that lined either side of a long aisle. The aisle ended at the altar and a podium mounted on a dais. The tiled floor and paneled walls were stark white, contrasting the dark wood of the pews, and the confessional booth to the right of the altar. Along the opposite wall stood a series of collapsible tables lined with candles. Some were lit and some were not.

I surveyed the scene and lifted my gaze to the high ceiling, which was adorned with paintings that represented stained glass windows. The effect was soothing.

Malcolm's hand slipped from mine. He stepped to the small well of water near the doors, dabbed his fingers, and crossed himself—his parents were devout Catholics—then turned his attention to the row of tables.

I couldn't see exactly what he was fixated on. I followed him.

He approached a table and pointed to a tall, lit candle elevated above the others by a silver holder. Before the candle sat a silver plaque engraved with fancy script and a pen beside a guest book.

The silver glimmered as if freshly polished and the candle looked fresh. "Someone must be lighting a new candle every day," Malcolm marveled.

Nodding, I leaned in and read the engraving.

Baby Judea - December 2, 1980.

"This baby has the same birthday as me," I murmured. Not until I reread the words did understanding hit. My jaw dropped. Gooseflesh rose on my arms.

This baby had the same birthday as me…because this baby *was* me.

"It's me. Malcolm, this memorial is for me, and they gave me a name." Unbidden, tears sprang to my eyes. More to distract myself than anything, I opened the leather-bound cover of the guest book and read the prayer neatly printed on the first page:

Most Holy Saint Jude, Martyr and Apostle, unyielding companion and servant to Christ Jesus, intercessor to all who seek to place themselves in your care in difficult times, we ask your intervention as the patron saint of hope. We ask that you pray for Baby Judea, now and in her time of need. Send comfort in her despair, courage in her trials, and wholeness in her suffering. We revere your promise to all who believe, and we praise Almighty God with you. We promise our faithfulness to you and our devotion to you as Baby Judea's patron in hope. Amen.

Beside me, Malcolm murmured, "The Patron Saint of desperate cases."

I clenched my jaw and breathed deeply to stave off the sobs that threatened.

They named me after him. As I read the entries on the pages that followed—thirty years' worth of prayers, well wishes, hopes, and thoughts—I realized that the entire church had adopted me. Each and every entry was dated. Members of the congregation prayed for my health and well-being. They prayed for my parents. They sent birthday wishes every year on December 2nd. As recently as a few months ago, several different hands wished me a happy twenty-ninth birthday and said a prayer for my continued happiness and success.

I stared at the flame of the candle for a long moment. Such a gesture meant so much more to me than I ever could have imagined. Had my birth really touched so many? Had I really mattered to so many people? Had these people really prayed for me, for my recovery, for my life? The most recent entry, dated nine days ago, prayed for my health and well-being.

I've never tended to displays of emotion and sentiment, a stoicism I learned from my dad. But now, I broke into sobs and cried hysterically for the next few minutes, overcome by the compassion and love shown to me by strangers who, when I hadn't had a name, gave me one so I would never be forgotten.

Malcolm wrapped an arm around me and half carried me to the nearest pew. I could imagine the people in the sanctuary casting glances at me.

Through tears, I tried to explain to Malcolm that I wasn't angry or sad, simply overwhelmed by the response of so many well-wishers. For more than twenty-nine years, members of this church had been waiting for me to find it again, had been waiting for me to come home.

I hadn't intended to break down, so I hadn't brought anything with which to wipe my face. Malcolm suggested that we step outside to get some air. I agreed, hoping the cold air would help me regain control.

A woman now sat at the reception desk outside the sanctuary. She jumped up as we neared. "Welcome to our humble parish! I haven't seen you here before." She looked more closely at me. "Are you all right?"

Malcolm, ever my anchor, explained that I'd become a bit emotional when I saw the candle lit for the baby.

The woman nodded, then surprised us by saying, "Such a sweet little thing she was. I remember the day she was found, as if it happened yesterday."

This stopped me cold in my tracks. "You were here when the baby was found?"

"Certainly! Held her and everything," the woman said proudly. She came around her desk and held out her hand. "I'm Una Braithwaite."

I recognized her name. After I was found, Mrs. Braithwaite had been interviewed by several newspapers. She spoke on behalf of the congregation, and appealed directly to the woman who had given birth to the newborn. She had held me as a baby.

Malcolm took her hand and introduced us. "You must be the Father's secretary," he said tactfully,

Mrs. Braithwaite beamed. "Indeed, I've served here at the Parish for almost forty years now." She tilted her head. "You must be new in town. Everyone who lives here knows the story of the baby girl discovered in Tome in the snowstorm of 1980."

Yes, I thought. The guestbook gave evidence of this.

"I would be happy to tell you the story," she offered. She ushered us to the row of chairs lining the wall and we sat, Malcolm between us, as she began. "I can't believe it's been thirty years."

"Was the current Father here then?"

"Father Clement? Oh no. He's only been here...." She rolled her eyes to the ceiling, squinted, then frowned. "Eight or nine years. Back in 1980, Father Patrick was our priest, God rest his soul. He wasn't here that night."

"Were you?"

She bit her lower lip and shook her head, seeming almost disappointed. "Not when she was found, no. Poor little dear. If I had been here, we might have discovered her sooner. But, see"—she leaned forward conspiratorially—"there was a snowstorm that day, and Father Patrick—God rest him—sent everyone home early. I left late that morning, and Father Patrick cancelled choir practice that afternoon before retiring to the rectory." She pointed out the far window to a rundown building on the edge of the property.

"That's the original rectory, and hasn't been used since he passed, God rest him. Father Jessup—he came after Father Patrick passed—started living in the new rectory on 1st Street. The original rectory was built at the time of the original church, in 1876. Of course, that church burned down after a lightning storm back in...well, it must have been '73 or '74."

I nodded politely.

"But let's see, 1980. The only one here at the church that evening was Bernard, our caretaker—his son took over from him years ago—and he found the little girl. He arrived just as I was leaving and found the baby in the late afternoon, so we can only guess how long she was there or when she'd been left. Drifting snow had filled in any footprints. It was a Tuesday. And the way Bernard told it, he'd locked up the church and started walking away when he heard the cries, faintly, over the wind. Thought it was a cat at first and took him a bit of searching to find her. But then he saw the bundle and realized it wasn't a cat. Well, he scooped her up and brought her inside quick as you please, and hugged her to his chest to keep her warm and comfort her. He had seven children of his own, he and Mrs. Beardsley. And first thing, he calls my house. The rectory didn't have a phone," she explained. "My husband drove as fast as he could in the snow to get us back here, and I held the poor dear and rocked her while the men started calling folks. Word spread like wildfire! Even in the snow, we had Doc Wilby and Ms. Bain —she's a nurse—come all the way over. They called the police before the storm took down the lines.

"We don't have a hospital here in town," she went on, almost apologetically, "and back then we didn't have any medical facilities to care for a baby, at all, really. It was two of our emergency volunteers who decided they were going to drive through the night, through the storm, to get her to the hospital in Prince George. Got her there just in time, too, we found out. She was such a sweet thing, and so small, and so sickly. They think she was premature and dehydrated and might have had frostbite. We were all so afraid she wouldn't make it," she confided sadly.

She did, and she's sitting in front of you, I thought, but I couldn't bring myself to say it. I just wasn't ready to reveal that the story she was telling was my story.

"We stayed here most of the night and into the morning. Father Patrick opened up the sanctuary for an all-night vigil, praying to the Lord and the Blessed Mother and all the saints to intercede on her behalf."

I thought I saw tears in her eyes.

"The next morning, we got word that they'd made it. The police started searching best they could for the mother, but they had to wait till the next day for the storm to subside. By then, any trace had been erased and we never found her. We heard the baby went to wonderful parents and moved away, but we never heard of her again."

She fell silent and looked at us expectantly, and I offered a guttural, "What a story." All the while she had been speaking, the name and face of Marcia Garvey had floated in front of me. I was reminded of how quickly Inspector Chilton had recognized my features the day before. I wondered if someone in the community might possibly recognize me, as well. We hadn't yet eliminated the possibility that my biological mother was from Tome or the surrounding area. "Do you remember what the baby was wearing when you found her? Or what she was wrapped in?"

"Oh, heavens yes!" Mrs. Braithwaite exclaimed. "I remember because she wasn't wearing hardly anything, really. She had a towel for a diaper and was wrapped in a girl's t-shirt and a girl's coat. We always figured the mother must have been young and poor, but no one was able to find her. We don't think she was from around here. But we don't know where she came from or where she went."

I began fitting these pieces into my partially formed puzzle. My mother was young and poor and hadn't been prepared for my arrival.

"Mr. Braithwaite and I wanted to take her, poor thing," she added. "We never did have children. But in a way, she belonged to the whole town. We all adopted her, and we still pray for her. I change the candle and light the new one every morning and clean the wax and buff the name plaque. Father Patrick—rest in peace—started the practice the day she was found, and Father Jessup continued the tradition."

"Why 'Judea'?" I asked after a moment of quiet introspection.

"It rather fits, don't you think? Father Patrick declared that no child of God is a lost cause."

I felt a rush of affection for the old priest who had loved me so much, for the paramedics who had driven through the night, for the caretaker who had found me, for this woman who had held me and comforted and warmed me. Without warning, tears rushed to my eyes again and I wiped desperately at my cheeks.

"Oh dear, please don't cry," Mrs. Braithwaite urged. "I'm sure Baby Judea has had a loving and cherished life."

I could have admitted that I was the baby she had held thirty years ago, tiny and helpless and not expected to live. I could have confirmed that I'd been raised by two loving people and given a happy home and a successful future. But I couldn't bring myself to speak, to reveal my secret to this woman. Instead, I rose abruptly and pulled her into a hug.

"I don't know what's the matter with me," I said, addressing the deep concern evident on her face. "I'm sorry for being so forward. But thank you for taking the time to tell us this story." Then I turned to Malcolm with a watery smile. "I want to leave a note in the guest book in the sanctuary. I'll be back in a few minutes."

As I stepped away from them, a question occurred to me and I turned. "What is Mr. Braithwaite's name?"

"John," she said in surprise.

"And do you remember the names of the men who drove the baby to the hospital?" I knew Thomas Chance's name from the articles Mom had given me but had never learned the second man's name. This seemed the safest way to ask without evoking questions I wasn't prepared to answer.

She considered for a moment. "Thomas Chance and Michael Plummer."

I thanked her again.

I left Malcolm there with her and returned to the sanctuary, passed the pews, and hesitated before I headed for the candle that burned for Baby Judea. I picked up the pen next to the guestbook, flipped to the next available page, and scrawled my message to the family I hadn't realized I had here.

I came seeking and received the most loving and gracious welcome. I am overwhelmed and humbled by your caring thoughts and loving prayers for my health, happiness, and well-being. I wish to give my most humble thanks to each and every one of you who have cared for me in every way since the day you first found me. I would especially like to honor Father Patrick, Bernard Beardsley, and John and Una Braithwaite for rescuing me and ensuring I would never be forgotten. I would also like to thank Dr. Wilby and Ms. Bain, and to honor Michael and Thomas for driving through the storm during great peril to ensure my life could be saved. Thank you to the medical staff at Prince George Hospital for giving me life, and to Dr. Bradley for giving me a future. I will never forget you. With deepest respect and the humblest of appreciation,

I signed the message "Baby Judea" and added "February 2010."

To the farthest left of the table rested a stack of fresh candles and a donation box. I dropped all the change I had in my wallet into the box, lit a new candle, and set it beside Baby Judea's. Then I wrote a name on the card that would accompany it: Jane Doe. I silently promised to never forget Jane Doe, even if it turned out she wasn't related to me. Somewhere, she'd had family, someone who cared for her, and who must have wondered what had happened to her.

None of us wants to be forgotten. Everyone wants to be remembered. She and I were joined in solidarity.

Chapter Nine

I FULLY EXPECTED TO LIE AWAKE THAT NIGHT, MULLING over what we'd discovered. Instead, both Malcolm and I slept soundly until after sunrise. I awoke feeling better rested than I had in days.

Malcolm was already sitting up in bed next to me, flipping through my notebook, casting an occasional glance at the TV. A map lay across his lap as well, which bore several pencil marks of a hiking route to a giant X. I recognized the X as the location where Jane Doe had been discovered. It would take us perhaps three hours to reach the site, but we were both experienced hikers and in good shape, and had sturdy hiking boots, weather-appropriate attire, and backpacks.

It wasn't supposed to rain, but the overcast sky bore a scattering of dark clouds. I tucked a slicker into my pack just in case, next to our granola bars, water bottles, and Malcolm's folded map.

Over cereal, yogurt, and juice, Malcolm broached the subject of the letter I'd begun drafting two nights prior. He suggested, "What if you included something to the effect of, 'I respect your privacy and understand if you don't wish to speak with me, but I would appreciate any information you might be able to share about Marica Garvey'? It gives the option of opening dialogue about her childhood, her family, her home life, and whether they knew were she went after high school while still being respectful. If they don't want to talk, they won't answer."

His line conveyed everything I wished to say but hadn't been able to phrase. I quickly jotted it in the notebook underneath my scribbles before we left the hotel room.

I babbled about inconsequential things on the drive to the lake. I needed to keep from thinking about where we were going and the reason we were going there. The realization that I was in Tome, the place of my birth, looking for information about my biological family, terrified me. This venture was a drastic departure from the comfortable, predictable life we had built together. As with our visit to the church on the previous day, I didn't feel ready to face the fact that I would soon be standing over Jane Doe's shallow grave, but I felt that we had come too far to go back without seeing the site for ourselves. This was the next step, regardless of how difficult it was.

I desperately wanted this puzzle solved so we could go home and fall back into our comfortable routine. To this end, I grasped for the easiest solution, which was that Jane Doe was Marcia Garvey, and Marcia Garvey was my mother. All that remained was to prove this was true, and in my mind, that was a minor detail.

Of course, I had no reason to feel so confident about my belief. I was relying on a gut feeling and wishful thinking. I clung to this solution fiercely because it required the least amount of effort, and because it neatly explained everything we had found thus far. The DNA test would prove that Jane Doe was my mother, and then we would find a way to prove that Jane Doe was Marcia Garvey. I couldn't put my obsession to rest and return to the life I'd suspended for Jane Doe until I had the answers I sought.

I looked forward to the physical exertion of the hike. We parked in the gravel lot just north of the campsites on the northern edge of the lake. Our route would take us through the campgrounds and into the underbrush.

The provincial park was much like any forest in the dead of February. Snow lay in frozen clumps, littered with plant debris and animal tracks. The campground entrance was gated for the season, but we skirted the metal bars and passed through the deserted campsites. Cabins dotted the gravel road to our right, and to our left, we caught glimpses of the lake through the bare trees. I could imagine how magnificent this place was in summertime.

Malcolm took the lead and set an easy pace on the worn trail. I followed on his heels, growing impatient, wanting him to walk faster. More than once, he reminded me that our trek wasn't a race, but I wouldn't have stopped even for water if he hadn't made me.

We trekked through the abandoned grounds to an unpaved utility road. Malcolm climbed over the barrier and waited, ready to assist me if needed, but I hauled myself over and dropped to the ground. As we walked, I searched for signs of life. Occasionally, a bird called, and the wind rattled barren branches, sounds barely audible above the crunch of snow under our boots. We might be alone in the world.

After walking for perhaps an hour, we left the utility road and plunged through underbrush onto a footpath.

After another hour, Malcolm studied the map again, then led us through a break in the trees toward the lake's southern shore.

I took comfort in the fact that Jane Doe had laid in such a serene, beautiful place. Even though the landscape was gray and bleak with deep winter, the lake was surrounded by distant purple mountains covered with white caps of snow. The calm, reflective surface of the lake was incredibly soothing.

Malcolm stopped for a water break.

The occasional rumble of passing traffic drifted through the silence of our surroundings. I glimpsed patches of ice in the shallows close to shore. I might have enjoyed the scenery more if not for the reason we made this hike.

"How are you doing?" he asked.

"I wish I could turn my brain off," I admitted. "I just can't stop thinking."

"At least it's beautiful out here."

I appreciated his attempt to reassure me.

He checked his watch. "We're about two-thirds through our hike, give or take. You okay to keep going?" The sun's glow barely pierced the cloud cover, which cast the landscape in tired, pale light.

I nodded and hoisted my backpack a little higher on my back.

The last portion of the hike veered off the beaten path. As we struggled through dense underbrush, angry red welts and scratches appeared on our faces and the exposed skin on our necks. I'd be sore later, but now, I welcomed the effort of dodging and avoiding branches. The activity distracted me from the dark thoughts crowding my mind. Still, relief flooded me when we stumbled into a clearing. Tired, sweaty, and panting, we squatted and rested for a few minutes before getting our bearings.

"This is it," Malcolm said softly, staring at the map. "It's *this* clearing."

Malcolm's declaration left me stunned. I hadn't expected to arrive so abruptly.

I scrutinized our surroundings. The clearing photographed in 2005 wasn't this overgrown in brush.

"Where?" I asked quietly.

Malcolm pointed to a spot to our right.

The cedar trees had been cut down. Their stumps, several feet in diameter, rose a foot or two above the ground. The missing trees must have stood there for centuries before the discovery of Jane Doe. When had they been cut down? The stumps' exposed surfaces were weathered, so the trees' removal hadn't been recent. Indeed, a quick glance around told me that we were likely the first to come here in a long time. Perhaps the first visitors since the authorities left five years ago, taking their clues and evidence and her remains with them.

How had the killer found this place—well away from any regularly traveled road or path? Had Jane Doe been alive when he brought her here?

Chills raised the hairs on my arms and neck. I abruptly stood up.

I wanted to flee, but instead, slowly approached the tree stumps. I stared at the ground where the earth dipped just enough to form a shallow trench.

I looked around for Malcolm. He hovered close enough that I knew he was there if I needed him, but he gave me enough space for a quiet moment of reverent contemplation.

I returned my gaze to the trench. Other than the slight depression, no trace remained that anyone had ever been here—not the girl who had been buried in this spot, nor the men who found her, nor the authorities who retrieved her remains and searched for clues of her identity and fate.

I brushed the soggy leaf rot and strewn branches away from the hollow, then looked around the overgrown clearing. The need to do something to mark this moment, the significance of this space, tugged urgently at me. I began to collect the few stones within arm's reach and stack them into a pile.

"What are you doing?" Malcolm asked.

My actions must have answered his question, for he stooped and began picking up more of the weathered, flat gray stones that sparingly littered the ground.

I knew the gesture was silly and sentimental. The cairn we built, exposed to the weather and wildlife, would eventually fall. Still, I needed to do something to show that Jane Doe hadn't been forgotten. Her life had passed so quickly and ended so abruptly. No one seemed to remember her or miss her or even know who she was. But none of us want to believe that our lives are so insignificant that our passing isn't noticed by anyone.

We laid the foundation in the shallow trench where Jane Doe had lain for so long, and perhaps even spent her last moments alive on earth.

I positioned the final stone and gestured to Malcolm that I was through. The rough structure stood slightly less than half a meter tall. Like the surroundings, the cairn was cold and hard, but not desolate. Its significance gave the structure a warmth and comfort I hoped Jane Doe might appreciate.

I stared in silence for a few minutes. I did not want to think of Jane Doe's final moments. In the dark hours of recent mornings, when I lay awake, unable to sleep, I had pictured this clearing a hundred times. I imagined the dark night she might have been brought here. In my mind's eye, that night was cold and raining, ominous and frightening, and in my nightmares, a hulking figure silently stole into the clearing, abandoned the girl, erased the evidence of his crime, and skulked away into the gloom.

I couldn't rid myself of that image now.

A sudden gust whipped about me, sending shivers through my body and returning me to the present. Several twigs and leaves blew past. A leaf snagged between two of the stones. I looked up. A storm cloud blocked out the weak sunlight. The place lost its peaceful, beautiful feeling. In the gray bleakness of the day, with debris blowing about, the clearing became the place of my nightmares, ominous and threatening, isolated and full of despair.

Malcolm stepped forward and embraced me from behind, arms wrapped securely around my waist. As I inhaled his familiar scent, I pictured our home back in Vancouver with its comforting accents and familiar furniture, all of which we'd picked out together. I thought of the cookbooks and wine glasses on the shelves in the kitchen. I thought of the pictures on the walls. Our home, peaceful and cozy. It was where I felt safe, with my husband beside me and my parents nearby.

"I want to go home," I mumbled, sounding like a child even to myself.

Malcolm turned me to face him and searched my face.

I couldn't stop the tears that fell. "I want to go home," I repeated.

He nodded. "We can check out this afternoon and be in Vancouver tonight, if you want."

I knew he was offering this option for my benefit, that he dreaded driving six hours after our long day of hiking.

"Tomorrow will be soon enough," I said, wiping my eyes on the back of my sleeve. I refused to look around the clearing again as we left. Instead, I concentrated on the forest floor until we reached the utility path. There, I accepted Malcolm's proffered hand. He held on tight and didn't let go until we reached the parking lot.

We checked out of the hotel early the next morning. I didn't look back as we left Tome, and barely glanced up as we passed through Cold Lake and then 100 Mile House. I ached to get back to the life we had built for ourselves, a life that made sense and fit together neatly. I wanted to immerse myself again in everything that was routine and normal and comfortable. I wanted to forget about Jane Doe and Marcia Garvey and all we had learned, and to forget that I'd ever seen that newspaper article. I knew that wasn't possible, but even for a few hours, I needed to not think about it.

When we arrived home, I welcomed the familiar smells of fresh paint, thick carpet, and lightly scented air freshener that greeted us when we trekked up the three flights of stairs and down the hallway to our condo. The smells were so much more comforting than I had realized.

As soon as we stepped inside the condo, I found an inner reserve of energy. I pulled a bag of soup from the freezer to thaw for supper, gathered soiled clothes from our duffel bags, started the washing machine, and found other mundane chores to do that kept me from dwelling on the trip.

Malcolm had been incredibly supportive and encouraging, but I could tell he was reaching the end of his energy. He needed some time to himself, particularly after the long drive. I didn't mind when he stretched out on the couch to watch an old movie.

I poured a glass of wine and selected a book from my bedside table— a romance novel loaned to me by a friend who'd been going through a trial separation. I curled up next to Malcolm and tried to lose myself in the story. When my mind wandered, I whispered aloud the words on the page to disengage from the intruding thoughts. I was determined to put Jane Doe on pause for the rest of the evening.

Shortly before dinner, I realized that my parents would want to know we had made it home safely, and I dutifully called and spoke with them. Dad was interested in the facts we had discovered. I relayed all we had found to be true, what we suspected to be true, and what we still needed to determine. Mom was more concerned with how I was holding up, and I reluctantly admitted that I was emotionally exhausted and needed a break from the puzzle of Jane Doe, at least for the night. Mom would have been content to make suggestions and trade theories all night, but, luckily, Dad picked up on my reluctance and started winding down the conversation.

Tomorrow I would begin again, I told myself. I would start tracking down the individuals belonging to the names we had found. Then I would make time to write and send the letters I'd drafted. No other viable course of action lay available to me, and maybe this in itself would prove to be a good thing.

But tonight, I simply wanted the comfort of Malcolm's arms and a warm cup of soup.

Chapter Ten

Malcolm left for work late Monday morning, having taken the first few hours of the day off after so strenuous a weekend. I woke briefly when he kissed me goodbye, and though still groggy, I hovered between sleep and wakefulness for another hour before giving up on sleep.

After a shower meant to invigorate me, I poured a cup of coffee and carried it to the kitchen island, where my laptop was plugged in, positioned beside the notebook.

A new plan had started to take shape as I drifted to sleep the night before. The first step that made sense to me was to search for Marcia Garvey. If I could find her alive and well, or find some recent trace of her, I could eliminate the possibility that she was Jane Doe. That might also answer the question of whether she had given birth to me thirty years ago.

Barring any success finding Marcia Garvey, I would proceed to the second step. I had thirteen points of contact: all twelve of Marcia Garvey's classmates, as well as the Garveys I found in the phone book. I would try to find both physical and email addresses for all the names and send letters to everyone. I had copied down a few addresses from the phone book, which greatly encouraged me.

I searched social media for Marcia Garvey and found a woman of the same name living in a small town in England. Her profile picture showed a white-haired woman with a small dog. Her advanced age and location left no doubt that she couldn't be the woman I sought.

I plugged Marcia's name into several internet search engines. The new matches didn't uncover any clues or trace of a Marcia Garvey that looked like me—not an engagement announcement, a census, or an obituary. I reminded myself that this lack of presence on the internet didn't necessarily mean anything. If Marcia Garvey was alive, she would be approaching the age of fifty. That alone might explain her lack of presence on social media.

For the sake of thoroughness, I checked newspaper archives of publications from Prince George to Vancouver, including 150 Mile House, Tome, Cold Lake, and 100 Mile House. I hoped to find a birth announcement or a transfer of property that mentioned her, but her name did not appear.

I crossed Marcia Garvey's name off my contact list and repeated the same process with the next entry on my list, Todd and Louise Garvey. Their names appeared together in the phone book, and they had the same physical address, so it was easy to conclude that they were husband and wife. I quickly discovered that neither Todd nor Louise Garvey had a social media account or an email address. Given their lack of internet presence, in tandem with their appearance in the older edition of the phone book, I assumed they were elderly. Perhaps they were Marcia's parents–or maybe my grandparents. If this were true, they would be quite advanced in years.

I searched for them in the various media archives and found Louise Garvey's obituary in an edition published in 150 Mile House. The article stated that she was born in 1915 in 100 Mile House and resided there her whole life, passing away in 1970 from heart failure. She was survived by Todd, her husband of thirty-five years, and her two children, Allan and Eleanor Garvey.

I added Allan and Eleanor to my list and scratched out their mother's name. Louise had been dead for more than forty years and besides, she was too old to have been Marcia Garvey's mother, if Marcia had indeed been born in 1960.

Todd Garvey's obituary appeared in the same publication in 1986. He lived his eighty-one years in 100 Mile House and passed away due to complications from diabetes. He was a noted citizen of 100 Mile House; his many achievements and contributions to the community listed under a black and white photograph of a man with a rather stern smile. Allan and Eleanor were mentioned in this obituary, as well, though the article noted that Allan Garvey had predeceased his father in 1974.

I scratched off Todd's name, noted that Eleanor Garvey had married sometime between 1970 and 1986, and added her married name, Reinhardt, to my list.

I turned my attention to the son, Allan Garvey. Already knowing that he had passed away in 1974, I looked for any information about his short life. Did he marry and have children? Where had he lived? What was the cause of death and where did he die? I could find neither an obituary nor any other mention of the adult Allan in any archives. Save for a birth announcement in 1939, his name was entirely absent, as was information regarding family or descendants.

Reaching a dead end after unearthing such a strong lead frustrated me. I was working on the premise that Marcia Garvey was descended from either Allan or Eleanor. In 1960, when Marcia was born, Allan was twenty-one years old and Eleanor was sixteen. I wanted Allan to be Marcia's father rather than her uncle. The thought of a sixteen-year-old Eleanor bearing a child didn't sit well with me. It also didn't explain why, if Marcia was Eleanor's daughter, she was given her mother's maiden name. If Marcia was conceived out of wedlock, hasty efforts would have been made to cover up the circumstances of her birth. While such things don't matter as much now, they carried heavy stigma in the 1960s and 1970s.

I reached for the phone book and flipped to "R." Three different listings for Reinhardt were recorded, though none included first names or initials. I copied all three addresses under Eleanor's name, then typed her name into my search browser. Though she was advanced in years, it was possible that she had a social media account. One Eleanor Reinhardt popped up, but she currently studied at a university on the prairies. A publication in 100 Mile House announced Eleanor's engagement to George Reinhardt in July 1971, and the same publication announced the births of three children to the couple, in 1973, 1975, and 1979.

Eleanor Garvey Reinhardt would receive only a letter then, not an email or social media request. I thought perhaps hers was the most promising prospect to gain information regarding Marcia.

I took a break for lunch and a short power nap, then turned my attention to the names and yearbook photographs of Marcia Garvey's classmates. I couldn't help thinking that this venture might prove futile. After all, their interactions with Marcia had taken place more than thirty years ago. How much would they remember? Would they be able to give me any information about where she came from? What were the chances that any of them might know what had happened to Marcia after she disappeared from the 1977 yearbook?

Six males and seven females, counting Marcia, comprised the grade ten class of 1977. I had physical addresses for seven of the classmates—Chad, Shelly, Mary, Albert, Reggie, Leslie, and Will. A quick search on social media turned up email addresses for Chad, Albert, Will, and Leslie. I copied this information into my notebook and highlighted those four names, indicating I had all the information I needed for them.

I found email addresses for Tammy and Joe on social media, but nothing for the remaining three classmates, Kenny, Kacie, and Jackie.

I turned again to media archive searches and scanned for notices regarding marriages, deaths, births, or sale of property. I found an engagement notice for Jackie to her classmate Will. They married in the summer of 1979, right after graduation. I already had both a physical and an email address for Will, and joined their names on my list.

My next discovery was an obituary for Kenny, dated 1983. The short article mentioned only that he had been twenty-three years old and moved to Vancouver in the summer of 1977. No cause of death was mentioned. Kenny had apparently been one of the young and restless who moved to the famed, far-away big city with a pocket full of dreams. I crossed his name off my list but found myself staring at the phrase "summer of 1977." That was the last trace I had of Marcia Garvey. Was it possible that Marcia had gone with him? Had they been an item and moved to Vancouver together, and that's why I lost her trail? I quickly scribbled down that possibility, intending to follow up after I finished the current search.

Was it possible that Kenny and Marcia had intended to move to Vancouver together, but Marcia never made it? Had Kenny been the one to do away with her? I shook the thought away, not bothering to write it down.

I studied the face of each classmate from the photographs on my phone as I tracked them down. I memorized features and invented personalities for each. The last one, Kacie, was a sullen, dark-haired beauty who looked at the camera. Her melancholy expression made her beauty all the more devastating. But if a trace of this young woman existed after 1977, I could not find it.

Of the original thirteen classmates, ten were confirmed alive and I had contact information for each of them. I located my drafted letter and began typing.

My name is Nora (Quinn) Devrey. I live in Vancouver, BC, but was born in the town of Tome in December 1980. I was adopted as a baby and am now looking for my biological parents. In commencing my search, the name of your former classmate, Marcia Garvey, has arisen as the next person to speak to. I have reason to believe that she has information regarding who my parents are. I saw your name and picture in a high school yearbook dating from 1977 as part of her grade 10 class. I hope that you might remember Marcia, or some information about her past, or that you might know where she is now.

I respect your privacy and do not wish to intrude if you do not feel comfortable speaking to me. I would greatly appreciate any assistance you might be able to give me.

I listed my name, phone number, and email address, printed eight letters, and copied the text into six different emails. Before

I could change my mind, I sent all six. Then I signed each letter, folded them, and sealed them into envelopes bearing the names and addresses of Marcia's former classmates.

In the final letter, the copy that would go to all three Reinhardt addresses, I greeted Eleanor Reinhardt specifically and used the same introduction but altered the body.

I found your name when tracing your family's surname. I found the obituaries for your parents Todd and Louise, as well as your brother Allan, and I would like to offer my sincere condolences for your losses. I respect your privacy and do not want to trouble you if you do not feel comfortable speaking to me. I wonder if you might know who Marcia Garvey is, and whether you know where she is now or if you could provide any information to aid in my search. I greatly appreciate any assistance you can offer me.

I included my contact information, printed three copies of the letter, and placed stamps on each of the eleven envelopes.

I yawned, stretched, and glanced at the clock. Even though mail wouldn't be picked up until tomorrow morning, I walked down three flights of stairs to the main lobby. At the alcove that housed our mailboxes, I hesitated. Before I could talk myself out of doing so, I slid the envelopes into the Canada Post slot. Although they would sit there overnight, I wouldn't be able to retrieve them.

As I slowly climbed the stairs to the third floor, I considered that once again, I had no viable course of action before me. Malcolm might joke that I no longer had distractions from finishing the marking I had postponed. Considering my classes resumed the following morning, that was just as well. But even with the return to routine, waiting might prove more difficult than action.

During the ensuing days, Malcolm described my behavior as that of an excitable puppy who kept racing to the window to see if his human had come home. I reluctantly agreed with his description. I obsessively checked my email and stared at my phone, willing a notification to pop up. Even though our mail was delivered only once a day, I trekked downstairs every morning and evening to see what had come. It became my way of seizing control of something I had no power over.

In the first week of March, not quite ten days after I sent the inquiries, the first response came. It was an email from Will and his wife, Jackie.

I was exhilarated, but dreaded reading their response. At worst, they might demand that I never contact them again. Or perhaps the worst might be that they didn't remember and couldn't help me.

The email appeared to have been written by Will. Neither of them remembered much about Marcia or knew where she came from, where she went after she left school, or why she left. He mentioned that Marcia had lived with one of their classmates, either Shelly or another girl named Terry (I assumed "Terry" was actually "Tammy"), and had dated a classmate named Chad for awhile. Will provided Chad's email address and wished me luck with my search.

Might Chad have been the one who'd gotten Marcia pregnant?

In the yearbook photographs, Chad was a stocky youth with light eyes, skin, and hair, and a cocky grin. If Marcia was indeed my mother, and Chad my father, I hadn't received any of his light-toned genetics.

I received Chad's response next, also in email form, a few days after Will and Jackie's reply. Given the close proximity of their responses, I wondered if Will and Jackie had gotten in touch with Chad, sparking his action. With very little preamble, Chad cautioned that he didn't think he knew anything, but if I asked my questions, he would answer what he could.

My heart pounded as I tapped "reply," wondering if this would prove to be the first of many exchanges between me and my biological father. This also made me think of the impending results of the DNA test. I pushed both of these thoughts away.

I didn't take time to correct misspelled words and grammatical errors as I typed out the questions that drove me. Did he know where Marcia came from, or anything regarding her family and upbringing? Was it true that Marcia had lived in town with a girlfriend? Did he know why, and who it was she'd stayed with? How long had he and Marcia gone together? Did he know why Marcia left school? Did he know where she went after leaving?

After I hit "send," I realized how brusque I'd been. I quickly sent a follow-up email thanking him for his willingness to speak with me and apologizing for the brazenness of my questions.

Because I had replied so quickly, I hoped that he might still be online and promptly respond to my emails. He didn't.

Almost a week later, Chad's second email came. Whereas his first had been short and concise, perhaps indicating a man of few words, his second email was longer. He explained that he and Marcia had gone together for a few months before she started dating another guy, Kenny. He'd lost track of Marcia shortly after the summer of '77 and hadn't heard her name again for thirty years.

While they dated, Marcia had expressed a desire to get away from 100 Mile House, but didn't talk much about her home life or family. Soon after her father died, she moved in with one of their classmates, a girl named Shelly. After two years at school, Marcia, Kenny, and another friend, Tammy, dropped out of sight. He'd heard rumors that they had gone to Vancouver but couldn't confirm that. A few years later, the entire town was stunned to hear that Kenny had died of a drug overdose in Vancouver. As to what became of Tammy and Marcia, he didn't know.

I read through his email several times. So many pieces of the puzzle started to come together, but even more mysteries emerged.

Though I relied on speculation and guesswork to reach many of my conclusions, I still didn't know much about Marcia prior to 1976. If Allan Garvey was Marcia's father, this fit the date he'd passed away.

I also had reason to believe that Marcia left 100 Mile House in 1977 and fled to Vancouver with Kenny. Chad's recollections fit with the information I'd found in Kenny's 1983 obituary. Also, it seemed unlikely that Chad was my biological father.

Kenny couldn't help me, but Tammy might prove to be a fount of information if she'd gone with the duo to Vancouver. *If* she was willing to speak with me.

I thanked Chad profusely for his help. I could think of only two more questions to ask, though I knew it was a long shot that he would have the answers: Did he know where Marcia Garvey lived before moving to 100 Mile House? And could he think of any reason she might have traveled to Tome or the surrounding area around the year 1980?

In his final email, Chad said he couldn't be sure exactly where her hometown was. He knew it was a smaller community farther north, not far from 150 Mile House. As for her travels to Tome or the surrounding area, Chad didn't know whether she'd gone to either place but couldn't imagine she would have. She wanted to leave the small towns where she grew up, not return to them.

I studied the notes on Malcolm's white board and shifted tidbits of information among the respective columns of confirmed, suspected, and unknown facts. I color coded the information to easily cross-reference the sources, then stepped back to consider and contemplate.

Had Marcia made it to Vancouver in 1977? If everything I had learned so far was true, and that was assuming a lot, then Marcia went from 100 Mile House to Vancouver in the summer of 1977 with her boyfriend Kenny and close friend Tammy. Assuming Marcia was my mother, she had returned to the northern interior in the winter of 1980 to leave me at the Parish in Tome.

What about the town had she wanted to escape? Jane Doe ended up buried near Cold Lake sometime prior to 1985. If the timeline was correct, she returned north in or before 1980, gave birth to me, then abandoned me at the church in December of 1980.

Did she stay in the Interior until she was killed, or leave the area and then return yet again? If so, why?

Maybe Marcia returned, wanting to find the baby girl she left behind. Although the thought was comforting, I didn't think I'd be able to bear knowing that her last act on earth had been to find me, which led to her demise.

Or, had Marcia died soon after my birth?

Were Marcia and Kenny still going together in 1980? Was Kenny my biological father?

The thought that my father might have died from a drug overdose three years after my birth did not appeal to me, but I had to face the reality that there almost certainly would be things in my past that I would find disheartening.

Shelly's eagerly anticipated email came in the third week of March, as the spring solstice arrived and I administered midterms to my students. In my office, in between a lecture and office hours, I read the long letter.

Shelly explained that Marcia came from a small town called Lachlan, located northeast of 100 Mile House.

The girls met at a dance hall in 150 Mile House when they were eleven or twelve years old. Marcia used to hitch rides west, and Shelly hitched rides north from 100 Mile House as 100 Mile didn't have any decent dance halls in those days. They dressed provocatively, did their makeup, put their hair up, and danced with strangers until the dance hall closed down in the early morning hours. That's the way things were done in the days of sex, drugs, and rock 'n' roll, even at such a young age.

The two stayed in touch when they could, but Marcia's family didn't have a telephone, and because Lachlan was so isolated, letters often took weeks to pass hands.

Once or twice a month, the girls met up at the dance hall. They bonded over the hair styles and clothes fashions of the day. They smoked weed together in the alley behind the hall. Marcia confided that her father had passed away when she was younger, but that he hadn't really been around much anyway.

Marcia's mother remarried within weeks of her husband's death. By the time Marcia was twelve years old, she often ran away from home, hitched rides to 100 Mile House, and stayed with Shelly for days, saying she just needed to get away. She would arrive in a dark mood and cry herself to sleep or smoke weed in the backyard with Shelly, but she always returned to Lachlan. She said her younger siblings needed her. Shelly had a feeling that Marcia's home life was horrible, but Marcia never talked about it. From the few bits that slipped out here and there, Shelly learned that Marcia didn't get along with her stepfather and her mother didn't seem to want her as Marcia was a reminder of her late husband.

Marcia ran away from home for the final time at the age of fourteen, hitched to Shelly's house in the middle of the night, and begged Shelly to ask her parents to let her stay. They agreed.

Marcia lived with Shelly for the next two years. The girls were inseparable. They attended high school together, though Marcia often fell behind in her studies. They smoked weed together, attended dances, got drunk, flirted with boys, went on double dates, and snuck out to meet their lovers. All the while, Marcia spoke determinedly of running away. Shelly quoted Marcia as having said, on multiple occasions, "leaving this bullshit behind" and "getting out of this backwoods hellhole."

During their grade ten year, Marcia started dating Kenny, who idolized her, and Shelly dated an older boy who became her husband. Marcia and Kenny made plans to leave for Vancouver at the end of the school year. Marcia begged Shelly to come, but Shelly didn't want to leave her beau, and the girls parted on amiable terms, saying goodbye at a gas station near the freeway in 100 Mile House in June of 1977.

Though they promised to keep in touch, Marcia sent only one letter that summer, and Shelly's response was returned unopened and marked, "Addressee does not reside at this address." Thus, their contact ended. Because Shelly married, she figured that Marcia also married, settled down, had children, and didn't have time for long-distance friendships. Shelly thought of Marcia often.

I printed Shelly's email, then underlined dates and circled names and locations and facts to help me process everything. Then I wrote a reply to Shelly, thanking her for her willingness to share her life story with me and for the information she provided. I asked whether she could think of any reason Marcia might have returned to Lachlan, Tome, or 100 Mile House. Had she heard anything about Marcia being pregnant in 1980?

This last was highly unlikely, as the girls lost touch three years before my conception. Also, I was fairly certain that Shelly would have insisted that Marcia look her up if she returned to the Interior, but I wanted confirmation.

Afterward, I began an internet search for Lachlan.

The town was two hours away from 100 Mile House, accessible by a single road heading east from 150 Mile House and surrounded on all sides by wilderness. Its population was less than a thousand residents.

How many people had lived in Lachlan in the 1970s? A small town would surely remember its past residents.

That Marcia came from Lachlan explained why I hadn't had much success finding Garveys in the Tome phone book. Perhaps most Garveys who left Lachlan settled farther north, in 150 Mile House. Maybe Eleanor Garvey Reinhardt was a distant cousin, remotely connected to Marcia Garvey. I still held out hope that the letters I'd sent in search of Eleanor Reinhardt would bear fruit.

Meanwhile, I had a second place to search, and more pieces of the puzzle to add to the whiteboard.

Internet research revealed that Lachlan had neither a newspaper or a school, and so fell in the catchment for 150 Mile House. Although Malcolm and I didn't find records of her in the schools' archives, she would have attended elementary school in 100 Mile House. Based upon Shelly's remark about Marcia's school performance, I suspected that, if Marcia had been educated at all, her studies had been pre-empted by farm labor and family obligations. I suspected that the two years she spent at the high school in 100 Mile might have been the most stable years of her life, and at that age, she would have been behind her classmates and struggled with her studies. I struggled against my anger for the young girl who hadn't seemed to find favor or fortune anywhere she turned.

What had Marcia been running so hard to get away from? All clues pointed to a conclusion I didn't want to reach.

I placed the printed copy of Shelley's email in my notebook for later perusal.

As with everyone who had replied to my correspondence, Shelly lost contact with Marcia after 1977. Only Tammy might be able to shed light on that later period of Marcia's life. For this reason, I was most eager to hear from her, but the next email I received came from Joe, in the third week of March. His reply was similar to Will and Jackie's response. Joe knew little about Marcia and hadn't heard anything from or about her in thirty years. He was sorry not to be of help and wished me luck in my search.

When not checking emails, our postal box, or obsessing about Marcia Garvey, I managed to maintain a semblance of a routine. In evenings and on weekends, Malcolm and I went snowshoeing on the trails of the North Shore Mountains. During the week, I prepared lectures and notes for the three classes I taught, answered emails, attended office hours, and graded papers. As final exams approached—three weeks away—my students grew panicky over the term papers due at the end of March. When my summer teaching schedule was finalized, I became keenly aware of the passage of time. Each week brought me closer to the DNA test results.

I had two weeks off at the end of April before the summer semester commenced on May 3rd. I began preparing lesson plans and outlines for my new classes, an activity intended to keep me busy as well as prepare for the upcoming months.

Late at night, when I wasn't distracted by work, I tried to keep myself from thinking about the DNA test and the responses I hadn't yet received. Five weeks had passed since the test had been submitted. My search was stagnant until I heard something more, and I grew impatient with Tammy and Eleanor and the medical examiner.

When I made the decision to contact Marcia Garvey's friends and possible family, I vowed that I would send a single, initial letter to each person to protect their privacy concerns. I didn't want to badger and hound. I decided this in the optimism of believing that everyone I contacted would be happy to speak with me and would reply quickly. Reality severely tried my patience. I was tempted to send follow-up letters, even knowing it wasn't fair to do so.

Another week went by without a single new email or letter, taking me into the final week of March.

The silence was deafening. I wondered if my other letters had been received, or if they'd simply been ignored. Might a person I was trying to contact have passed away, leaving me without a crucial source of information?

On Tuesday morning, March thirtieth, I lectured to a late morning classroom full of first year students when my phone vibrated in my pocket. Certain it was either Malcolm or one of my parents calling, I discreetly pulled the phone from my pocket, slipped it onto the podium, and glanced at the lit screen.

The name displayed contained four letters—RCMP—and a long-distance phone number. The call I'd eagerly anticipated and secretly dreaded had arrived, though earlier than I had expected. I didn't know if this meant good news or bad.

I couldn't take the call with sixty faces staring at me, pencils poised to jot down whatever I said next. The class had already taken its break and wouldn't end for another hour. The news would have to wait.

With heart in my throat and palms sweating, I clumsily tripped through a recitation of facts and dates and names significant to the October Revolution of Tsarist Russia and the downfall of the Provisional Government in 1917. After reviewing what could be expected on their final exam and reminding my students that their term papers were due the following Tuesday, I ended the class as quickly as I dared. After the last stragglers trickled out, I fairly sprinted to my office.

Alone at last, I listened to the voicemail message from Inspector Chilton. He asked me to return his call as soon as convenient and rattled off a phone number that I hastily scribbled down on the ledger on my desk. I couldn't tell from the inflection of his voice what the news might be. Indeterminably vague and unfailingly polite, he might very well have been inquiring about the weather in Vancouver. The results of my DNA test weren't due back for another two weeks.

I dialed the number.

A pulse pounded in my head when Inspector Chilton picked up after the second ring. I identified myself and politely inquired as to how he was doing, laughing perhaps a bit too loudly at his response, having not heard a word he said. He shared some anecdote and I responded appropriately in the right places.

Finally, he said that the results of the DNA test had come back. The results showed a 99.9 percent match between my profile and that of Jane Doe, proving that we were, in fact, related.

"Even more conclusive," he went on, "is the presence of mitochondrial DNA in your profile. This is the DNA passed between a mother and child through the mother's genetics. And yours fully matches Jane Doe's."

I almost dropped my phone. Even though we still didn't know her name, even though I couldn't yet connect Marcia Garvey to Jane Doe, I now had the proof we'd been waiting for.

Jane Doe was my mother.

Part Two

THE SEARCH

Untitled

Part Two -The Search

Chapter Eleven

A Season of Marcia

April 2010 became a whirlwind of interviews, conversations, and questions. The police investigation began a new line of inquiry into Jane Doe's identity. I still harbored the belief that Marcia Garvey and Jane Doe were one and the same. I still couldn't prove it, but the confirmation of my biological mother lit a new fire in me.

Most of my conversations with the RCMP investigators took place over the phone or via video conference. The police were now as interested in finding my birth parents and biological family as I was, if not more so. They took charge of our amateur investigation with fervor. Though I couldn't be made privy to everything they uncovered, Inspector Chilton and his team took every care to keep me as informed as possible.

In light of the conclusive DNA results, Malcolm and I planned a second trip to the Interior to take place the third week of April, after the exam period ended.

I did learn one key thing from Inspector Chilton soon after our

March call. He explained that the RCMP had been following a different theory as to Jane Doe's identity with what little information they had available. Initially, Inspector Chilton had believed that she was another victim of one of the so-called Highway of Tears murderers, a dark chapter in the history of our province. Northern BC has a highway that runs through remote and isolated communities between Prince George and Prince Rupert, and throughout the previous decades, serial killers picked up hitchhikers along this route. The victims were always women, usually young, and often of Indigenous descent. In the absence of any real proof otherwise, Inspector Chilton believed that Jane Doe was one such victim and that, due to mistrust of the authorities, she had never been reported missing. Tragically, these women and girls were often destitute, runaways, or both, having fallen through the cracks of a system that utterly failed them.

His team had now revised this theory and wanted any information I could give them about where I had come from and what I had learned. That was the purpose of the video interview scheduled with investigators on April fourth. Malcolm sat and sipped tea with me on the couch in our living room. When the video call connected, Inspector Chilton greeted me like an old friend and thanked me for my time.

I assumed that the interview would be similar to the first conversation we'd had with Inspector Chilton in early February. Unlike that meeting, this one included several members of Chilton's team who sat at the conference table, in view of the webcam, pencils poised over legal pads.

I expected to be nervous or anxious, or have trouble keeping my thoughts coherent, but I was strangely calm. Receiving the definitive DNA results served to sooth my obsessive compulsion of the past few months; I was entirely confident and steady as I began speaking.

I introduced my husband and explained my profession to help establish my credentials as a reliable and resourceful researcher. This provided a perfect segue into the story of how Jane Doe came to my attention. I detailed my research and how I'd compiled everything I could get my hands on pertaining to Jane Doe. I spoke in great detail of the conversation with my parents and the box of newspaper clippings my mom gave me. I explained how I'd been found on the Parish steps in Tome and later adopted. I finished my narrative by outlining my upbringing in Vancouver.

I'd been speaking for almost an hour at this point. They questioned me closely, but after a few extraneous inquiries, they seemed to run out of steam with this particular portion of the story, and so I told them about the trip to Tome in February—why we went, the places we visited, the people we talked to, and how we discovered the photographs of Marcia Garvey in the 1976 and 1977 high school yearbooks. I pulled up those photos on my phone. "This is Marcia Garvey." I turned my phone toward them. Their amazed reactions spoke volumes. It was clear they saw her uncanny resemblance to me.

I read aloud the emails and letters from Marcia Garvey's former classmates, allowing the investigators time to scribble down names, dates, and facts. I promised to forward this correspondence to Inspector Chilton.

Mentally exhausted and starving, I wanted the call to end, but I wanted information even more.

"Do you have any questions, Nora?" Inspector Chilton asked.

I didn't hesitate. "I know you can't share details, but can you tell me if you've had any other tips on the hotline?"

The investigators shared glances. Inspector Chilton seemed to consider his response before carefully stating, "Up until this time, we haven't had any tips that are worth pursuing."

I was elated that he told me that much. "Okay, thank you. My next question is about the lack of records that are available for Jane Doe. Obviously, you can't say for sure because she hasn't been identified, and so we don't know anything about her specific situation. But how often does this happen? In cases you investigate, someone not having official records anywhere in the country has to be rare. Right?"

Inspector Chilton tilted his head and considered. "I wouldn't say rare. Actually, the lack of records available was one of the reasons we so strongly suspected that Jane Doe might have been a Highway of Tears victim. The autopsy proved that she was of Caucasian descent, but prior to having that knowledge, and given where she was found and the circumstances that seemed to surround her death, we believed she was from a remote community. Oftentimes, especially in isolated towns, records are incomplete, inaccurate, or simply missing. So no, I'm afraid it's not necessarily rare. Why she doesn't have records is not something I can speak to at this point."

I took a moment to process what he had said. Then I nodded and took a deep breath. "What can you tell me about how Jane Doe died?"

"We are giving you this information on the understanding that it will be kept confidential and not shared with anyone," Inspector Chilton said. "Are we agreed?"

Malcolm and I agreed.

One of Chilton's team members explained that Jane Doe had been between the ages of seventeen and twenty-one when she died. They were able to narrow down her time of death to a three-year period, between 1980 and 1983, based on the clothing she wore, as well as other forensic factors that meant little to me. He mentioned that her clothes suggested the mild weather of late spring or early fall. The remnants of the blue windbreaker jacket matched a generic clothing manufacturer that sold products to the mass market through large department stores. That made it difficult to pursue this lead.

Inspector Chilton then cautioned me, "The details that follow might be difficult for you to hear." He sounded as if he hoped they could skip this information.

I needed to hear those details. "Since learning that Jane Doe gave birth to me, I've been plagued by images of what might have happened to her. The truth can't possibly be worse than what I've imagined," I murmured.

Chilton's colleague said, "Jane Doe died by strangulation and was then transported to the burial site. Evidence points to sexual activity taking place prior to death. Trace samples of DNA were badly deteriorated and don't match any individuals on file, but we're following up potential leads. Her remains were damaged postmortem, likely by wild animals, which explains why certain bones are missing."

As the officer spoke, Malcolm discreetly slid his hand over mine. "We know that Marcia hitchhiked quite a bit," he said. "If she is Jane Doe, it makes sense that she was picked up along the highway."

"But why was she in Tome in 1980, at all?" I was frustrated, but not at Malcolm. I wasn't handling my emotions as well as I would have liked. "She moved to Vancouver in 1977, and we can't find any reason that she would have willingly returned to the Interior."

The same officer continued. "The medical examiner discovered evidence of childhood injuries. She'd fractured her leg and would likely have walked with a slight limp. Also, she had an unhealed crack in her right collarbone."

The picture painted by this information chilled me. I wanted to believe that my biological mother, like me, had simply been a clumsy tomboy. I wondered what a medical examiner might make of the broken arm I'd sustained at the age of ten. What must Jane Doe's parents, my grandparents, have been like?

Chilton's colleague concluded, "This is all the information we have about the demise of Jane Doe."

The pronouncement was met with stunned silence from Malcolm and me. I was wrung out. I wasn't sure what else his team could divulge, and by all indications, the conversation was drawing to a close. I offered a heartfelt, "Thank you. I intend to keep investigating."

"Please keep us informed if you uncover anything new," Chilton requested. "We'll do the same."

I hoped we would be speaking again, and soon.

The next day, Inspector Chilton telephoned my parents and set up an interview with them on the following Saturday afternoon. For this video call, I went to my parents' house, both at my mother's request and because I wanted to be part of every step of the investigative process.

My parents, seated side by side on their living room loveseat, faced the laptop propped open on the coffee table. I sat on the rug, my cheek resting on the hand my mother placed on my shoulder.

Inspector Chilton knew the story of Baby Judea before he met me, and the details of my stay in the hospital weren't really pertinent, so Inspector Chilton's questions focused on the facts of my adoption.

"We were granted temporary guardianship of Nora that very morning, as soon as we arrived at the hospital," Dad explained. "That was December 3, 1980."

Mom added, "At approximately 6 a.m."

Dad went on, "It was arranged by the hospital's social worker, Sherry Keegan."

"I have copies of all of these documents," Mom said, reaching for the few papers on the coffee table next to the laptop. "Do you need them?"

"Thank you, but not at this time," Inspector Chilton answered. "I appreciate you preparing them though, and if they become necessary in the future, I'll let you know." He consulted the legal pad in front of him. "And the order of legal custody?"

"Signed two weeks later, on December 17th," Dad said promptly.

"Do you need the name of the Justice who signed the order?" Mom asked, again reaching for the papers.

"Honey, if he needs it, he'll ask," Dad soothed with a teasing smile.

Mom threw an apologetic look toward the screen, where Inspector Chilton shook his head with a patient smile. "Not at this time but thank you. And the date of the adoption?"

There was a slight catch in Dad's voice when he answered, "April 11, 1983. Early Monday morning."

"I put her hair in pigtails for the hearing"—Mom patted my shoulder —"and put her in a cute purple dress. But she was a little cranky that morning, and when the Justice looked at her, she cried." Both my parents chuckled.

I hadn't heard these details before. I pictured the scene in my mind and smiled, then cringed when Dad added, "To celebrate, we went for ice cream afterwards, and she dribbled ice cream all down the front of her dress."

This anecdote led to other stories from my childhood, making me blush and roll my eyes. Mom told tales of me drawing on walls with markers, and covering my face with Dad's shaving cream so I could shave just like he did. Then came the infamous incident that occurred when I was five years old.

"I had lit some candles in the living room while Nora was playing with her toys," Mom began, and I groaned, recognizing the opening to the story that had been told to friends and family for years. "Nora put down her dolls and marched right out of the room. I asked her where she was going. She said she was going to the kitchen to get a drink so I didn't bother following her. Well, I tell you, less than ten minutes later, a great big fire truck comes screaming down the street and pulls up in front of the house. Nora had her face pressed to the front window, and I went out onto the porch to find out what was going on." Mom tousled my hair. "Turns out this monkey had called the fire department to tell them I'd lit the house on fire and planned to burn it down!"

"In my defence," I teased, "you did light a fire. At least, I was a responsible child!"

"We had a serious talk about supervised and unsupervised fires, and not calling 911 for unimportant things." Mom gazed at me fondly.

I smiled and shook my head.

Inspector Chilton smiled indulgently, and I thought she might continue telling embarrassing stories from my childhood, but Dad nudged her. "I'm sure the Inspector has more questions for us."

"I do yes, thank you," Inspector Chilton said. "I would imagine that you wanted to know everything possible about Nora's biological family. Obviously, there was nothing to be found through official channels. Did you ever search for the family yourselves?"

My parents exchanged a look, and Dad said, "We thought about it several times, but there never seemed to be a need. So, no, we didn't."

"It wasn't our responsibility," Mom chimed in, her tone slightly defensive. Her hand was in Dad's, her grip so tight that her knuckles turned white.

"No, it wasn't," Inspector Chilton soothed. "Investigations are conducted by the Ministry of Child and Family Development. They're responsible for identifying and contacting family members and determining if they have a legal claim to the child."

After the interview ended, tears welled in Mom's eyes, but she dabbed at them. "I'm all right. It's just…it's overwhelming. How are you doing, honey?"

Her concern for me was evident in the deep lines on her face. In that moment, I realized how much she and Dad had aged.

I joined them on the sofa. "This doesn't change anything," I said. "You are my family. I am the luckiest person in the world."

During the second and third weeks of April, I spoke with Chilton on numerous occasions. Upon reopening the investigation into Jane Doe, his focus had been on tracing Jane Doe's movements leading up to her death. The police had been seeking anyone who might remember seeing her during the period she was estimated to have been in the Tome, Lachlan, or Cold Lake areas. They had also sought information about her movements leading up to her death, which included information on persons known to have frequented Highway 97 between Vancouver and Prince George.

I knew from talking to Mom that, mere hours after I'd been found, the RCMP began looking for any woman who had recently given birth, and in light of my connection to Jane Doe, Doug resolved to delve into those archived files to pursue any uncovered leads. I decided to continue my search by trying to find where Marcia Garvey had come from. Malcolm agreed that finding where Marcia Garvey came from was just as important as discovering where she went after leaving 100 Mile house in 1977. Shelly's letter gave me a new place to dig—Lachlan.

Malcolm and I made plans to fly to Prince George on Thursday, April 22nd, and rent a car for the drive south—first to 150 Mile House, and then east to Lachlan. I hoped to find some remnants of Marcia Garvey's family. I also wanted to meet Dr. Bradley in person. I called to arrange a meeting date, time, and location with him.

The night before we left for Prince George, we were dozing on the couch in front of the TV when my phone rang. I didn't recognize the number and couldn't imagine who might call so late. In my groggy state, I prepared to let the caller go to voicemail.

Then I remembered that I had included my phone number in my outreach to Marcia Garvey's classmates, and I picked up just in time. "Nora speaking."

The woman cleared her throat nervously. "It's Tammy. Tammy Robbins. You sent me a letter?"

The warm fog of my catnap instantly disappeared. "Yes, Tammy, hi! Thank you for calling me." I rose from the couch and hurried into the bedroom to keep from disturbing Malcolm. I didn't know how long this conversation would take or how intense it might become.

"Why are you looking for Marcia Garvey?"

"I'm trying to find my biological family." I closed the bedroom door and sat on the edge of the bed. "I think Marcia knows who my mother and father were, but I haven't been able to find her. I hope you might have some information that helps."

"Don't know about that. Haven't seen her for years."

Yet another person who hadn't heard from or of Marcia Garvey for a long time, and another indication that Marcia and Jane Doe could be the same woman.

"We left for Vancouver in June of '77," Tammy went on. "The day after school ended."

"You and Marcia and Kenny?" I asked.

She hesitated as if surprised that I knew this, then her tone of voice lifted. "We wanted to leave 100 Mile House for good. I wanted to be a singer and an actress, or maybe even a model. Kenny wanted excitement, dreamed of the fast life and endless entertainment in the big city. He'd nibbled at a taste of that life in the dance halls of 150 Mile House, and he was hungry for more." Tammy fell silent, as if trying to remember.

I prompted gently, "And Marcia?"

"Just wanted to get away," Tammy's voice went flat. "She wanted to disappear into a city of faces where no one knew her or her family or her past. She simply wanted to run.

"We hitched a ride with Kenny's uncle. He was a rancher who drove cattle between 70 Mile and 100 Mile. There's a general store on the south end of 70 mile, and that's where we climbed out of the back of the pickup and said goodbye. Spent the rest of the morning and some of the afternoon on the side of the road. I played guitar and sang while Marcia danced and smoked a joint, and Kenny stretched out to take a nap." Her voice held a trace of nostalgia, as if she longed for the good times of days long past.

"It took the better part of two days," Tammy went on, "but we managed to hitch all 400 kilometers to Vancouver. Landed in the heart of downtown with no job prospects and no money, but we knew we'd make it just fine. We slept on the beach in English Bay that first night, a few meters from the water. We woke with the sun, and it was beautiful. We had so much hope."

The edge in her voice filled me with a sense of foreboding. I knew how Kenny's tale ended, and I guessed how Marcia's had. I was left wondering which direction Tammy's story would take.

"We made our way to a hostel to start our new life. Found a shower, found a place to wash our clothes. We drifted for a few days until we landed on West 4th Avenue, on the stretch between Burrard and MacDonald."

I knew the neighborhood, the heart of hippie and commune culture in Vancouver in the '70s and '80s.

"We joined a commune and lost two years in this neighborhood to marijuana and alcohol and free love. We shared everything with everyone, and we never wanted for anything we didn't need. I earned money playing music on street corners and in parks and at bus stops. Kenny joined a band and played a coupla gigs every month."

"Marcia just…drifted. She was lost. She didn't thrive, at all. The city just crushed her. She went from weed and alcohol to ecstasy and LSD, and then heroin. Woke up in houses all over the city, disappeared for days at a time. Always looking for the next high.

"Within a few months, she got arrested on minor charges, which were dropped. Probably public drinking or weed or something like that. But then she was arrested again and again and the police always brought her back to the commune, which drew police attention to us. The cops despised the hippie movement and started harassing our members. So the commune voted for Marcia to leave. She stormed off, and Kenny followed her.

Why didn't Marcia Garvey's criminal records appear in any of my internet searches? As far I knew, court documents were a matter of public record.

"I stayed." Tammy sounded almost wistful. "I didn't see either of them for a year. I later learned that Kenny had gone to prison, and Marcia was on the streets. I saw her for the last time maybe two years after she left the commune. I was working various nightclubs and strip joints—I was a singer only, never anything else. And in the early morning hours, I was walking home, past the First United Church at Gore and Hastings on the Downtown Eastside, when I saw her. Sitting on the sidewalk, unresponsive, high as a kite. It took a few minutes for her to come out of it, but she greeted me like nothing had happened.

"She denied she was in trouble, but broke down and admitted she'd hit rock bottom. She was addicted to heroin, facing charges for prostitution, and under court orders to dry out and clean up. She cursed the cops, insisted they'd trapped her. Ranted against the judge, the parole officers, the rehab workers who tried to tell her how to live her life.

"Finally, she started crying, and I'll never forget what she said," Tammy's voice went hoarse with emotion. "Marcia said she had to get away. She had to get clean and make a fresh start. She said she'd change her name and start over someplace new. Said she was afraid that if she didn't leave town, she was going to kill herself with the drugs, and she wasn't so sure that would be a bad thing.

"I never saw her again. I want to believe she turned her life around. I really do. I want to believe that she is in some far away city, and that she got clean, and she found peace. I want her to have fought against her demons and won. That's my hope. It's what I tell myself to make myself feel better. For all I know, she died of an overdose, just like Kenny did, or was beaten to death by a john and dropped off the Lions Gate Bridge. I don't think I'll ever know, but I tell myself she's happier, wherever she is."

I considered telling her what I suspected happened to Marcia Garvey, to give her some closure, but the information wouldn't bring any measure of peace. I said nothing. I didn't know for sure if Jane Doe and Marcia Garvey were one and the same.

"Could you say when this meeting took place?" I asked. "Do you remember the approximate year?"

"I was working at the Leo downtown, and hadn't met my second husband yet, so maybe in '82? '83?"

My heart leapt. This was the first indication I had found that Marcia had been alive past 1980. I was mentally fitting together the pieces of the story when Tammy said, "No, wait. My son was born in 1981, and it was the summer before that, right before I got pregnant. So that would have made it around early summer of 1980. Maybe May or June?"

Those words burst the balloon of hope swelling inside me. In that moment, I realized how utterly I believed that Marcia Garvey and Jane Doe were the same person. If true, I wanted Marcia to have lived those extra years, to have had that extra time to get clean, to find love and peace. She had died young, and I couldn't change this fact, but perhaps the blow would be easier to handle if her last years had been happy.

I hastily reviewed the story Tammy had told. "Do you know what Marcia was running from when she left Lachlan?"

"You mean specifically? She didn't really talk about her life before high school. So no, not really. She was very unhappy."

Yet another person who mentioned Marcia not talking about her past. I wondered if anyone would be able to shed light on her childhood. Part of me wondered if I really wanted to know.

Realizing that my silence had gone on too long, I stammered out my last question. "D-do you know if Marcia might have been pregnant when you last saw her?"

Tammy's pause was heavy. "In your letter, you said Marcia was the next person you needed to talk to. Do you think she's your mother?"

None of Marcia's other classmates had me asked this, and I answered cautiously, "I think Marcia is related to me in some way, either through my birth mother or my birth father."

"If Marcia was pregnant, I couldn't see it. She had protruding ribs, stick-thin legs, and wore minimal clothing. She probably hadn't eaten in awhile. Or maybe it was the drugs. She looked like she was wasting away." Tammy ended on a small sob.

When she got her emotions under control, she asked, "If you ever find Marcia, could you let me know?"

"Yes, of course," I said. "If I have more questions, would you mind speaking with me again?"

"I dunno. Maybe. I'm sorry, kiddo, it's really hard."

I couldn't ask more than that of her. It had taken courage for her to reach out when she so easily could have ignored my letter. I thanked her, ended the call, and then sat on my bed and stared at my phone in the dark. Marcia had been so young. Had she ever known love, contentment, happiness, peace? Had she always been running away?

And what had she fought against for so long?

Chapter Twelve

It took me forever to fall asleep that night. I woke the next morning in a black mood, having been plagued by nightmares of shadowy figures on the dark streets of Vancouver on cold, rainy nights. My mood didn't improve as I went through the motions of the morning. Breakfast was a cup of coffee, bitter, as I'd forgotten to add sugar and couldn't be bothered to rectify the situation. I helped Malcolm load our bags into the car. At the airport, I handed over my boarding pass and stumbled after Malcolm, duffel bag in hand.

All the while, the unwanted implications of what I had learned weighed heavily on me. Marcia had landed in Vancouver, her faraway promised land, only to fall into the pitfalls of drug addiction. She had prostituted herself to support her heroin habit, and lost her boyfriend, first to prison and then to an overdose.

I wanted to believe, as Tammy did, that Marcia had gotten clean, changed her name, and started fresh in another city. I knew this wasn't likely, and that knowledge depressed me.

I wondered, too, if Marcia had taken drugs while pregnant. If she was my mother, had I been a heroin baby? I discarded the thought as quickly as it occurred. If that were the case, Dr. Bradley would have known and informed my parents. But another, equally unpleasant thought arose.

Marcia had been a prostitute. I might never know who my birth father was. She herself might not have known.

I realized I didn't care as much about finding my birth father. He didn't seem as relevant to me. Instead, I fixated on Marcia, the tragic teenager who lived and most likely died decades ago.

Jane Doe might not be Marcia Garvey, I chided myself. Marcia Garvey could have rebuilt her life and had no connection to the young woman who gave birth to me and died a few short years later. Perhaps this trip to Lachlan would help to illuminate the truth. Perhaps Malcolm and I would find a member of Marcia Garvey's family, someone who could tell us what had become of her and who would submit a DNA sample that would conclusively reveal that Jane Doe was their relation.

While Malcolm slumbered in the seat next to me, I leaned against the airplane's window and stared at passing clouds without really seeing them, replaying the conversation with Tammy. What had happened to Marcia after that last encounter? Where had she gone? Would I ever be able to find the answers, and how could I even go about doing so? What came next? Eventually, I fell into a fitful doze.

I woke with a start when Malcolm shook my shoulder. Passengers around us were standing and stretching and reaching for overhead luggage bins. I was slow to move. We'd been on the plane for over an hour. I felt hungover and couldn't think straight.

Malcolm dealt with the agents at the rental car counter while I went in search of badly needed coffee. Before leaving Prince George to drive south to 150 Mile House, we would have lunch with Dr. Bradley, my parents' friend and the doctor who had saved my life.

Malcolm and I arrived first at the small café Dr. Bradley had recommended. The menu promised amazing home-cooked soups and stews and sandwiches. I inhaled the warm aromas and stared through the window at the dead flowers in the window boxes around the deserted patio.

I had never met Dr. Robert Bradley in person, but I'd known of him since hearing Mom's and Dad's anecdotes from their college days. Every year, I'd been obliged to sign my name in the Christmas card addressed to him. They had described Dr. Bradley as tall with a large personality, but I was not prepared for the giant with a large, booming voice who swept in and greeted everyone in the diner by name.

Malcolm chuckled at my surprised expression and rose as Dr. Bradley, face half-hidden by a bushy beard, strode toward us, the only strangers in the café. Malcolm's hand disappeared into Dr. Bradley's grip, but the doctor was a hugger. He pulled Malcolm into a one-armed embrace and pat on the back. Then he turned to me, his green eyes wide above the wrinkles of his red cheeks.

"Nora," he bellowed, and his arms crushed me. My face landed somewhere around his middle. My arms couldn't span his width to return the embrace. He released me and stared down into my face, eyes sparkling. "Dear girl, you're all grown up! Last time I saw you, you fit easily into this palm!" He held up a hand nearly the size of a dinner plate.

I could only marvel at him, overwhelmed by his incredible energy. "It's—it's so nice to finally meet you, Dr. Bradley," I stammered.

He slapped my back jovially. "Call me Doc Tiny. Everyone does. It makes the kids laugh."

"Thanks for meeting us, Doc Tiny." Malcolm and I squeezed into the same side of the booth. I don't think I would have fit comfortably beside this man, and Malcolm certainly wouldn't have.

"I cannot believe this pretty young lady is the same wee tiny baby I held thirty years ago," Doc Tiny boomed.

I cringed when several faces turned in our direction.

"How are your folks?" he continued at the same volume, signaling the waitress for coffee.

"They're great. Mom's loving retirement. She raises swans and paints and plays tennis. Dad says he'd be too bored if he retired and plans to work till he drops at his office. Even jokes that he hopes he has time to write his own obituary."

"Dan always did have a twisted sense of humor," Doc Tiny said drily.

I giggled at the accuracy of his description.

"When did you last see my parents?" I asked.

The waitress arrived to take our order.

"You folks like steak sandwiches?" Doc Tiny asked us.

We nodded.

"Three steak sandwiches, Dot," he told the waitress, "and sides of the chowder to start." He looked back at us. "Now, where were we? Ah, yeah, when I saw your folks. Woulda been two or three years ago. I was heading to San Diego for a conference and popped in on my layover. Think you two were outta town at the time; otherwise, I woulda insisted on an introduction. Your mom said you're a college professor."

I swallowed a hot sip of coffee and nodded. "I teach history."

He laughed. "You're Dan's kid all right. He woulda majored in history if he coulda. But he got bit by the investigative reporting bug. This was the seventies, of course, when draft dodgers mixed with flower kids and the Vietnam protesters. And Watergate broke. Your dad couldn't wait to wade into the thick of things."

Doc Tiny was regaling us with a rather juvenile prank my dad had orchestrated in their second year of college when Dot brought over three steaming bowls.

"This is the best chowder you'll get on this coast," he promised. "Clam chowder just like you'd find in Boston."

The chowder was quite good, a perfect antidote for drafts of cold air that passed through the diner every time the front door opened.

"Why did you move north?" I asked.

Doc Tiny explained that he'd been accepted into a prestigious program here in Prince George. He'd figured on spending a few years gaining experience before searching for a position closer to home. But he'd met a local girl, Beth, and they'd married in 1978. They had three children and two grandchildren. "My youngest daughter, Kristen, was born about six months before you were."

Dot arrived with three open-faced sandwiches topped with steaming onions. The men attacked their steaks eagerly, but I picked up and put down my utensils several times.

Finally, I took a deep breath. "Did my mom tell you—"

"About why you two are in Prince George? Yeah, she filled me in." He lowered his knife and looked at me in solemn concern. "I'm really sorry about your birth mom."

"Thanks," I murmured. "I appreciate it. But learning about her was more of a shock than anything. Dan and Maureen are my real parents, and I wouldn't have it any other way."

Doc Tiny smiled warmly and took a large bite of steak.

"Would you mind telling me a bit about the night I was found?" I asked, lifting a morsel to my lips.

Doc Tiny paused mid-chew and rolled his eyes to the ceiling. "Yes. December second, right?"

At my nod, he continued.

"I was working in Emergency that night. Had just started on the floor when the call came in from Tome that they'd found a newborn baby girl. Authorities couldn't land a chopper in the snowstorm so two guys drove you to us. Gimme a minute and I'll think of their names."

"Michael Plummer and Thomas Chance," I supplied.

"Right, thank you, sweetie. They took turns driving while the other held you to keep you warm. You barely cried, and a few times they thought you'd stopped breathing and pulled over to revive you." He smiled gently. "They were incredible. Considering the conditions, they got you here in record time."

My expression must have betrayed my emotion because he reached across the table to cover my hand entirely with his.

"The three of us sat with you into the night, monitoring your vitals and making sure you were hydrated. We were scared you wouldn't make it. You were so small. We didn't want you to be alone. I held you for several hours, imagining you were my Kristen. You finally opened your eyes and wailed, a good, strong wail, and you wouldn't stop squawking until we got some food into you." His face creased into a broad smile and his eyes lit with joy. "That's how I knew you'd be a fighter. You lifted your arm outta your blanket and wrapped your tiny hand around my finger." He waggled his right pointer. "You had a strong grip, and your skin was finally warm and pink. You stabilized, and your vitals looked good, and we administered steroids to help your lungs develop. But you were outta the woods, and it seemed like a miracle.

"The hospital social worker—Sherry was her name, Sherry Keegan— had a list of possible foster parents. I told her I knew just the right couple. I handed you to Michael and stepped to the nurses' station to call your folks." He sat back, his plate empty, and grinned at me. "I walked the floor with you all night," he blustered.

I appreciated his teasing.

"You didn't want to be put down. Michael and Thomas were exhausted and napped in chairs, but you wanted to be held, and if I sat down, you started wailing. Kept me working hard all night, you did."

I grinned. "When did my parents get there?"

He considered. "Round breakfast time, I think. My shift had ended but I stayed till they arrived. Later that morning, church folks from Tome started trickling in to visit and pray for ya. Those ladies were disappointed they weren't allowed to hold you. You were the center of attention and everyone fell in love with you.

"When your parents finally met ya, your mom started bawling. You did too. It was so perfect. Kinda wish I'd gotten a picture of it. And of your dad holdin' ya for the first time."

I had finished my meal while he spoke. "It's all so overwhelming." I met his gaze and smiled through welling tears. "Thank you. Truly. For staying with me and saving me."

Doc Tiny squirmed. "It was a pleasure. Only too happy to. You've grown into a fine woman." He glanced at Malcolm. "I'm kinda mad you found her first. My son needs a good woman."

"That's not much of a recommendation," I joked, and Doc Tiny dissolved into roars of laughter.

After another hour of coffee and anecdotes and gawking at photographs of his grandchildren, we said our goodbyes. I was reluctant to leave. The days ahead loomed in stark contrast to the comforting warmth of Doc Tiny's presence. For a few hours, I'd been able to forget my foreboding black thoughts and enjoy myself.

Outside the diner, I hugged Doc Tiny one last time.

"Good luck to ya, kid," he boomed, opening the car door for me. "Travel safe. There's snow on the road to 150 Mile, even in April. Come by anytime you're in the area. I'd love for you to meet my wife. And drop me a line from time to time. Let me know how you're doing."

I promised to do so and waved through the window as Malcolm aimed the car south toward Highway 97.

.   .   .

IN 150 MILE HOUSE, MALCOLM HAD RESERVED A CABIN, located on the edge of a large cattle ranch, that doubled as a bed and breakfast. The owner, Brad, carried our bags onto the porch, unlocked the front door, and let us know that his wife served breakfast in the main house. Then he shoved his hands deep in the pockets of his overalls and asked if there was anything else he could do for us.

"Yes." I turned from admiring the golden-brown beams of the cabin's high ceiling to smile at him. "We're trying to trace some of my ancestors."

"Hobby of yours, eh?"

I held his gaze. "I've got reason to believe my grandfather might have hailed from hereabouts. Did you ever hear of a family named Garvey?"

Brad ran a hand over his stubbly chin and squinted. "I don't think so, but I'll ask the Missus. Any idea what line of work they was in? Did they have property local, or…?"

I shook my head. "I'm afraid we haven't been able to find out much about them."

"Do you perhaps have a phone book?" Malcolm jumped in.

Brad produced one from a kitchen drawer then bade us good night with a cheery, "If you need anything, come rap on the kitchen door. We're awake till ten and up again with the sun."

After such a large lunch, neither Malcolm nor I was very hungry. We snacked on peanuts and veggies and flipped through the phone book—a recent edition in surprisingly pristine condition. Listings included Big Lake Ranch, Lachlan, Soda Creek, Toosey, Dog Creek, and the Williams Lake Indian Band. No Garveys were listed.

I had wondered if Marcia Garvey's parents were still living or if the sibling she'd mentioned to Shelly might have stayed in the area. The lack of information in the phone book only indicated that any remaining family members didn't live in the Williams Lake region, or had married or passed away. This made our task much more difficult.

Perhaps her parents had a different last name, though I couldn't make that make sense. Perhaps they hadn't wanted to be listed in the yellow pages. Given that, in Vancouver, telephone books were nearly obsolete, I had no idea what went into being included. But here in the Interior, where neighbors lived great distances from each other, towns were small, and internet connections were spotty, it made sense that phone books were still in use.

I looked to Malcolm for help. I had counted on having a physical address in Lachlan to go. Without one, I had no idea where to start. "I'm not sure what happens first," I admitted.

Malcolm flopped onto his stomach on the bed next to me, which made me chuckle. "Well, if movies and books about small towns are to be believed, Lachlan would have some sort of central hub where all the locals gather—pub, church group, coffee house, library. So why don't we have breakfast with Brad and his wife in the morning, then make the half-hour drive into town? If nothing else, we can grab coffee at a restaurant and ask questions there." Then, with a wry grin, he joked, "They have to have at least one Tim Hortons."

Charming the locals for gossip about the Garveys was a good plan, but I couldn't pretend excitement at what local gossip might reveal about Marcia's family—the family I believed to be mine.

Chapter Thirteen

The following morning, Malcolm and I enjoyed a hearty rancher's breakfast of steak, scrambled eggs, and fried potatoes before setting off for Lachlan, a town so small, only three pictures turned up on my website searches. I drove so Malcolm could doze off his breakfast lethargy.

After half an hour, I turned onto Chesamore Way, a hard-packed dirt road pocked with potholes and lined with cattle guards, forests, and patches of melting snow. According to GPS, this muddy road was the only access to Lachlan. I could only imagine the isolation experienced by residents of such a remote community.

We were the only car on the road, though we passed men and women walking in the opposite direction.

I shook Malcolm awake when we came to a gas station with pumps that dated from the early 70s. "I think we're entering Lachlan's town center." I eased past two abandoned fruit and vegetable stands and glanced down narrow driveways. The homes resembled junk yards, complete with rusted car shells, tires, and outdated farm equipment, fenced by barbed wire and chain link fence. Beyond the houses rose wilderness. Past a white church with a cross above its double doors stood a windowless pub, its parking lot empty. A train's boxcar converted into a 1950s-style diner called Thelma's marked the end of the "business district." Lachlan had everything its inhabitants needed and not one thing more.

Malcolm and I exchanged glances. I could tell we were both thinking the same thing: no wonder Marcia ran away from this place.

"We should just keep driving," I said. Instead, I circled back, parked in front of the diner, and we left the warmth of the car.

Those born and raised in Lachlan might not notice the biting wind, but the chill added to the desperation that seemed to hover in the air. I had a hard time imagining this place appearing welcoming even in idyllic weather.

Thelma's neon arrow was turned off or not working, and the outdoor seating was covered in old snow. Movement through the glass window was the only indication that the diner was open—a waitress making her way from table to table, chatting with customers.

I hesitated, overwhelmed by foreboding as Malcolm opened the diner's door and gestured for me to precede him. I would rather have returned to the car and driven to the café in Prince George where we'd eaten with Doc Tiny. The warm, cheery atmosphere of Dot's contrasted the dim, dank solemnity of Thelma's.

The waitress turned when the chime above the door sounded, her brows knit in puzzlement even as her mouth twisted into a version of a welcoming smile. She jutted her head toward a table and several chairs on the far left of the boxcar. Malcolm nodded and smiled back.

Every face in the diner turned toward us. I didn't make eye contact with anyone and let Malcolm sit with his back to the wall so he could survey the room. The waitress passed behind the counter and disappeared through a doorway before returning with two plates of food that did not steam as one might expect.

The waitress delivered the food to a table, returned to the counter and hollered across the room, "Whatdywant?"

I cast a furtive glance around.

"Coffee," Malcolm called back, and she nodded as if this were a correct answer.

Soon, she plopped two cups of coffee on our table. The mugs were stained and chipped. The china was only slightly warm in my hands when I pulled a cup toward me.

"You folks ain't from around here," she said.

"Just passing through," I murmured.

She snorted. "Nobody just passes through Lachlan, love." Her long, red nails matched her shade of lipstick. "Where're you from?"

"My wife and I are from Vancouver," Malcolm said.

"You're a long way from home." She tapped her pencil against her notepad.

Malcolm ordered toast for both of us, though after the breakfast we'd enjoyed at Brad and Penny's, I doubted I could swallow a single bite.

"White or wheat?"

"Wheat."

The waitress hollered over her shoulder, "Kitty! Two wheats!" She stuck out her hip and rested a hand on it. "What are ya doing in Lachlan?"

"My wife might have family in the area that we're trying to track down."

"Oh, eh?"

I pasted a smile on my face. "That's right. I don't suppose you know anybody named Garvey?"

She wrinkled her nose. "Garvey? Nah, ain't nobody named Garvey in town."

Was it possible that the Garveys had been forgotten? "Are you sure?"

She rolled her eyes. "I've lived in Lachlan all my life and ain't never met nobody named Garvey."

I decided to try flattery. "My grandparents would have lived here before the eighties. You're probably too young to remember."

She practically beamed, her grin showing teeth stained by years of tobacco use. "Bless your heart, dearie, ain't you sweet. But I'm a gramma, ya know."

"Surely not!" I feigned surprise. "You're my age, aren't you?"

She still beamed as she yelled over her shoulder, "Jack!"

Three tables away, a man with hunched shoulders, graying hair, deep wrinkles, and blue veins on his nose from years of heavy drinking looked up. "What?" Both he and his companion, another old-time townie by the looks of him, faced us, lit cigarettes dangling from their lips.

The waitress jerked a thumb at me. "She's looking for family. Ya'll ever hear of a Garvey?"

Jack shrugged, shook his head, and lifted his coffee cup. His companion took a long drag before removing the cigarette and coughing. "Garvey—could that be Belham's old lady's first husband?"

"That was Garver, Frank," Jack said.

Frank shrugged. "Same shit, ain't it?"

"Sorry, Belham?" Malcolm repeated.

Everyone in the diner, even Kitty from the back kitchen with her stained apron, was now paying attention to the conversation, all pretenses that they hadn't been eavesdropping forgotten.

"Gordie Belham," an older woman sitting at the far end of the diner spoke up. The slur in her words made me think she might be nursing a hangover or perhaps still drunk from the night before. "Gordon. Ol' Crazy Gordie."

"You remember, Jack," Frank said. "Cracked up and bought it back in '81."

"Shot hisself and his old lady, Renee," the woman slurred.

Our waitress jumped in. "I heard *she* was holding the gun and shot him and the kids before she offed herself."

I cringed, both at the details and the cavalier way the diners discussed the family.

Kitty narrowed her eyes. "Why are you two looking for the Belhams? They ain't your grandparents, are they?"

I shook my head. "I don't think so. My grandparents would have been named Garvey." I didn't know this for sure but figured a little white lie wouldn't matter.

"Wasn't Gordie's old lady named Garvey afore she married him?" Kitty asked. "What was her name? Rena?"

"Renee." The old woman was pouring something into her coffee cup from a tarnished flask. "Landed here in the sixties with her man."

Our waitress shook her head vehemently. "Nobody *moves* to Lachlan. You're born here and you die here, and that's life."

"They moved here," Frank insisted. "He worked odd jobs for my uncle for a few seasons. Bought that small shack out near Bennett's place."

"The one that burned down in '83?"

"That's the one."

"I remember Renee," Kitty said darkly. "Odd one, she was. You ask me, she were hiding something."

Malcolm and I didn't need to ask questions. These folks knew how to tell a story with plenty of details, though I couldn't separate fact from rumor. Before one person stopped to draw breath, another was finishing their sentence.

Kitty frowned. "That Garvey, he took off, didn't he?"

"Few years after they got here. Wife like that, I ain't surprised."

Malcolm quickly jumped in. "What was Garvey's first name?"

"Alvin or Allan or something like that," someone suggested.

"Allan," Frank confirmed.

My jaw dropped. In my research, I'd come across the name Allan Garvey in the obituaries. He had died several decades ago, though I couldn't recall the date. I made a mental note to find the information.

"Allan and Renee kept to themselves, didn't they?" Frank asked.

"Couldn't get two words outta them unless he was drunk. But she was too good for the likes of us." Kitty sniffed. "Nobody asked her to move here."

"Do you know *why* they did, or when?" I asked.

There came a collective shaking of heads and murmurs of denial.

"They weren't here, and then they was," the old lady said. "Snuck in in the middle of the night and bought Bennett's shed and set up house."

"Allan took off in '66 or '67. Finally had enough of his old bitch and said fuck it," Frank said.

"Horrible woman." Kitty grunted. "Spiteful, malicious little toad. She'd say anything and do anything she pleased. Drinking and taking pills and raising hell."

"Not surprised she couldn't keep him," Frank agreed. "He was a good man."

"What happened to him?" Malcolm asked.

Frank shrugged. "Went back to where he came from, I s'pose. Probably waited until she was deep in her cups, then took off."

"How good a man could he have been to run out like that?" the waitress asked.

"Jesus himself woulda smacked her, and she deserved it," Frank snapped.

I wanted to ask if Allan and Renee had had children, but Jack jumped in. "Then she shacks up with Crazy Gordie a few months later, don't she?"

"Why do you call him Crazy Gordie?" I asked.

"Cuz he weren't right in the head," Kitty said. "He got religion in a bad way and went stark raving mad with it. Joined a cult. Didn't believe in government and running water and electricity. Called them tools of the devil."

"Had an episode in the late fifties. Took an axe to the church." The woman in the corner shook her head. "Hacked through the front wall, yelling about offing the minister 'cause he was the antichrist or some shit. Took five men to arrest him. The authorities tried to have him committed, but the only charge they could make stick was destruction of property, and that got dropped. Think the prosecutor couldn't be bothered. So, he slunk back to his rat hole."

"Fucking nutter, that one."

"They both were." Frank grunted. "Gordie comes into town one day and announces he and Renee are married. Wanted everyone to take him serious, but everybody knew better. She and the girls moved into his shack up there in the woods."

"They wasn't proper married," Kitty said. "Prolly got drunk one night and took a tumble."

"She was a spiteful one. Controlling and domineering. Don't know who started the fights, but they'd take to beating each other up and hollering and raising hell. The cops were called more than once."

"Had the kids taken away, too, didn't they?" Jack asked.

The woman in the corner shook her head. "Nah, they tried, but Renee threatened to poison the kids so they couldn't take 'em. Gordie drove the police off with a shot gun."

Frank grinned and shook his head. "He never was stable to begin with. She just sent him over the edge."

"They aren't around anymore?" I wanted to believe the folks in the diner were exaggerating, but something in their manner convinced me there was more naked truth than embellishment in what they said.

Jack shook his head. "Nah, they bought it years ago."

The waitress sat on the chair next to mine. "One day, dead of winter, back in '81 or thereabouts, one o' their kids comes running into town—one of the only ones left; the others all run off as soon as they could. He ain't got shoes or a coat, or even a shirt. But he was bawling, saying they were both dead."

"He shot her and then himself," the drunk woman said.

"Nuh uh, she killed them both," Frank said.

"In any case, Constable said it was a murder-suicide. They're both buried on the edge of town, and good riddance to them both."

They traded more stories of Crazy Gordie and his even crazier wife, Renee, but I stopped listening. I needed time to process Allan's, Renee's, and Gordie's lives. If they were Marcia Garvey's family, I had a better idea now of what she had run from.

"Who lives there now?" I asked the waitress.

She looked surprised. "Where?"

"The house where Gordon and Renee lived."

"It wasn't a house," Frank muttered. "More of a shack."

"It ain't there anymore. A group of kids went on a rampage back in the spring of '83 and burned out a bunch of abandoned places. The rathole Gordon had were one of 'em." Jack lit another cigarette.

"And funny enough," Kitty mused, "the first place, out near Bennett's, where Renee lived with Allan. It got burned out that night too."

"Prolly weren't much of either place to burn out. They lived like pigs. Ceiling falling in, mold, water everywhere, broken windows. And that's before the shacks were abandoned." The waitress shrugged and then looked at my plate. "You gonna eat that toast?"

I took a large bite of cold toast to save myself from talking, chewed, and swallowed. The food tasted like ash.

Malcolm looked at me and I nodded, signalling my desire to leave. At a break in the chatter, Malcolm caught Jack's attention. "How do we find the sites where Renee lived with Allan and Gordie?"

Jack obligingly sketched a rough map on a napkin, marked the town limits, and drew the route between the two former homesteads.

Frank looked at me and grunted. "Bennett owned the land way back when, and Allan leased the property from him while he worked there as a ranch hand. But now the property's owned by a different family. Bennett passed away long time ago, so you won't be able to ask him anything.

I nodded.

As we left Thelma's, I felt sure every person inside watched us until we got into the car.

I wanted to turn west on Chesamore Way and forget all about Lachlan, but if I didn't visit the locations where Marcia had once lived, I might have to return later in search of closure. That was something I absolutely did not want to do.

I was disappointed to learn that Old Bennett was long gone, though I wasn't surprised. Decades had passed since anyone connected to Marcia had lived in Lachlan. I wondered if Bennett might have been able to tell us why Renee and Allan had landed here in this tiny town all those years ago, especially since their arrival was shrouded in mystery. If what the diners had said was true, the couple had avoided townsfolk, leading to speculation that still ran rampant, even though everyone concerned was long gone.

Bennett's place was about a kilometer north of Thelma's, where the wilderness gave way to pastures and farmland. A kilometers-long, wooden fence enclosed the farm property. A two-story farmhouse sat at the end of a long drive but we weren't interested in introducing ourselves to the current owner or requesting a tour. Instead, we drove slowly on the main road until we spotted the remains of a small outbuilding on the property and came to a stop. Neither of us made a move to exit the car.

The Garvey's shack was little more than a foundation. The remnants of its blackened eastern and southern walls stood barely taller than the weeds and brush that had reclaimed the site. Even those standing remains seemed isolated, derelict, and full of despair.

"Let's go," I murmured.

Ten minutes later, we arrived at the second wreck where Marcia had lived with her mother and stepfather. As at the Bennett place, we didn't leave the car, but stared at a cluster of blackened stumps that outlined the rectangular shape of the building. This dwelling, too, had been small, judging from the foundation, and surrounded on three sides by untamed forest. The yard was filled with mangled metal and twisted barbed wire overgrown by weeds and underbrush. Broken glass and cigarette butts littered the few patches of bare ground.

On several nearby trees and boulders, spray painted graffiti and images made reference to or depicted lewd acts. I could picture the local youth coming here to drink and smoke and hang out, swapping stories of the Belhams intended to induce fear.

Though I wanted to deny the evidence, I began to believe that Allan and Renee were Marcia's parents. This made Crazy Gordie the stepfather Marcia had fled from. Even if only half of what the folks at Thelma's had claimed was true, I could understand why she ran away so often. I understood more of Marcia's story now, though most of my conclusions were speculation and conjecture.

In any case, all three of these individuals were now dead. If Marcia was Jane Doe, that explained why no one came forward to identify her. I also suspected that Gordon and Renee hadn't cared that Marcia ran away in 1976.

But my conclusions didn't explain why she'd been found dead in a clearing two hours south of Lachlan, in a town she'd had no reason to visit. Surely, she hadn't come this far north when she left Vancouver. I could readily believe that nothing would compel her to return to the town of her childhood.

Though it was entirely possible that Renee was my grandmother, I felt nothing but loathing toward her. The townsfolk might have exaggerated their depictions of her, but I was inclined to believe them. Marcia had run away from something, after all.

For several minutes, I imagined the life Marcia must have lived, having been born into her parents' dysfunctional marriage; her father dying when she was a small child. She was then thrust into a powder keg situation with an unstable stepfather and a high-strung, alcoholic, possibly drug-addicted mother. Gordon sounded like one of a thousand religious conspiracy theorists who adhered to inflexible ideas of what constituted sin. What must it have been like to grow up without running water, electricity, modern plumbing? To be isolated without friends, relations, a support structure?

Kitty mentioned that Gordie and Renee had several children. No one seemed certain how many, much less their names and ages, only that the children had all disappeared. Had they run away or been turned out to fend for themselves? Either way, like Marcia, they were victims of two people whose selfishness and instability turned me cold with anger.

I might never know the full story.

Perhaps I didn't have a right to judge those long dead individuals, but I did. I thought harshly of the adults who had failed Marcia. I had become fiercely protective of the woman I believed to be Jane Doe.

With no relations left in Lachlan to take a DNA test, no way existed to confirm whether or not Marcia Garvey was Jane Doe.

As Malcolm drove back to Brad's bed and breakfast, I stared out the window, emotionally drained.

"I wish we hadn't come," I said as we entered the cozy rental cabin.

"I'm sorry, babe," Malcolm said quietly.

I lay on my side on the bed, back to him, curled into myself. The bed shifted as Malcolm settled next to me and wrapped an arm around my waist.

"I wish I'd never seen that newspaper," I murmured. "I don't want to know anymore. I want to unlearn everything."

Malcolm ran a hand over my arm.

Tears streamed down my cheeks. For the first time since finding Marcia Garvey, I hoped fervently that she wasn't Jane Doe. Like Tammy, I wanted Marcia to have fought her demons and won, to have moved away and found happiness and contentment and peace and love. After learning how her story had begun, I didn't want her to have died alone and buried in an unmarked grave, unmourned and forgotten.

"She escaped, babe," Malcolm murmured. "Marcia got away."

"But she didn't," I sobbed. "She never really got away. She was trapped by her past, and she used drugs to try to escape."

"She did what she had to do. She was strong enough to run, and she deserves respect for her resilience."

I knew he was right.

"She deserves our sympathy," he continued. "She was a victim of other people's choices, but she started to make her own way, and she was strong enough to run."

I nodded.

"Look, it's completely your choice whether you keep looking or walk away from Jane Doe," he said. "Her life, her death, doesn't define who you are. You've gotten yourself to where you are."

"My parents helped," I mumbled.

"You're strong, too. And you get to make choices moving forward. We've discovered some things that are horrible, but we've also found some things that are pretty incredible. Doc Tiny and the story of how you were saved, and the paramedics who drove through the snowstorm, and the parish in Tome that still lights a candle and prays for you."

I rolled over and offered him a weak smile.

He wrapped his arms around me. "What if we forget about Lachlan for now? How about tomorrow we drive to Tome and have another conversation with Una Braithwaite? We could ask to meet Father Clement, and maybe Michael Plummer, the paramedic who saved you."

Malcolm's reminders of the decent people we had met coaxed me out of my dark thoughts. My eyelids grew heavy. Safe in his arms, and with the promise of a better day tomorrow, I drifted off to sleep.

Chapter Fourteen

Malcolm and I returned to the Parish of St. Raymond early the next morning. Una Braithwaite required a few moments to place us, but did so when Malcolm reminded her of our previous meeting in February.

"Is Father Clement available?" Malcolm asked.

Una ushered us into the main office. "Father, this is Malcolm and Nora Devrey, all the way from Vancouver," she said as if we'd been friends for a long time. "This is their second visit to the Parish, and they're eager to meet you."

Father Clement, a young pastor who exuded warmth, spread his arms to indicate his surroundings. "You are most welcome here. It's a pleasure to meet you both."

"Your church is beautiful," I said. "I felt at home here right away."

Una gestured toward the chairs in front of the Father's desk, and Malcolm and I sat. "I can bring coffee or tea, if you like."

"No, thank you," I said. "We don't want to impose. But I would love to chat with both of you."

Una looked a little surprised to be included but took a seat.

"What can we do for you?" Father Clement asked, resuming his own chair behind his desk.

I took a deep breath and smiled shyly. "Actually, I think there's something that I can do for you. My husband and I came to Tome last February because I'm looking for my family. I was adopted when I was little—just a baby."

Father Clement nodded politely, but Una leaned forward, eyes wide.

I looked at her. "My mother gave birth to me here in Tome on December 2, 1980. She left me here at the Parish during a snowstorm. I–I'm Baby Judea."

Una's hands flew to her mouth and tears sprang to her eyes. She left her chair, pulled me into a hug, and sobbed as if I were her prodigal daughter. "I held you as a baby," she exclaimed. "I can't believe you're here in front of me now."

Father Clement clasped his hands. "Let's give thanks to the Almighty for this blessed reconciliation. He truly does have plans for each of us. As he says in Jeremiah 29:11, 'For I know the plans I have for you,' says the Lord, 'Plans to prosper you and not to harm you; plans to give you hope and a future.'"

"Amen," Una murmured, crossing herself.

Malcolm did the same, and I quickly mimicked his gesture.

"There are so many people who would love to meet you," Father Clement's eyes shone with tears of joy.

This wasn't something I had foreseen. "Thank you, but we were hoping today's meetings might be more quiet and intimate. I wanted to meet you, of course, and to see Una again." I turned to her. "And I hoped I might meet your husband, John. If it's not too much to ask."

"Of course not," Una exclaimed. "No trouble at all. I'll call him right now." Without missing a beat, she lifted the receiver from the Father's desktop phone and punched in several numbers. A brief moment of silence followed before she said, "John, you must come to the church straightaway! No, nothing's wrong, I have a lovely surprise for you." Her eyes found mine and twinkled, "Hurry up and get here. Your keys are in your overalls pocket."

"Tell us about your parents," Father Clement urged as Una replaced the receiver.

In the middle of an anecdote about my parents, someone entered the outer vestibule of the church, then a man tapped on the open doorway of the Father's study.

"John," Una exclaimed, rising and rushing to pull him into the room. "You will not believe who has come to visit us today!"

John Braithwaite's small face went bright red when Una led him over to where Malcolm and I had risen from our chairs. "This is Baby Judea."

I smiled shyly and offered my hand. "Nora Devrey, and this is my husband, Malcolm."

John dipped his head and murmured, "It's a pleasure to meet you, ma'am." He shook Malcolm's hand in turn and said to me, "There was a time when we thought we'd be the ones to adopt you."

"Una told me," I said warmly. "You are both so wonderfully kind, I would have been lucky to have had you as parents."

"Oh, if only Father Patrick were here to meet you. And Thomas. And Bernard. May they rest in peace," Una said with a sigh. "But they see us. They know."

"Amen," Father Clement murmured. "Do you have any idea what might have become of your birth mother? No trace of her was found in Tome that winter, as I understand."

Malcolm looked to me.

"We're still trying to find her," I said. "We believe she went to high school in 100 Mile House and moved to Vancouver in 1977. We don't know why she came to Tome in 1980 or where she went after. But we have a few leads to follow up on."

"Are you helping the police look for her?" Una asked. "A few weeks ago, we got a call from the nicest police investigator. Oh, what was his name?"

"Chilton," John said. "Something Chilton."

I pressed my lips together. I wasn't ready to reveal my involvement with the investigation.

"He asked all sorts of questions about the night you were found," Una went on. "Of course, I was only too happy to help. He wanted to know about your birth mother. I wonder what the police want with her."

If they sensed that we knew more than we were telling, they gave no indication.

Malcolm glanced at me. "We were hoping that we might be able to meet Michael Plummer."

"Michael lives with his daughter and son-in-law a few blocks away," Una said. "Let me give him a call and see if you can drop by." She picked up the phone on Father Clement's desk and punched in a number from memory.

After Una hung up, she said Michael Plummer was home and invited us to stop by. John volunteered to show us the way. Una and Father Clement wished us the best of luck in our search for my birth mother and begged us to let them know what we discovered.

I promised to do so.

We followed John's white pickup truck a few short blocks to a neatly kept, one-story home with children's toys scattered about the front porch. John gave a series of toots on his horn to say goodbye, then drove off.

An older man I assumed was Michael waved to us from the front window as we got out of the car. When we knocked, a young woman holding a small boy opened the door. She stepped back so we could enter.

"Hi, I'm Emily, Michael's daughter. This is Neil. Michael's in the living room, just there." She gestured with her elbow. "Please make yourselves welcome. I'll bring you some tea."

Michael Plummer stood shakily as we entered the tidy living room. He must have been at least seventy and was slightly stooped. I glimpsed a medical alert bracelet on his wrist and a hearing aid in one ear. But he still stood taller than Malcolm and his handshake was firm.

Malcolm introduced us and took my hand. "Thank you for letting us drop in on you on such short notice."

Michael waved the air. "I love having visitors. Besides, Una was most mysterious when she called. But any friend of John and Una is a friend of mine."

Emily entered with a tray of tea and cookies. "Shortbread, Dad, your favorite."

I was reminded of the closeness I felt to my dad.

She set down the tray and excused herself, saying it was time for Neil's nap.

"Emily's my youngest," Michael said. "My oldest, Lucy, became a nurse and moved to Prince George a dozen or so years ago. I came to stay with Emily six years ago, after she married a lawyer. Chris—that's her husband—works at his father's firm here in town. My Theresa had passed by then, and I wanted to be closer to family, especially with grandkids coming." The pride in his family was evident in his smile. "So, what is it I can do for you two?"

"We heard that you and another volunteer, Thomas Chance, saved a baby's life in 1980. I hoped you might tell us more," I said.

Michael seemed to shrink and the tips of his ears reddened underneath his thinning white hair. "We were just glad she made it, the poor tyke. It was a miracle. It really was. But it was no more than any one of us would have done. It just happened that Thomas and I were on call that night for emergencies."

"Could you tell us about it?" I asked.

Michael paused and nodded. "Tome gets a lot of snow in winter. It often starts snowing in October and, most years, keeps on right through March. We get ice storms, windstorms, rainstorms, and then spring floods. In every major weather event, most everybody in town loses power, and phone lines go down.

"In this particular storm, Tom and I were going door to door making sure everyone had blankets, wood, and bottled water," Michael recalled, "when John Braithwaite called us on the radio. Una and Father Bernard found a baby on the church steps. Tom and I did a quick dash to the snowmobiles at the end of the block. I say 'dash,' but really, we were swimming down Main Street through two feet of fresh snow. We ripped to the church. Doc Wilby and Nurse Bain were there, and told us the baby would die if she didn't get to the hospital. Well, we don't have a hospital in town, which is why Lucy lives in Prince George. And the hospital in 100 Mile didn't have the facilities for preemies. So, she had to go to Prince George. We would have flown there, but you can't land a chopper in that kind of weather. That baby was so small and sickly, and oh so cold that me and Tom, we look at each other, and we knew without saying that we were going to drive that little girl wherever she needed to go. I told Una to tell Theresa and Nancy—Nancy Chance, Tom's wife—where we were going. I picked up that baby girl and tucked her into my coat, and Tom got the keys to John's pickup truck, and we headed to the highway.

"Couldn't see your hand in front of your face. Temperature was down to twenty-three below zero and the windchill was even worse. Your breath froze on your lips." He pointed to his top lip. "Tom drove the first bit because he knew the roads better than he knew his own backyard. I rocked the baby and patted her back and kept checking to make sure she was breathing. Two or three times we thought she'd stopped breathing, and stopped to resuscitate her, and all the while we were thinking we weren't gonna make it. Hospital was a two-hour drive in the best conditions. The storm stopped just outside of 150 Mile, but the plows hadn't been through, so the road hadn't been plowed or salted, and we didn't see another soul that night. The only thing that changed was now we could see, though we had no idea where the road was." Michael shook his head. "It's a great story now, but the whole way there, we were scared. We'd trade off every so often, so Tom held the baby and I drove, and then back again."

"And you made it," I murmured, wholly enthralled. I'd heard the end of the tale from Doc Tiny, but I still sat on the edge of my seat, caught up in the moment.

"We made it," he confirmed. "Left Tome around five or so and got into Prince George around nine. No idea to this day how we did it, but we did. And we stayed with the little girl till we knew she was gonna make it. Sat with her all night, praying. And she made it."

He laced his fingers over his stomach and sighed. "I think about her from time to time. I heard she went to good parents. I hope she grew up and lived happily ever after."

Malcolm glanced at me with a question in his eyes.

"Go ahead," I said. "Tell him."

"Tell me what?" Michael asked.

Malcolm squeezed my hand. "Nora was adopted as a baby." He

paused. "She recently learned that she was found here in Tome on December 2, 1980."

Michael had been smiling politely at Malcolm. Now his jaw dropped. He stared at me and sputtered, "You're the baby girl?"

Tears spilled onto my cheeks as I nodded, and then Michael was laughing—a high-pitched cry of joy. "Dear girl," he exclaimed, reaching for me. I met his embrace, and he kissed my cheek.

"It's been quite an emotional visit," I said, wiping my cheeks. "I'm not normally a crier."

"Oh, if only Thomas were here to meet you." He searched my face. "Look at you! All grown up. And I held you!"

"Thank you," I said with all the sincerity and depth and warmth I felt toward this man.

He called to his daughter.

Emily rushed into the room. "What's wrong?" she cried, alarm on her face.

"It's a happy reunion," Malcolm hastily assured. "Your father rescued my wife when she was a baby."

"She's Baby Judea," Michael choked out.

Emily's eyes went wide and she looked at me in astonishment.

"I'm still getting used to this myself," I joked.

Michael clapped in delight.

I took both his hands and looked deeply into his eyes. "Thank you, Michael. Thank you for making the drive to save my life."

Some time later when the door opened and the Braithwaites entered Michael's living room, we were still sipping tea, chatting, and reminiscing like old friends. Not quite an hour later, Emily's husband, Chris, came home to find his living room full of happy, emotional people.

I suggested that we make a visit to the cemetery to visit the graves of the others who had rescued me. The idea was met with enthusiasm. Malcolm and I made a quick stop at a florist and caught up with the others at the front gates of the Garden of Eden cemetery in Tome.

We laid flowers on the graves of Father Patrick, Thomas Chance, and Bernard Beardsley. I thanked each of these men for their part in my story. And I thanked my newfound friends in Tome for being there with me.

Before Emily took Michael home, he begged us to visit anytime we happened to be in the area, and we promised to do so. Then we hung on each other and hugged and teared up again, as if we didn't expect to see each other again.

After such emotionally reinvigorating interactions, I felt brave enough to revisit the painful part of my story. I asked Una Braithwaite if she knew how to contact the two hikers who found Jane Doe. She was only too happy to provide the numbers for their families. Then I gave her a final, fond embrace before we said goodbye.

As we drove back toward 150 Mile House, I turned to Malcom with a smile, entirely contented and refreshed. "You were right about coming here and meeting these people. Thank you."

He smiled as he signaled a turn and slowed. "What do you feel like doing tomorrow?"

After a slight hesitation, I said, "I thought we might return to Jane Doe."

His jaw clenched. "Are you sure that's a good idea? You were pretty upset yesterday."

"I know. But you were right. There were positive discoveries, as well. I have to take the good with the bad, right? I want to contact Terry and Scott Duggan."

"The men who found Jane Doe," he said.

I nodded. "I'd like to see if they'd be willing to meet me."

Scott was. Terry wasn't. Scott explained that Terry was a man of few words who had shied away from the media attention surrounding their hike in the summer of 2005.

We arranged to meet at a restaurant in Tome for breakfast at nine thirty the following morning before Malcolm and I drove back to Prince George for our flight home at five. It had been a struggle to get Scott to see us that early. He finally agreed when we said we'd pick up the bill.

I recognized him when he stumbled into the restaurant a few

minutes before ten. He'd aged since giving those media interviews five years earlier, but he had the same wiry build, small beer gut, bald head, and goatee. He looked and smelled hungover. His nose ran and his eyes were red rimmed.

The waitress arrived soon after Scott reached our table. She refilled the coffees Malcolm and I had ordered to hold us over while waiting. We quickly placed our breakfast orders and she hurried away.

"So, you want to hear about that hike," Scott said with some satisfaction, sprawled on the other side of the booth, arms outstretched along the top of the bench seat. His attention shifted about the restaurant, then lingered on a young lady who walked past headed toward the restroom.

I hid a smile. Scott exuded superciliousness and inspired ridicule.

Malcolm shook his head.

Terry gave exactly one interview in the summer of 2005. Scott talked to anyone with a camera who would put his face on the news.

"Yeah, I'm kinda famous around town," he said, casually flicking a bit of lint off his left shoulder. "Something like a celebrity or a TV personality. Everyone wants to hear how I found that body. I think I should write a book about it. Maybe they'd even turn it into a movie."

Rather than being offended by his cavalier attitude, I found myself biting my lower lip to keep from laughing. "I saw the interview you gave."

"Which one?" he asked, preening a little. "I was made for the camera. Wasting my time in a small town like this."

"So, tell *us* the story," Malcolm said.

"Well, see, I'd been working real hard leading up to that weekend, and just needed a break. Always working, and little sleep, and my pregnant wife getting on me all the time with her nagging...." He hesitated as if he realized his statement might offend me, then turned to Malcolm and added, "You know how it is."

"Fortunately, I do not." Malcolm smiled, his hand lovingly on my arm. "Tell me, what line of work are you in?" His tone, though polite, contradicted the glimmer of mischief I noticed in his eyes.

Scott's smile seemed frozen in place. "Well, I-I'm in between opportunities right now," he hedged. "Big things coming around the corner. Are you in business?"

"I'm in marketing," Malcolm answered. "And my wife is a researcher and lecturer."

I guessed from his expression that Scott held unfavorable opinions about females who held careers, in spite of his polite, "That's nice."

We were spared having to respond by the return of the waitress. After she passed out plates of eggs, bacon, and toast, and Malcolm assured her we didn't need anything else, I said, "So, you and your brother took a weekend away."

Scott talked with his mouth full. "I'm rather an avid outdoorsman. I love hiking in the summer and camping and really roughing it in the backwoods. I'd been to that clearing many times, used it to camp in the winters when I go ice fishing."

Braggart that he was, I wouldn't have been surprised if he'd launched into a story about catching a record-breaking fish.

"My brother, Terry, not so much. He doesn't really leave town, more of a homebody. But I thought it would be good to get him out into the great outdoors for the weekend, so I persuaded him to come out with me. Not to the campsites or the cabins. You can fend for yourself if you have the right gear and know what you're doing."

The exaggerations were so entertaining, I leaned forward in encouragement. "You packed up all your gear and hiked out there? How long did it take? That must have been quite difficult."

Scott smiled condescendingly. "Perhaps for you city folk. But we're used to roughing it. True, it's a tough hike, fighting back country wilderness and battling uphill most of the way. Took us a good five or six hours, it did, and with heavy gear, it was quite the workout. But I work out all the time."

We had completed that same hike. Considering that almost half the distance had been along a level, dirt-packed utility path, I allowed myself a private smile. I had no doubt that it had taken Scott and Terry six hours to reach the clearing when it had only taken us three. Scott struck me as an amateur who'd stumbled in circles while battling underbrush.

"I knew exactly where I was going, but I had to slow my pace to match my brother's or I would have left him behind. He's not an experienced outdoorsman, otherwise we might have made it in half the time. Of course, when we get to the clearing, he's exhausted and needs to rest for a spell, so I start putting up the tent. And his dog—oh, he brought his dog along just in case we ran into anything, bears, or cougars, or anything. I told him he didn't need to bring the mutt. I had my gun and I'm a crack shot. I can hit a bullseye every time. Once dropped a bear with a single shot. But I left my gun in the truck. Any experienced outdoorsman would know you wouldn't see bears or cougars or wolves on that part of the lake edge. Too close to the highway."

"You were saying about the dog," Malcolm prompted.

"Oh yeah—the dog trots over to the other side of the clearing, underneath these great bloody trees, and starts digging at the underbrush. I figured it was something nasty, so I hollered at Terry to get his dog."

I noticed Scott's contradictions but resisted the temptation to point out his glaring inaccuracies. I worried he might take offense and clam up.

"But Terry's still a bit tired, so he sits on the stump, and I go over to grab the dog and drag him off. And that," he lowered his voice to a near whisper, "is when I saw it." He paused dramatically, clearly waiting for us to ask.

Malcolm indulged him. "Saw what?"

"The skull," he whispered.

I had been laughing inwardly at this ridiculous man, but now the solemnity of the moment hit me. That skull, I wanted to shout, had belonged to my mother. I stared at the table.

"The skull looked like a rock at first," Scott continued. "Couldn't see the eyeholes or teeth. She must have been lying face down when she was—"

"We don't need the details or your opinions," Malcolm interrupted. "Just tell us what happened next."

Scott appeared offended. I imagine most of his audiences had been hungry for every detail.

"I threw the tent into a backpack, and we took off out the far side of the clearing."

"Not back the way you came?" I prodded.

"Nah. It was faster to hike an hour or so to the highway and flag somebody down. I used the guy's cellphone to call the police and tell them what we found, and we waited about half an hour for them to drive up from 100 Mile. The cops brought ATVs, so it took less than twenty minutes to get back to the spot. Then some reporters started showing up, and they put up all kinds of barricades so no one could see them dig up the rest of her. We gave our statements to the cops. And then the reporters wanted to talk to us."

I'd heard enough. A pounding had begun in the base of my skull that threatened to erupt into a headache. I pushed my plate aside and turned to Malcolm. "I'm not feeling well." The air was suddenly too stuffy, and I needed to step outside.

Malcolm signaled the waitress for the bill.

"Thank you for meeting us," I told Scott politely, though I wanted to snap at him.

He looked me over, seeming elated at having gotten such a reaction, and disappointed that his retelling had been cut short.

As I walked away, Scott asked Malcolm, "She get squeamish?" I didn't hear Malcolm's reply.

I was resting in the passenger seat with my head tipped back and my eyes closed when Malcolm rejoined me. After a moment of silence, he snorted. "Wasn't he charming?"

I looked at him and smiled vaguely.

"You okay?" he asked.

Closing my eyes again, I shrugged. "I know I wanted to meet him, but I can't think of a single good reason why. We didn't learn anything new."

"Maybe not, but you can cross him off your list and go home knowing he's an arrogant ass."

His attempt at humor cheered me slightly, but another dark mood was settling. I couldn't change Jane Doe's story, but I could ease into it more slowly, as I would immerse myself in a cold ocean or a really hot bath.

Our flight left Prince George in a little over six hours. We gassed up the rental car and hit the highway north out of Tome. I looked back as we left, not sure if I would ever return. I had appreciated meeting the Braithwaites and Michael Plummer and the Davies and Father Clement. If I found myself in the area again, I would be thrilled to visit them, and I knew I'd be welcome every time. But I couldn't think of another reason to return. I wasn't sure of the way forward from here. We'd learned everything we could about my birth story, the discovery of Jane Doe's remains, and Marcia Garvey's childhood, and we'd hit a dead end.

Perhaps Inspector Chilton might have some new information. I had promised to keep him apprised of anything we learned, and resolved to call him the following day. Then I would meet my mother for tennis and lunch and forget about Tome and Lachlan and Marcia Garvey and Jane Doe.

At least for now.

Chapter Fifteen

APRIL QUICKLY TURNED INTO MAY, AND THEN MAY INTO June. For a while, I spoke with Inspector Doug Chilton once a week by phone, but as weeks passed without new developments, two weeks and then three went by without contact. These conversations were the only interjections of the Jane Doe investigation into my life. By July, when another infrequent telephone call came in, Inspector Chilton and I were on a first name basis.

"Nora, we got a tip from the hotline, from someone who might have seen Jane Doe. He's not sure it's the same girl, or the right time of year, or even what year he saw her, so don't get your hopes up."

The tip, Doug said, came from a man who'd worked in his father's grocery store on the outskirts of 150 Mile House as a teenager. One night while helping an elderly woman load groceries into her station wagon, he watched a really pretty girl wearing a blue rain jacket who could have been Jane Doe.

The girl limped across the parking lot and entered the store. Her long black hair spilled past the hood that lay flat against her back, and her blue jeans were tucked into well-worn boots. She entered the store, bought something, and stood at the counter talking to the informant's father for a few minutes.

During that time, a long-haul truck driver named Dimes pulled up in his rig. The informant had no idea where the nickname came from or what Dimes' real name was and could only describe him as short with black hair, a beard, and a moustache.

Dimes entered the store, and he and the girl exited together a few minutes later. Both got into his truck. Dimes hadn't forced or coerced her to go with him. The truck chugged out of the lot and made for the southbound ramp to the highway. The tipster reported having never seen either of them again.

"He admitted to smoking a lot of weed in those days, so his story might not pan out. We're following up, though," Doug said. "Especially since we believe Jane Doe was hitchhiking, and the store is situated an hour or so from where her body was found."

I listened in silence, visualizing the pretty girl with the long black hair climbing into the man's truck. Was the girl Marcia? Marcia had been living on the streets of Vancouver for a few years by then. She'd hitchhiked for most of her teenage life. She wouldn't have had any qualms about getting into a truck with a stranger.

Doug sighed. "Everyone assumes they won't fall victim to a predator, that bad things happen to someone else but not to them. We have several persons of interest connected to other missing persons cases. We haven't found any matches from the DNA samples we collected from Jane Doe's remains, but we're still looking."

I wondered about Jane Doe's killer. Who had taken such pains to hide her in a clearing where they hoped she'd never be found? Was her murderer a short, dark-haired trucker nicknamed Dimes? A shiver crept up my spine.

"We corroborated what you learned about Kenny with records from the Correction Service of Canada and Vancouver Police Department. Kenneth Stephen Gates was arrested for armed robbery in late 1978 and sentenced to seven years in prison. He was released for good behavior after serving five. His criminal records note that he was a quiet young man who suffered withdrawal from heroin and cleaned up reluctantly. In 1981, he obtained his high school diploma through their education program. His parole officer notes that Kenny planned to go into construction or another trade that required little schooling. But three weeks after his release, he died of a heroin overdose."

Kenny's incarceration in 1979 made it highly unlikely that he was my birth father. He was simply another young kid with big dreams in a world of limitations who had partied too hard and made some bad choices that proved fatal.

"Marcia's criminal record also arrived," Doug continued. "Her first arrest in 1977 was confirmed and occurred weeks after she joined the downtown commune. They were minor charges of mischief and vandalism, which were dropped."

I remembered my April conversation with Tammy. "I discovered the possibility of Marcia having a criminal record from an old friend of hers, but couldn't find a trace of those records through internet search. Do you have any idea why that might be?"

"It's possible," he said, "the convictions happened so long ago that any official records were buried on the back page of the search. It's also likely that human error played a factor if her last name was spelled wrong when the files were digitized. But I think it's likeliest a matter of the search engine you used. Criminal records aren't a matter of public record, but court documents and convictions are, subject to certain caveats."

"What do you mean?"

"Any records that occurred before the age of majority would have been sealed. But in Marcia's case, most of her convictions occurred after her nineteenth birthday. Any public record verdicts or rulings have to be accessed through the BC government website. They have a database for online court services through which you can search by individual name, date of birth, date of arrest, court file number, and so on. I doubt a general internet search is able to pull information from this database."

"That fits. So, getting back to her history, can you tell me what a charge of mischief entails? Does the arrest record say what she did?"

Doug hesitated. "Her juvenile records are sealed, but a charge of mischief and vandalism could have been something as minor as participating in an anti-war protest, or a rally to legalize marijuana, or equal rights for women and homosexuals."

Knowing the charges filed against Marcia in subsequent years, it was difficult to give her the benefit of the doubt.

"She was arrested for possession soon afterward, resulting in a slap on the wrist and probation," Doug continued. "A few weeks later, she was back in court for minor theft. From there, the charges get more serious. Her earliest drug offenses are recorded in early 1979—drunk and disorderly, disturbance of the peace, theft, assault, drug possession and distribution. Later that year, she was charged with prostitution, though the charge was dropped when the john invoked his right against self-incrimination. In the spring of 1980, she was caught in an undercover prostitution sting, and the court offered her a choice. She could dry out, clean up, and sober up, or face prison time. She opted for rehab.

"According to her probation officer's monthly reports, after getting clean, she entered a recovery house on the other side of the Fraser River, away from Vancouver and her old haunts. She attended twelve-step drug and alcohol programs several times a week. Her probation officer notes she found employment in the fall of 1980, and for several months, she didn't miss a check-in or appointment. Until January, 1981, when she disappeared. A bench warrant went out for her arrest, but she was never found. Though"—Doug hesitated—"I can't see the authorities actively searching for her. In the seventies and eighties, repeat offenders often fell back into the system with very little effort exerted on our part."

If Marcia was my mother, her timeline fit with my birthday. She could have landed in Tome in late November or early December, given birth to me, and then…what? She hadn't stayed in Tome. There was no trace of her having been there. Had she continued north for some unknown reason, or gone back to Vancouver and eluded the authorities?

Or, was it possible that Marcia was murdered before her January check-in with the probation officer?

"So, there's no official trace of Marcia after 1981," I said.

"No record of her after 1981 that we've found yet," Doug clarified.

I bit my lip. "Doug, tell me the truth. Do you think Marcia Garvey is Jane Doe? Do you think she's my mother?"

He sighed. "Without a living family member to submit a DNA

sample, we can't conclusively prove that Marcia Garvey is Jane Doe. But hang in there. We aren't beat yet."

My search for Jane Doe remained on hiatus for the rest of the summer as the flow of information had stagnated and I had no motivation to continue looking. My days somewhat resembled my pre-Jane Doe days. I stopped compulsively checking the mail and let two or three days go by before collecting it. I read emails from old friends from our university days without wondering if I'd ever hear from Marcia's classmates. Malcolm and I attended a friend's wedding. We went camping. We bought new balcony furniture and, together, assembled it one Saturday evening over drinks. We repainted the bathroom. We frequently visited our parents.

At the university, the familiar routine of lectures, office hours, tutorials, exams, and term papers made the weeks fly by, and I began planning lessons for the fall semester.

Finally, in late August, I adjudicated my final exams and summer classes ended. The following day, Friday, Malcolm and I planned to leave for a camping trip to a special secluded spot, one of our favorite summer traditions. I was in the kitchen, airing out the hiking backpacks we'd used in February, when my phone on the counter began vibrating. I didn't recognize the number and was tempted to ignore the call. Instead, I answered with a terse "Yes?" expecting a telemarketer to launch into a scripted sales pitch.

After a moment of awkward silence, a woman ventured a cautious, "Hello. I'd like to speak with Nora Devrey, please."

"Yes, speaking." I shifted the phone to my shoulder and braced it against my jaw so I could zip up Malcolm's pack.

"Ms. Devrey, my name is Eleanor. Eleanor Reinhardt. You sent me a letter."

The hairs on my arms stood on end. Eleanor Reinhardt, born Eleanor Garvey, was Allan Garvey's sister and the woman I believed to be Marcia Garvey's aunt.

"I apologize for not getting in touch sooner," she said. "My husband and I summer in Nova Scotia with his sister. Our oldest son house sits for us, but he left several weeks ago when that forest fire broke out north of Calgary. He's a firefighter," she explained. "He inadvertently tucked your letter into his bag when he left, and he finally returned home the day before yesterday. So, you see, your letter only just came to me yesterday." Her slightly muted voice, sweet and full of warmth, shook with the effects of age. She coughed quietly every few minutes. "I called as soon as I had the chance, but to be perfectly honest, I don't know how much I can tell you. My few interactions with Marcia happened so long ago, I can't be sure I have anything that might help."

"I appreciate that you've taken the time to call me, I'm very pleased to meet you. And please, again, let me extend my condolences for the loss of your parents."

"Oh, thank you, dear, though they passed away some time ago. You do miss them as you get on, but my parents had full lives. I think Dad, especially, was ready to go. He missed Mom. They'd been together since childhood and practically grown up together. How do you go for so long without your soulmate after being together for almost fifty years?"

I thought of Malcolm and shook my head. "I can't imagine."

"I had married and had children of my own, and Dad was able to meet his grandchildren and tell his stories. My brother was already gone by then, as well. So, you see, I do miss my family, but I know they are together and that someday we'll be reunited."

"Yes I-I'm very sorry about your brother, as well."

"Ah, Allan." She sighed. "I adored Allan. He was four years older than me. Growing up, he told me how Dad went off to fight in the war, leaving him and Mom at home. Then Dad came home, and I was born shortly after."

"Your parents sound like they were fascinating people."

"Ah, yes, you mentioned you found my name in their obituaries, and are trying to find your own parents. Is that right?"

"That's right." I had given the bare bones of my story in my letter but explained again that I had been born in or near Tome and found at the parish before being adopted and raised in Vancouver.

"And you think Marcia Garvey will be able to help you find your parents?"

I hesitated. "I have reason to believe that Marcia Garvey knows who my birth mother and father are. I'm afraid that every other lead I've pursued has been more or less a dead end."

She clucked her tongue. "Marcia Garvey is my niece, Allan's daughter."

At her use of the present tense, a jolt of excitement raced through me.

She went on, "I'm afraid I haven't seen her since she was very young. I'm so sorry I can't help you."

Disappointment washed over me. "No need to apologize. But I wonder if there is anything you can tell me about her. Or maybe about your brother and his wife? If you wouldn't mind."

Eleanor was silent for so long that I worried the call had dropped. I was opening my mouth to say something, to see if she was still there, when she sighed.

"Nora— May I call you Nora? I'm sure you can appreciate that you're asking about a deeply personal matter." Her tone was kind but firm. "And I'm sure you can understand why I would be hesitant to share the intimate details of my family with anyone, particularly a stranger, and particularly over the phone."

I felt properly chastised. "I didn't mean any disrespect," I said meekly.

"Of course, you didn't, dear. But I would feel more comfortable sharing information if you were able to tell me why you believe Marcia's connection is relevant to your search."

I took a deep breath. "Mrs. Reinhardt, you're right, you have a right to know, but what I have to say isn't all pleasant." I searched for a kind way to break the news and failed. "I believe your niece may be my birth mother."

She didn't say anything.

I filled the growing silence with a simple, "I'm sorry."

"I suppose you have good reason for this ruse," Mrs. Reinhardt said at last. "I can't expect that you would want to confide in a complete stranger, either. But tell me why you believe my niece is your birth mother."

"It's a bit of a long story," I said.

"Go on."

I decided not to mention the newspaper article and the tragic demise of Jane Doe, as Eleanor seemed to believe that her niece was alive. Instead, I described our trip to Tome to see where I'd been left as a newborn, and how Malcolm and I searched the yearbooks for people who looked like me.

"Sounds as if you were searching for a needle in a haystack," Eleanor said.

"We actually got very lucky," I replied. "We found pictures of your niece in the 1976 and 1977 yearbooks at 100 Mile House. Her photos look just like me."

"100 Mile House?" she repeated. "She went to school in 100 Mile?"

"For a year or two," I answered. "She was living with a girlfriend there. Shelly gave us more of Marcia's story, and said Marcia was born in Lachlan. That's where the search took me next."

"Lachlan. So *that's* where Allan and Renee went," she mused.

My breath caught.

"Did you find Renee?"

"I'm afraid we didn't. From what we were able to gather, Renee took up with a local man who wasn't.... He had a reputation about town; didn't appear to be emotionally stable. They both died in 1981."

She sighed. "Oh dear."

"Marcia went to Vancouver with friends in 1977. I believe she came back to the Interior sometime at the end of 1980, and in December of that year, she gave birth to me and left me in Tome. Then she seems to have vanished."

"No one has seen her since 1980? Oh dear," Eleanor repeated. "Could she still be alive?"

"I–I hope so, I really do."

Eleanor fell silent again. When she finally spoke, her voice was full of sorrow. "I hope so, too. I loved my brother despite his faults, but I was always wary of Renee."

I opened my mouth to inquire about her sister-in-law when she asked, "I don't suppose you know what happened to the other girl, Ellen?"

I snapped my mouth shut as her question sank in. After a moment, I stammered, "I'm s-sorry. Ellen?"

"Yes. I last saw them in 1963. I've always wondered what happened to those two little girls I played with that day." Her voice seemed strained, as if she were trying to control strong emotions.

I struggled to process what she'd said. "Do you mean Shelly? Marcia and Shelly?" Even as I asked, my questions didn't make sense to me. Eleanor hadn't seen her niece since Marcia was very young. Marcia met Shelly when they were eleven or twelve. It wasn't possible that Eleanor had known Shelly, and even less likely that she would be concerned what had happened to her.

"Shelly, the girl Marcia lived with in 100 Mile? No, dear." She sounded confused. "I mean my other niece. Allan and Renee's younger daughter."

Part Three

A SEASON OF ELLEN

Chapter Sixteen

Allan and Renee's younger daughter, I repeated to myself, struggling to process what Eleanor had said.

"Ellen would have been born in.... Oh, what was it? Late 1962, or early 1963, I believe."

"Allan and Renee had another daughter?" I repeated in disbelief.

"That's right, dear." Eleanor sounded puzzled. "You mean you didn't know?"

The significance of this new piece of information was hitting me slowly. I knew it was of vital importance, but it took a minute to understand why.

No one had mentioned a younger sister. Not Tammy, or Chad, or anyone in Lachlan. Shelly had mentioned younger siblings, but in a very off-handed comment, as one of the few things Marcia mentioned about home and the reason she felt compelled to return home after running away. Was it possible no one knew of Ellen's existence outside of her family?

Marcia was born in 1960. Ellen followed about three years later. She lived in the same small cabin with Allan, Renee, and Marcia, and later, with Gordon, Renee, and Marcia. Ellen had likely endured the same traumatic childhood as Marcia. Marcia had run away. Had Ellen done the same? If so, where would she have gone? Most importantly…where was she now? Which girl had lain in that shallow grave for twenty-five years? "So, it could be Ellen," I said at last.

"I'm sorry, dear, I'm confused. You mean you think it's possible that Ellen is your mother?"

"I didn't know there was a younger sister," I whispered.

"But you seemed confident that Marcia was your birth mother. Perhaps you could explain what made you believe this."

I sat down heavily on the kitchen floor and leaned against a cabinet, hand covering my mouth as I tried to settle my thoughts.

"Mrs. Reinhardt," I said at last, "I don't quite know where to begin. Please bear with me. I've known since I was young that I was adopted. My parents are wonderful people, and I was never interested in finding my biological family until six months ago. I think you need to know the whole story. It's going to be difficult to hear, and I can only say I'm sorry it has to come from me."

I began by describing my height, weight, hair, eye color, and distinguishing features. Then I told her about the cold case the RCMP were trying to close and the police sketch of a woman who looked identical to me.

"A police sketch?"

"Yes. The police were asking for help in identifying this girl. They were calling her Jane Doe. She was the victim of a homicide at least three decades ago. Her remains were found in a provincial park in the Interior in 2005."

She gasped.

"The sketch made me question where I came from. I was found as a baby in Tome, the town closest to the park where this girl was buried."

"And the police think the girl was one of my nieces." Her voice was resigned.

"They're still searching for positive identification. I am so sorry. This is the worst way to learn this news, from a total stranger."

Somehow, Eleanor kept control of her emotions. "Which girl do they think it is?"

"Until now, I thought Jane Doe was Marcia," I said. "But all I know for certain is that a DNA test proved that Jane Doe was my biological mother."

"And the police sketch of Jane Doe looks exactly like you."

"Yes."

"As do the pictures you found of Marcia in the yearbooks."

"I'm afraid so."

She was quiet for a long time. "So, if Marcia or Ellen was your mother…." she faltered. "Then one of the girls was murdered."

"I'm so sorry." A remote chance existed that I was wrong, that Jane Doe was neither Marcia nor Ellen, but it seemed cruel to give Eleanor false hope.

"I only met Ellen once, when she was a baby," Eleanor said. "I met Marcia three times. Renee never forgave my parents for not accepting her, you see, and she insisted that Allan sever all ties with us, just as my father forbade me to have anything to do with my brother. But Allan and I exchanged letters when we could, and I met Marcia when she was slightly more than a year old. She was a darling girl, wary of me our first visit—I was a stranger, after all—but she warmed to me. She cried when her father carried her away. A year later, she didn't remember me, but she was less shy, though more stubborn and independent. I wanted to give her a present that Christmas—it would have been 1962—but Allan wouldn't let me. Said Renee wouldn't take kindly to knowing that he had brought Marcia to see me, and he would just have to throw the teddy bear away. I saw Marcia again when she was three. That's when I met Ellen.

"Ellen was a darling infant. She had the same facial features as Marcia. The eyes, the hair, the perky little nose, even the expressions that crossed her face. I wasn't allowed to give her a present either, but I hugged those girls fiercely, and played with Marcia all afternoon. Then we said goodbye, and Allan said he would arrange another visit sometime. I didn't see my brother again for three years, and when I did, he was alone. He didn't say where Renee and the girls were, just that they were gone."

"I'm sorry," I said.

"Do you know where the girls went after Renee left?"

Maybe Allan hadn't outright lied and said his wife left him, but he apparently made it appear this way. Eleanor said she loved her brother. She wouldn't be eager to learn that he had abandoned his wife and daughters. "I'm afraid it was Allan who left, not Renee," I said carefully.

"Part of me always wondered," Eleanor said quietly. "I didn't question him too closely because I didn't really want to know. It was easier to believe that Renee had left. My family already disliked her so. But then again, it doesn't make sense that she left. She would have stayed married to Allan if she'd had her way. She married him because she thought he stood to inherit quite a sum when my father passed."

"I know it isn't easy to hear."

"What happened after Allan left?" She spoke with a note of finality, as if determined to push past this unpleasant fact about her brother.

"Renee took up with a local man who was unstable. I-I'm sorry, but from what we've been told, Marcia and Ellen were neglected, maybe even abused. Marcia ran away from home several times. That's how she ended up in 100 Mile House in 1976."

"I wish I had known. I've lived right here my whole life. But she wouldn't have known that, and I might not have recognized the teenager she grew into if I ran into her."

I recognized traces of bitterness and regret.

She sighed. "Doubtless, Renee poisoned the girls against their father and his side of the family. If they knew about us, at all."

Eleanor seemed to confirm the Lachlan townsfolks' opinion that Renee had been a malicious woman. "Allan and Renee seem so ill-matched. Can you tell me how they got together in the first place?" I held my breath. Though she'd gently chastised me for my intrusiveness, I hoped that she would feel comfortable telling me the lesser-known facts of her family, especially given the possibility that she was my great-aunt.

In response, she asked slowly, "Renee is dead, you said?"

"Yes."

"Do you know how?"

"From what I could learn, Renee was a deeply troubled individual."

"You could say that," she replied wryly.

"It would appear that her second husband was, as well. My husband and I were led to believe that he killed her in a murder-suicide."

I allowed her a few minutes to digest this information. Eleanor had been acquainted with her brother's wife, and perhaps she needed time to grieve the woman she might once have called friend. I picked at a stray thread on my jean shorts and waited patiently.

"I haven't thought about Renee in years," Eleanor said at last, "but there isn't any harm in sharing the circumstances of their marriage. You have a right to know, I suppose. Besides, everyone directly concerned is gone now. Long gone, in some cases."

I let out my breath.

"But, Nora, my own children don't know some of this family history, simply because I believe in protecting the dignity of other people and allowing them their decisions. I will tell you these things if you can promise to be discreet."

"I understand, and yes, I can promise my discretion." .

Eleanor took a deep breath. "My parents, Todd and Louise, grew up on the same street in the heart of 100 Mile House. They married shortly after my mother finished high school in the mid thirties. My brother was born in 1939, and I followed in 1943, within a year of my father returning from the war. He almost lost his leg during the Italian campaign, around the time Mussolini was dismissed. Father carried shrapnel just below his knee for the rest of his life and walked with a cane and a noticeable limp.

"When he was discharged, Father used his government grant to buy a large plot of land on the outskirts of town. He built a sturdy, two-story home that we moved into in 1946. Father worked the land and found success first in small-scale farming and then in corporate agricultural ventures. He bought much of the surrounding acreage, and as the town expanded, he leased to local ranchers. By the end of the 1950s, he was able to semi-retire and leave much of the daily operations to hired farmhands.

"We were one of the better-off families in 100 Mile House. After I married, and my mother died, Father sold the house and land to the government and retired for good.

"I have very positive memories from our childhood, but I expect it wasn't so for Allan. My father was hard on him, but only because he expected Allan to learn the family business from the ground up. But Allan wasn't interested in learning the business. By the time he graduated from high school, he was withdrawn and introverted. It was only natural that he'd be drawn to anyone who paid him attention and hung on his every word. Somehow, he met the daughter of the town drunk, and when he was nineteen, he told our parents that he'd fallen in love and planned to marry Renee Macy, even though they'd only met a few weeks before. Renee was fifteen years old, the same age as me.

"To say that my parents were outraged and scandalized is an understatement."

"Why were they so opposed?" I asked. "Was it Renee's father's reputation?"

Eleanor drew a deep breath. "Are you sure you have time for this?"

I glanced at the camping equipment. "You're not interrupting anything important. Please go on."

Eleanor paused as if to collect her thoughts. "The legend about town is that the first Macy who came here once led a gang that robbed banks and trains across the Canadian prairies. He went by the name of Joseph Sandeen then. With his ill-gotten gains growing and the death count rising, the Mounties set a trap to capture Sandeen and his accomplices. When the smoke cleared, three criminals lay dead and two Mounties were killed in the shootout. The government howled for blood and the Mounties were bent on avenging their own. That's how Joseph Sandeen landed in 100 Mile House in the late 1800s, a few steps ahead of the Mounties.

"He changed his name to Macy and for almost two decades, hid in the dense, snake-infested swamp in the lowlands. During that time, he built a house, married a local whore, and sired a brood of little Macys, each one exhibiting their parents' moral ambiguity.

"The authorities finally caught up to him in 1905," Eleanor explained. "I don't know if someone on the street recognized him, but he was arrested and tried for the murder of the two Mounties. Whether he held the gun that killed them was never proven and didn't matter; he was the leader and his conviction was the one that mattered. A jury found him guilty and sentenced him to hang. Some of his associates here in town, along with two of his four sons, tried to break him out the night before his execution. He was shot and killed along with his sons. The authorities declared themselves satisfied, having saved the expense of arresting and trying the lot of them."

Eleanor coughed and then cleared her throat. "Even after the gutting of the patriarchy, the next generation attempted to form a criminal syndicate. During prohibition, they distilled whiskey and tried rum-running to Vancouver. Their brew was as likely to poison a man as get him drunk, so the distillery quickly went bankrupt. The youngest Macys were often arrested when their bumbling efforts at thievery were thwarted.

"As the decades passed, the numbers of Macys dwindled away. Their founder's cunning and stealth gave way to paranoia, delusions, and infighting. In 1925, a Macy was indicted for the murder of his brother. His defense was that the 'son-of-a-bitch had deserved it.' The courts disagreed and executed him.

"By the 1940s, only one Macy family was left, the rest having drunk themselves to death or rotted away in prison. Arn Macy and his mother, Tess, both drank like fish and reminisced about the good old days when the Macy name inspired fear and respect. Arn's hoard of brats were raised with a misguided sense of entitlement. Sharing the names of their ancestors meant they were superior to the townsfolk in 100 Mile House, and the reason they were looked down on was envy, not distaste. Macys didn't go to school. They didn't need to work for a living. The government owed them for wrongfully executing their family members. This was why they collected welfare and harassed the townsfolk and drank whenever, wherever, and whatever they wished.

"So when my brother announced that he, the son of a wealthy land owner and one of the most prominent families of the time, intended to marry Arn Macy's daughter, my father put his foot down. No Macy would get the name of Garvey or a cent of the fortune he'd built with his own hands.

"The truth finally came out after hours of arguing. Allan believed he'd gotten Renee pregnant and thought he was doing the right thing. My father was furious. He didn't believe there was a baby, or if there was, that it was Allan's. He threatened to disinherit my brother, certain that the pregnancy was a ploy by the girl and her family to get their hands on the hard-earned Garvey wealth.

"Allan left the house that night with only the clothes he wore. He and Renee went to the church the next morning, where they were turned away because Renee was too young. She threw a fit in the church, crying and screaming and carrying on. She insisted she would live as Allan's wife whether the church recognized them or not, and that if the pastor refused to marry them, they would be living in sin, and the baby would be condemned to an eternity in hell. The pastor reluctantly relented. Allan and Renee left 100 Mile House that same day.

"Father forbade my mother and I from having anything to do with Allan, and continued his life as if he'd never had a son. But Allan sent me a letter from a post office box in 150 Mile House to let me know they'd landed on a ranch up north where he'd been able to find steady work. I responded to that same post office box every time Allan wrote, which was every few months or so," Eleanor's voice trembled with emotion.

"He planned to work hard and buy the cabin they were renting, and then he would amass his own wealth to provide his wife and family with a comfortable living and prove our father wrong.

"In one of his later letters, Allan admitted that Renee was not an easy woman to have married. He excused her behavior by saying she was young, and women in the family way were emotional and irrational and high-strung. He joked about her accusations that he had ruined her and doomed her to a lifetime of unhappiness."

Unable to hug Eleanor and ease her distress, I drew my knees to my chest and wrapped an arm around them.

"Gradually, Allan stopped writing. I learned the truth about Renee during Allan's rare visits. She married him because she wanted the big house in 100 Mile, the pretty clothes, the dazzling jewels, the food and drink. My parents hadn't accepted her, but she fully expected that when they died, she would become mistress of the fortune and matriarch of the family. She had only to wait until Father passed away and Allan inherited, then she'd rule her weak-willed husband and everything she wanted would come to fruition. But several weeks after their marriage, Allan revealed that our father had disowned him. Renee screamed and howled. She threw his clothes into the fire, slapped and scratched him, and called him foul names. She threatened to report him to the authorities for statutory rape of a minor. Her final declaration was that there was no baby and never had been one." Eleanor stopped to draw a breath.

I exhaled loudly. "I'm speechless. I don't know what to say. Your poor brother."

She sighed heavily. "He'd always seen the best in people, even blinding himself to their flaws. Years later, when Allan confessed his wife's treachery to me, he refused to say Renee's name. He spoke in monotones, entirely devoid of emotion. He had sacrificed everything for this girl and allowed himself to be ridiculed and gossiped about. He hadn't truly loved Renee, but he had convinced himself that he was a good man because he had done the right thing in marrying the young girl he thought he had seduced. And it had all been a lie." Eleanor fell silent.

I stretched out my legs so they wouldn't fall asleep. I was surprised at how long we'd been talking, but many more questions remained unanswered. "Do you mind if I ask when you learned about Marcia?"

"Let me think," Eleanor trailed off. A moment later she said, "It must have been around the holidays, 1960 or so. In a letter, Allan told me I had a niece named Marcia. The earliest we were able to arrange a visit was the following summer. I made excuses with my parents, something vague about an afternoon with girlfriends at the lake. Allan drove south to meet me, and Marcia was in a cardboard box on the front seat of the truck. When I asked, Allan said Renee hadn't cared that he'd brought Marcia to see me. He added that Renee hadn't seemed to want Marcia anyway, though he was embarrassed that he'd let this slip."

I couldn't imagine. "She was lucky her father loved and wanted her," I said.

"He adored his girls," Eleanor said. "There were two more visits like this. He spent hours holding Marcia and tickling her to make her laugh. He was attentive to her every need. The same was true when Ellen came along. I met her during that final clandestine visit in 1963. But shortly after that, Allan's letters stopped coming and I didn't see him for years."

"What about the girls?" I asked, though I knew the answer. "Did you ever see them again?"

"No."

Goosebumps rose on my arms despite the summer warmth of the condo. I shifted my phone to the other hand and drew my elbows close for warmth.

"Early one morning in 1966, I was watching my father work on one of the cars in the large barn that housed a tractor and several older cars when Allan walked in. Father grunted at him and went back to the engine he was working on. Then he told me to go help Mother with the house. I didn't see either of them all day, but that evening, Allan accompanied Father into the house and sat down at his old place at the table as if the past eight years hadn't happened. Mother cried with happiness. I sensed that it wasn't the time to ask questions. We simply ate in silence. After Father left the table, Mother asked about Renee. Allan simply said that his wife had gone. The next morning, he dressed, put on work boots, and went with Father to the barn." Eleanor's hoarse voice fell silent.

She and I had been on the phone for almost two hours. Dredging up such a painful period of her family's history had clearly taken a toll.

"I am sorry for what you've been through," I said. "I appreciate your information and thank you for your candor. I promise to be discreet with what you've shared."

"Thank you, dear." She sniffled and blew her nose. "Though, if you are related to us, you have a right to know these things."

I hesitated to ask the question that burned in me as I'd listened to Eleanor's story. "I really hope you don't mind me asking. What are the chances that Marcia was not Allan's biological daughter?"

"I suppose it is possible, though I had no doubts at the time. Marcia looked so much like my brother, and my own children at that age reminded me of Allan's girls. I still believe that Marcia and Ellen were Allan's. But I suppose I could be wrong."

I wondered how closely I resembled Eleanor's children. "I'm sorry I had to ask. If Renee...strayed, then it doesn't make sense to continue my line of inquiry by tracing the Garveys."

"Yes, I suppose you're right," Eleanor murmured.

"I know this has been an emotionally draining conversation, Mrs. Reinhardt, but I wonder if I could make another request." I drew a breath. "If one of your nieces is my birth mother, and if they are truly Allan's daughters, this would make me your great-niece. Would you be willing to submit a DNA sample to determine if we're related?" I paused. "That same sample would also prove that Jane Doe is either Marcia or Ellen."

"Is there...? No," she said, answering her own unasked question. "I suppose since Allan and Renee are gone, and you can't find either girl, there isn't anyone else left who might be able to confirm Jane Doe's identity."

"Please don't feel obligated," I rushed to add. "I can search for Renee's family in 100 Mile House and perhaps—"

"Don't bother, dear," Eleanor interrupted. "They are the nastiest people you would ever meet. And a search would likely be futile. No one knows where they've scattered to, and good riddance to them."

I was relieved by that news. I felt nothing but disdain for the family she had described, and I was content to ignore the fact that they might be related to me.

"I don't ask for your help for selfish reasons," I assured. "Well, not for purely selfish reasons. I've felt an attachment to your niece, to Marcia, since I first saw the police sketch, and am determined to find the conclusion to her story, no matter how it ends. Whether she was my mother or not. I am also determined to give Jane Doe a name. No one deserves to be forgotten."

"Of course, I'll take the DNA test. It's the right thing to do." Eleanor said, almost interrupting me.

A knot of cold tension in my chest loosened. "Thank you. Thank you, thank you. I can't say how much your agreement means to me."

"Perhaps I could ask you to do something for me, dear. If you do find either of the girls, or both of them, could you please give them a message? Let them know that I loved them and…and I guess, that they can contact me and perhaps we can talk."

"I will," I told her fervently. "In the meantime, I'd like to stay in touch with you if that's all right."

"I'd like that," Eleanor said. "Perhaps we might even meet in person after I've had a chance to process all…this."

I promised we would talk soon, wished her well, and disconnected the call.

I felt like I was waking abruptly from a dream so vivid that I was left mentally exhausted rather than refreshed. Eyes wide, I glanced around the kitchen from my seat on the floor, taking in the scattered tackle boxes and hiking backpacks and propane tanks and sleeping bags.

Malcolm stepped from the bedroom wearing sweatpants, and I looked at the clock in shock. I'd forgotten that he'd planned to leave work early today, and had been so engrossed in my conversation with Eleanor Reinhardt that I hadn't noticed him enter, leave his laptop bag on the counter mere feet from my head, or enter the bedroom to shower and change clothes.

He greeted me with a kiss on my forehead and settled onto the floor next to me. "Who was that?"

"Eleanor Reinhardt, Allan Garvey's sister and Marcia's aunt."

He raised his eyebrows. "Really. What did she have to say?"

"You won't believe this, Malcolm. Allan and Renee had another daughter, Marcia's younger sister, Ellen. She was born in 1963."

He was silent for a moment. "So there are two possibilities." Then he brightened. "We may have discovered a potential solution. If Mrs. Reinhardt will submit a DNA sample—"

I nodded.

"—then some of our questions will be answered."

I nodded again. "She also said she might be open to meeting me."

Malcolm looked at me closely. "How do you feel about that?"

I exhaled loudly. "Confused. Nervous. Elated at the idea that I could sit face-to-face with a relative. I'm already fond of her, but it might just be wish-fulfillment, at this point. I don't really know." I got up and began fiddling with the camping gear. "I don't want to discuss this during our trip, okay? Let's just enjoy our time at Golden Ears. When we return, though, I'm going to dive back into the search for Jane Doe."

Chapter Seventeen

Which girl was Jane Doe, Marcia or Ellen? And what had happened to the Garvey sisters?

The questions turned over and over in my mind that weekend as I lay awake at night listening to the screech of insects and the rustle of wind through the trees. The answers were out of my hands until Eleanor took her DNA test.

Tuesday morning, I got in touch with Doug to tell him about Ellen. He was as stunned as I was and just as pleased that Eleanor agreed to the DNA test. He promised to connect with her that day.

I anticipated that weeks might pass before Eleanor and I spoke again, so I was surprised when my phone rang on Thursday afternoon and her number appeared. I was headed back to my office after having finished a first-year lecture about World History from 1900-1945 and hurriedly took the call as I quickened pace.

After an exchange of greetings, Eleanor said, "I spoke with Inspector Chilton earlier this week. We've scheduled an interview tomorrow morning. Then I'll be attending the hospital to have a DNA sample taken. I don't mind saying I'm a little nervous about both."

"Understandable," I said. "I was nervous too." I reached my office and unlocked the door. "Doug—Inspector Chilton—is a very kind man.

He'll set you right at ease. But is it the results of the DNA test you're nervous about, or the actual procedure itself?"

"Both, really, but the immediate concern is the procedure."

I explained my own experience: "It isn't painful or invasive at all. They run a cotton swab inside your cheek, twice. That's all. Are you going alone?"

"No, my husband George will go with me."

I leapt at this opening. "Tell me more about yourself and your husband."

"George is a retired electrician," Eleanor said. "We met in high school but lost touch in the early '70s when George relocated to Vancouver for his trades classes. We reconnected when he came back home to launch his own business. Six months after our first date, George proposed, and we married four months later. Grant, our oldest, the firefighter I told you about, was born in the first year of our marriage. Jeremiah came two years later, then Tabitha four years after that. While the children were young, I took correspondence courses to complete my teaching certificate, and began teaching grade three in 1984, the year Tabitha started kindergarten.

"I taught for twenty-two years before George and I retired in 2005," Eleanor said proudly. "We spend spring and most of summer in Nova Scotia with George's sister, and the rest of the year we're here in BC. My youngest two are both married, and we have five grandchildren that we adore and spoil. And since I've retired, I started writing historical fiction for young adults."

"Your family sounds wonderful," I said, acutely aware that they might very well be my family too. "Tell me more about your books! I would love to read them."

Eleanor shared the three titles that had already been published, and I jotted down the names, intending to check the public library on my way home that evening.

"How about yourself, Nora? What is your world like?"

"Coincidentally," I said with a chuckle, "I'm a professor of history here in the lower mainland. My focus is on Russian and Eastern European history, particularly during the Second World War and Cold

War eras."

Eleanor was delighted, and we spent several minutes swapping stories of our favourite historical figures and events. I shared several lesser-known anecdotes about famous people and events that caused her to laugh. Then she said, "I've almost completed a manuscript, written from the perspective of a Jewish family expelled from Russia in the pogrom on 1905. I don't suppose you'd mind having a look at it, for historical accuracy, before I turn it in to my editor?"

"I would love to," I said eagerly.

She promised to send the manuscript through email in the coming weeks.

"And what about family? Where did you grow up? Are you married?"

"I am! I grew up in North Vancouver with wonderful parents. My dad, Dan, is a journalist and my mom was a part-time librarian until I finished university. That's where I met my husband, Malcolm, and we've been married for nine years now."

"Do you have children?"

Rather than answering with my characteristically blasé "No, not yet," I admitted, "I don't think we're interested in having children."

"It isn't for everyone," Eleanor said. "I had children because it was expected. We didn't have as many birth control options back then. I did enjoy having children, and I am glad that we did, but I think if I'd had a choice, I wouldn't have."

I appreciated that Eleanor didn't attempt to change my mind or give the patronizing platitude that I might change my mind when I grew older.

I could have talked with her for hours, but my next class began in half an hour. "I'm afraid I'll have to say goodbye, but it's been lovely chatting, and I would love to again sometime. Good luck tomorrow, with everything. If there's anything you need, please let me know."

"We'll certainly keep in touch! And thank you, Nora."

She called briefly again the following day to let me know that she had spoken with Doug Chilton, who had requested that her DNA test be rushed. The results were expected within weeks. I tucked this information away and tried to settle into the familiar routine of the new semester.

Eleanor and I spoke by phone many Thursday afternoons in the weeks leading up to the DNA test results. I grew to look forward to our chats. We shared similar values, and the fact that she very well could be a family member added to my interest in her life. I was able to find two of her published novels, one told from the perspective of a teenaged girl in Halifax during the Second World War, and the second about a young man orphaned in Montreal in 1692 who became a trapper for the Hudson Bay Company before marrying an Aboriginal girl and siring a family. I stayed awake late into the night for almost a week to finish reading both.

As promised, Eleanor sent the draft of her latest book. I had studied the Russian pogroms under the Tsar, and I enthusiastically endorsed her book. When I asked where Eleanor got her information, or when she had time to research, she laughed and said that Grant had bought her a laptop with internet several years prior, so she had access to a wealth of information.

As was our habit, we ended our conversation with promises to touch base again the following Thursday.

During the fourth week of September, Eleanor called on a Tuesday afternoon when I was between classes. She was crying, her voice slightly husky and hoarse as she asked how my day was going and how the class had gone.

I suspected immediately why she was calling but couldn't tell if her tears were the result of happiness or stress. "Class went well. Eleanor, are you okay?"

She cleared her throat. "I don't quite know how to tell you this," she said. "I– I got a phone call from Inspector Chilton this morning. My profile is a confirmed match to the DNA profile of Jane Doe." She cried harder and inhaled shakily. "I thought you would want to know as soon as possible."

Tears flooded my eyes in empathy for Eleanor. The test result confirmed one of her nieces had died a horrible death.

"I'm so sorry, Eleanor. Part of me wishes it wasn't true. I'm so sorry."

"This is your loss as well as mine. I hope that having this closure brings you some sort of comfort, small though it may be."

"I-I suppose this makes us family," I said quietly.

"I suppose it does," she said. "Finding you has certainly been the silver lining to this ordeal. I don't suppose you'd want to meet sometime soon?"

"I would love to," I said. "I'd love to meet George, and to introduce you to Malcolm."

"What do you and Malcolm usually do for Thanksgiving? If you would like to celebrate with my family, George and I would be happy to host you for the weekend. Grant will be here, and Tabitha and her husband and kids. Please don't feel like you have to, though."

"Malcolm and I would love to come," I said.

We promised to talk again on Thursday before saying goodbye. I immediately dialed Malcolm's number, hoping he was taking his lunch break.

When Malcolm answered, I skipped a greeting and blurted, "I just talked with Eleanor Reinhardt."

"The DNA results came back," he guessed.

"She's my aunt. Jane Doe was either Marcia or Ellen."

"I'm sorry," he said, "But I'm also really proud of you. You've done something incredible."

"But it isn't enough," my anger escaped. "I still haven't given her a name. My birth mother. All this speculation and suspicion, all my guesses and fears. We're so close, but what if this is as far as we come?"

"It will come," Malcolm assured.

I wasn't finished being angry. "Everything we've learned. Allan, Gordon, and Renee. How could they? The parents who were supposed to have loved them but failed in every possible way." I lapsed into silence. As eager as I'd been to find the truth, part of me had hoped I was wrong about the Garvey sisters, particularly as details of their traumatic childhoods came to light.

"Babe? Are you okay?"

"I wish I had been wrong," I blurted.

"I'm sorry. What can I do?"

I shook my head. "I'll be okay. I love you."

"I love you too. How is Eleanor? Your…aunt."

"Overwhelmed. She invited us for Thanksgiving."

"We'll start making plans as soon as we get home tonight," he said. "You could even search the library's yearbooks for photos of Allan and Eleanor and Renee."

The last name made me wince. I was only too happy to embrace Eleanor as kin. Less so was I inclined to accept Allan, and I wanted to ignore Renee's existence altogether.

After our call, I placed the phone on the desk in front of me and stared at it. Then I lowered my head and surrendered to emotions I didn't understand but felt deep within my soul.

Chapter Eighteen

On Sunday, October 10, 2010, Malcolm and I drove to 100 Mile House for Thanksgiving and my first face-to-face meeting with the people who shared my family tree. The weekend had the potential to be fraught with tense emotion, but I was comforted by my easy telephone friendship with Eleanor.

Malcolm turned off the main road onto a long driveway lined with maple trees, their orange and red leaves brilliant in the afternoon sunshine. The house was perhaps half a kilometer back from the road, the long, green lawn leading to a two-story farm-style house with a sweeping porch and porch swing. Window boxes, empty now, lined the polished wooden railing. Close to the house, a tire swing hung from the low branch of a maple tree and wooden wagon wheels rested against the house. On the far side of the yard sat a decades-old, faded orange farm tractor. I imagined Eleanor and George's children and grandchildren climbing on it.

I had called from the highway to let them know when to expect us, and they were sitting on the porch swing waiting. Malcolm pulled in behind a vintage, lovingly cared-for pickup truck that appeared to have been freshly repainted and its chrome bumper recently polished. He killed the engine and looked at me.

I was mesmerized by the couple who descended the front porch stairs to greet us. I gripped the door handle and inhaled deeply before exiting the car. With a nervous nibble on my bottom lip, I smiled shyly and met Eleanor's eyes. "I can't believe this!"

Her eyes were watery, and she reached for me eagerly. "Aren't you just beautiful!"

I leaned into her embrace and blinked rapidly to ward off tears. "It's so incredible to meet you!"

We stayed in a hug for a long moment before pulling back. She was shorter than me, and almost too thin. I searched her face for familiar features that might leap out at me. Her complexion, lighter than mine, held lively bright gray eyes, and her short, silvery-white hair regally crowned her head.

Eleanor inspected my features with the same eagerness. "Turn your head."

I angled my head slightly to the right.

"I see him, just there." Eleanor gestured to her own features. "In your profile and your cheekbones. That's Allan." She squeezed my arm and turned to Malcolm, who stood behind me. "And this must be Malcolm. I've heard many delightful things!"

Malcolm ducked his head and grinned boyishly, accepting the hug Eleanor offered. "It's a pleasure, ma'am."

"Aunt Eleanor," Eleanor corrected with mock sternness, before turning to the man who waited at her side with a welcoming smile. "And this is Uncle George."

Uncle George was not a hugger, but he greeted us warmly and insisted on carrying our bags. When we entered the house, he disappeared upstairs to deposit our bags in their guest room while Eleanor ushered us on a tour of the main floor before bidding us to make ourselves comfortable in the carved wooden chairs at a small table in the kitchen. The large table in the adjacent dining room was already set in preparation for tomorrow's Thanksgiving dinner. Eleanor bustled around preparing tea until George rejoined us.

I was relieved that we weren't immediately inundated with her large family, who would arrive tomorrow morning. She was expecting Grant and Tabitha, as well as Tabitha's husband Finn and their teenagers, Larissa and Patrick.

Eleanor settled at the table and we chatted over tea, getting to know each other. I complimented the quaint décor of their farm-style home, which made both of our hosts beam with pride.

Later in the afternoon, the easy conversation stuttered as we ran out of small talk and the topic turned to the elephant in the room.

Eleanor had two things she wanted to show me, and while George boiled more water, she left the kitchen. When she returned, she handed me a photograph, its back facing me. In her careful handwriting, she'd written, *Allan and the girls, 1963*.

I flipped the photograph over and caught my breath. Allan, a very young man with an expression of solemn sadness, looked at the camera. He sat on a chair with a daughter on either side of his lap. Three-year-old Marcia wore a cute, flowered dress with her dark hair in pigtails. She had turned her head, apparently distracted by something out of frame, leaving her profile to be photographed. I recognized the profile, identical to mine.

The infant, Ellen, wore a t-shirt and diaper and sat cradled in the crook of her father's arm. I looked at the tiny face, the features, almost indiscernible, screwed up in preparation for a wail.

My attention returned to Allan, my grandfather. His eyes were melancholy, his jaw set in determination. His expression was that of a man who, despite his best intentions, had never found happiness. I recognized the cheekbones that I had inherited from him and, in turn, from one of the two girls on his lap—a family portrait frozen perpetually in time.

The photograph's edges were crinkled and the colors slightly faded. The photograph had been taken during the last visit Eleanor had with her two nieces, the first and only time she had met Ellen. This was also the only known photograph of Ellen Garvey.

I reluctantly tore my eyes away from the photograph to notice Eleanor's other offering: yearbooks of her time in school in 100 Mile House. The pages were printed on thin paper, their print and black and white photographs faded with time. Eleanor allowed me to peruse the four years of her high school career and in each, I found the young Eleanor Garvey. She had been a stunning beauty. I watched her mature from the age of fourteen to the age of eighteen.

"I'm afraid I don't have my primary school yearbooks anymore," Eleanor said, "which is a shame. Those had Allan's pictures, too. But they didn't survive. He graduated before this first edition." she gestured to the oldest book, stamped with 1956, when fourteen-year-old Eleanor attended grade 9.

Eleanor reminisced about her high school years as I flipped the pages. Page after page showed teenaged girls in poodle skirts and cardigans flirting with beaus who had shed tailored suit jackets in favour of white t-shirts. Between classes, boys and girls mixed in the hallways of the high school. I listened intently but also pored over the images. I was searching carefully for another face in the classes, since I knew that Renee Macy had been the same age as Eleanor. I didn't find Renee.

Then I remembered something else Eleanor said during our first conversation—Macys didn't go to school.

"I don't suppose you have any pictures of Renee," I asked.

Eleanor shook her head.

"That's okay," I said brightly, trying to mask the somber mood that threatened to overtake me. "Thank you for sharing these. You have some amazing memories." At a loss for a direction to take the conversation, I looked at Malcolm.

"I'm afraid we aren't sure how to move forward with our search from here," Malcolm said.

"You mean, because we can't concretely say which girl was the victim?" Eleanor asked.

I nodded.

George asked, "Wouldn't they be able to tell with medical or dental records?"

"I've seen that on true-crimes TV specials," Malcolm said. "They have the technology to identify homicide victims by comparing medical records to injuries found on the remains—broken bones, or fractures still evident on the bones. Didn't the forensic investigator tell us that

Jane Doe had a fractured collar bone and a broken bone in one of her legs?"

Eleanor shook her head. "Allan said that both children were born at home, and the births were registered weeks afterward. Renee hadn't gone to a doctor during either pregnancy, so the hospitals wouldn't have records. And I doubt the children received much medical or dental attention during their early years, if everything you've learned is correct."

"During one of my conversations with Doug—Inspector Chilton—he said they haven't been able to identify her through official records because she doesn't have any. He said this indicates that she never visited a doctor or a dentist anywhere in the province. In the whole country, actually." I fell silent. At some point, the Ministry had gotten involved with the family. This was evident in the attempted seizure of the children in the years following Renee's second marriage. What brought the family to the attention of the authorities in the first place?

"So, how do we find the other Garvey girl?" Malcolm asked.

When no one replied, he suggested, "We could go to the media."

"You mean, do an interview with a reporter?" I asked. I shared a furtive look with Eleanor, and could tell that her thoughts mirrored mine. Neither of us wanted that notoriety. We had just found each other and weren't ready to share our story with others outside the family. Not yet.

"Perhaps this is a good time to take a slight break, even if only to renew your strength," Eleanor said. "Especially heading into the holiday season. It's a time for family, for creating new memories with our loved ones." Her hand found mine on the table and squeezed it warmly. "You've come so far, and you have much to be proud of."

"Chin up," George said cheerfully. "There's a solution. We just need to be patient. These things have a way of falling into place."

I threw him a grateful smile. They were both right. I resolved to put aside the investigation and enjoy getting to know my newfound family, particularly as I would be meeting their children and grandchildren the next day.

After a delicious dinner of pork chops and roasted vegetables, most of which came from Eleanor's garden, we enjoyed an apple cider in the backyard, where George built a roaring fire in the fire pit and handed us cozy flannel blankets. I leaned against my husband and enjoyed the chill of the evening and the clear sky that showed hundreds of stars. It was a perfect way to end our first day together, and when I sluggishly followed George up the stairs to the guest room, I knew I would sleep well with the crisp air and the silence that surrounded us.

I awoke early and curled close to Malcolm for warmth. We dozed quietly until footsteps on the stairs woke us. When the grandfather clock chimed 8 a.m., we rose and dressed and descended, ready to help with Thanksgiving preparations.

I enjoyed peeling potatoes and root vegetables with Eleanor in the large kitchen while Malcolm helped George heap the smoker with charcoal and nurture the coals that would smoke the turkey for most of the day. Mid-morning, somewhere between the second and third cup of tea, Finn and Tabitha arrived with their fourteen-year-old twins, Larissa and Patrick. Before their arrival, Eleanor and I had agreed that she would introduce me as her great-niece through their uncle, who had passed away before the kids were born.

The kids were politely disinterested in Malcolm and I, and sat on the back porch chatting with their grandfather while sipping hot chocolate and snacking on potato chips. Finn and Malcolm found common ground and rehashed the recent football game between the Winnipeg Blue Bombers and BC Lions, predicting which CFL team would win the Grey Cup based on the preseason games.

Tabitha, a blonde beauty who greatly favored her mother, joined us in the kitchen to roll out pie crust and simmer the pumpkin her mother had grown. She stayed silent unless addressed, and spoke in single-word answers. She was understandably puzzled by my presence, and to put her at ease, I spoke at length about my family in North Vancouver, to assuage concerns she may have had about my intentions involving her parents. I had anticipated that she and her siblings might question who I was and where I'd been during their lives.

"I've known I was adopted since I was a child," I said casually, "but it wasn't until earlier this year that I had the chance to learn anything about my biological family."

This caught her interest. "Really?"

"More tea?" I held the kettle out.

She nodded.

"My adopted parents are wonderful, but I couldn't help wonder where I came from. I'm just so humbled that you all seem so wonderful."

Eleanor blushed, and Tabitha seemed to warm slightly. "So, you're my uncle's granddaughter."

The ice broke entirely with the arrival of Grant, the eldest son and a confirmed bachelor. Tabitha's kids rushed to greet him as he handed his father a twelve-pack of beer, greeted Finn with a raucous hug, and teased his sister until she blushed and could barely breath for laughing. He greeted Malcolm and I warmly, and flirted with me until Eleanor hushed him.

It was a scene of perfect domesticity that both comforted me and made my heart ache. Over a wonderful dinner filled with joking and laughter and some bickering between the teenagers, Malcolm and I were welcomed whole-heartedly. As we said our goodbyes in the early evening, we exchanged hugs and promises to get together again soon. Grant grabbed me in a bear hug, lifted me off my feet, and spun me in a circle.

"I'll call you on Thursday," Eleanor promised as we descended the porch stairs. "Thank you for coming. This has been so wonderful."

"Maybe we'll see you at Christmas," Tabitha said shyly.

"Don't be strangers," George called from the porch as the sun was setting.

As Malcolm turned the car and started away, I waved out the back window as the family receded behind us. Finally, I faced forward, full of warmth and contentment. I took Malcolm's left hand; his right clasped the steering wheel. After being a part of the interactions among George and Eleanor and their children and grandchildren, I found myself wondering if someday Malcolm and I might have children and grandchildren.

Malcolm navigated the highway in the darkness of the autumn night. I nestled into the seat, still full and a little sleepy. My thoughts started to wander as I imagined the pleasant memories we'd form with some of my new family.

Jane Doe was the commonality that brought all of us together. I knew that Eleanor and I wouldn't gain a definitive answer as to what had happened to her niece—my mother—until we found a trace of either Marcia or Ellen beyond 1985. But as Eleanor suggested, now was the time to rest and to appreciate family and loved ones as we headed into the holiday season.

As the final week of November arrived and I browsed in an electronic store to purchase one of Malcolm's Christmas presents, my phone vibrated in my pocket.

Doug's number appeared on caller ID. "Hi, Doug! How are you?"

"Well, thanks, Nora, and you?"

As we exchanged pleasantries, his slightly clipped tone caught my attention. I hoped he was calling to report a break in the case, but he was brisk and professional, as if in a rush.

"Sorry to bother," he apologized, "but I have a quick question. For the sake of formality and form, would you mind if I disclosed your name and phone number in situations where I think it necessary?"

I was puzzled. "What do you mean? To reporters and the like? I don't want to talk to media."

"Understandably," he soothed. "But if, hypothetically, a situation arose in which I received information from someone I thought you should speak to, would you be all right with my giving this person your contact information?"

I quickly connected the dots. "Is there someone who wants to talk to me?"

"Not exactly. But I have a duty to protect your identity and confidentiality, and I want to ensure you're comfortable if such a situation arose."

I was a little disappointed. I'd hoped new information had become available. "Sure, Doug," I said, trying to disguise my disappointment. "I trust you, I know you'll be discreet."

"Of course," he promised. "Hopefully, I'll be in touch soon. But I have to run. My best to Malcolm, okay? Take care."

I WAS GROCERY SHOPPING THE FOLLOWING DAY, ONE WEEK before my birthday, when my cell phone rang again. Caller ID showed a United States number. I accepted the call and wedged the phone between my chin and shoulder, greeting the caller as I reached for a jar of tomato sauce.

A low, melodic voice asked for Nora Devrey. When I identified myself, the caller went silent for a moment, as if gathering herself. "Ms. Devrey, my name is Caris Jones. I'm calling from Los Angeles."

I asked what I might do for her. I assumed she was calling in a professional capacity, perhaps something to do with my work at the university.

She spoke slowly, "I suppose you haven't heard of me."

This manner of speaking seemed to be her habit, as if she rehearsed her words before speaking them.

"No, I'm afraid I haven't," I said politely, wondering why she might believe I had.

"I was given your name and contact information by Inspector Doug Chilton."

I grabbed for my phone to keep from dropping it in my surprise.

She added, "He also gave me the name of Eleanor Reinhardt in 100 Mile House and said I should speak with both of you. Due to confidentiality, he was unable to tell me why I should get in touch with you, but he was very insistent that we needed to speak right away. Yours is the first number I called."

"Why did he give you my name?" I set my grocery basket down in the middle of the aisle and began walking toward the exit, knowing instinctively that the conversation shouldn't take place within earshot of strangers.

"Can you tell me why he felt that I needed to speak with you?" she asked.

I was struck by the oddity of the question. By my own admission, I hadn't heard of her and would have no idea why she might have called. Rather than say this, however, I cautiously said, "Inspector Chilton is the lead investigator on a Jane Doe homicide dating from the early '80s." I couldn't figure why a woman with the name Jones who lived in California would be involved. I was eager to hear what information she might contribute to this matter.

"Yes…." The word lifted slightly at the end, as if she were waiting for something more. After another moment of silence, she said, "I assume you have an interest in the homicide. What information have you provided to the police?" Her tone was slightly defensive, her question very loaded.

"I assure you, I have a very good reason for wanting to know who Jane Doe was," I told her, trying to put her at ease.

"And what is that?" her tone was less challenging now, as if she were genuinely curious. "Are you a relation?"

I had no idea what to say. I was lingering in the covered entryway just outside the store. I steeled myself against the driving wind and rain. "You don't have any idea why Inspector Chilton gave you my contact information?" I asked. "Or why you and I need to talk?"

"I can only assume one of us knows something the other needs to hear," she said.

When she didn't elaborate, I asked, "If you live in Los Angeles, how did you hear about Jane Doe?" I wondered if perhaps she knew Marcia or Ellen Garvey, or one of Marcia's former classmates.

"I used to live in Vancouver. I still maintain ties to the city." This response both answered and evaded the question. "And you?"

"I saw a police sketch of Jane Doe in the newspaper."

A moment later, after seeming to weigh her options, Caris Jones said, "I spoke with Inspector Chilton regarding some information I have about the woman who was Jane Doe. He told me that you had been working hard to identify her for personal reasons."

Before I could stop myself, I blurted, "You know which sister is Jane Doe? Is it Marcia or Ellen?"

"Marcia or Ellen," she repeated as if talking to herself. "I knew both girls."

My jaw dropped in shock. "How? When? Was it when they lived in Lachlan, or when Marcia moved to Vancouver?"

A couple walking past shot me a funny look. My voice had unconsciously risen.

Caris sighed into the phone.

I quickly said, "I'm sorry. How did you know the Garvey sisters?"

After another silence, she said tersely, "I'm a drug and alcohol abuse counsellor with a society called the Gathering here in Los Angeles. We are a recovery center for women who wish to walk away from abuse, addiction, and prostitution. I moved to Los Angeles from Vancouver in the 1980s."

"So, you met them here in Vancouver?" I asked. This solution made perfect sense. I knew that Marcia had fallen into addiction while living in Vancouver's Downtown Eastside. It made sense that Ellen might have followed the same path, though I couldn't say with certainty that Ellen had ever come to Vancouver. It was easy to imagine that she had followed her older sister.

The line went silent, and I was afraid the call had dropped. But then she spoke, so faintly I had to listen hard.

"I think that you and I should speak face to face. You live in Vancouver, right? I'll be there this weekend for a conference. Are you free Saturday at four?"

"Yes."

We arranged to meet at a coffee shop near her hotel.

Caris said, "Please describe your appearance so I know who you are when we meet."

"If you've seen the forensic sketch of Jane Doe, that is exactly what I look like."

"Just like her," she said quietly.

I was tempted to ask which "her" she meant. Instead, I admitted that I'd only ever seen a photograph of the girls when they were very young,

Chapter 18   199

and added that I would wear my hair in a ponytail, with dark jeans, rain boots, and a purple raincoat, so she would have no issue picking me out from the crowd.

"Saturday around four," she confirmed.

Although there didn't seem to be anything left to say, I wasn't ready to end this bizarre conversation. Caris knew something about the Garvey sisters, and I wanted to know what it was. "How did you know Marcia and Ellen Garvey?"

"How did you know them?" she countered.

"To be perfectly honest, I never met either sister. I– It's rather a long story. Did Inspector Chilton tell you about my DNA test results?"

"He did not."

I put all my cards on the table. "Jane Doe was my biological mother."

My words were met with a long silence.

She finally whispered, "That's not possible."

"I'm afraid it's true," I said softly.

"You can't be. You're her daughter?"

"I am. And I need to give her a name. Do you know which sister is Jane Doe?"

She finally said, "I do."

Chapter Nineteen

On Saturday afternoon, I brushed my black hair into a long ponytail, stepped into dark blue jeans and gray rainboots, and pulled on my purple rain jacket.

I was grateful that Caris Jones wanted to meet, and even more grateful that the timing had worked out so well, though my hands were clammy on the steering wheel. I drummed my fingers on my thigh at red lights, and I rolled my eyes at idiot drivers as I merged onto the freeway shortly after three o'clock.

Twenty minutes later, I parked near the hotel and walked through drizzling rain to the café. I picked my way to a table near the far wall and sat facing the door. Conversations murmured underneath the whir of the cappuccino machine and the smooth jazz playing from speakers on the ceiling.

At 4:00 p.m., I stared at the door expectantly. It opened right on the dot, but the girl who entered was young and accompanied by several friends. A man followed a few minutes later.

I grew restless. Had something happened, or was Caris running late? Had she changed her mind? I pulled out my phone and laid it on the table.

In the two days since Caris's phone call, I'd concluded that Caris

Jones had encountered one of the sisters sometime after 1985, and that was how she knew which sister had died. I still had her number, but I decided to give her a little more time before calling. Instead, I opened my shoulder bag, withdrew my Jane Doe notebook, and flipped through the pages. Soon, I was lost in my bizarre journey of the past ten months.

"Nora."

I sprang back in my seat as if electrocuted and knocked the table next to me. My mouth fell open in shock. How long had Caris stood in front of me without speaking?

Her eyes were full of tears, her face twisted in pain. "You look exactly like her," Caris said quietly.

I could have said the exact same thing to her. Caris stood about my height, with my eyes and facial features and hair. She was older than me, with a deeply lined face that spoke of years of hardship and hard-earned wisdom. Her dark hair, cut short, clung to her cheeks, sodden with rainwater. She stared at me with dark eyes, and I knew without asking who she was.

Caris Jones was either Ellen or Marcia. She was my aunt, directly related to me and to Jane Doe. She was my own flesh and blood.

Every assumption I'd made exploded in the presence of Caris Jones.

"Please, have a seat," I blurted, gesturing to the chair opposite.

She did, still utterly silent after her initial greeting.

I was too shocked to say anything more, and a little scared.

We sat for several minutes in silence, staring at one another. The intensity in her gaze didn't make me flinch. She had questions, as did I, and she deserved answers as much as I did.

"I didn't want to wait for a cab," she finally said. "The conference ran over by a few minutes and I thought it would be faster for me to walk over." Her tone was distant, dazed.

"It's all right," I murmured.

"I never thought—" she said, her voice barely more than a whisper. "I never imagined— I didn't think...." Her composure broke, and her voice choked with emotion. "I didn't think it could be true. When you said you were her daughter, I thought it was a cruel joke. I know there are younger half-siblings, some of them born after I ran away. I thought maybe that's who you were. But it's true. You are. You really are her daughter."

Caris stared at her hands, the fingers so tightly intertwined on the table that her knuckles turned white. "I have secrets that I don't want to share, but I'll tell you what I can," she said. "Are you sure you want to know?"

"I'm honestly not sure," I said. "I've been to Lachlan. I don't need to know more about that time. I am so sorry. Truly, for everything. For your loss. For your sister."

"I've spent almost forty years running from my past."

"I never meant to cause you or anybody any pain."

"I know. You deserve the truth as much as anyone. Maybe we can help each other. I've always wondered…." She bit her lip and shook her head.

"Let's start with something easy." I gestured to a server. "How do you take your coffee?"

A hint of a smile played around her lips. "Black."

We sat in silence as the server left to get our drinks. I wasn't sure which questions I could ask, which topics were safe, if there were any subjects that wouldn't evoke painful memories or intense emotions.

Finally, I said, "Tell me about the conference." My request seemed to surprise her.

"The Gathering, in Los Angeles, is a nonprofit agency advocating on behalf of marginalized women. We were the focus of a joint longitudinal study several years ago to examine the repercussions of decriminalizing sex work. Los Angeles has rather lax laws pertaining to sex workers," she explained. "We were approached by a similar non-profit here in Vancouver, and I became the liaison between the two in efforts to challenge the Canadian Criminal Code and decriminalize sex work." Settled into the comfort and familiarity of her passion, Caris's voice took on a more normal pitch and cadence.

I could easily see her speaking to a room full of people.

"The Criminal Code has three specific provisions pertaining to sex workers that we are trying to have struck down. The first concerns those who keep or are found in a bawdy house, the second concerns those who live off the avails of prostitution, and the third deals with public communication for the purposes of prostitution. Our team feels strongly that these violate Section 7 of the Charter of Rights and Freedoms—the right to security of the person. It will be quite some time before the Court decides whether they will hear this case, and even longer to have a ruling issued if they do hear it. But if these laws can be struck down as unconstitutional, we are confident that violence against sex workers will significantly decrease and focus will shift from prosecution to the plight that many of them face."

Her passion so drew me in that I found myself leaning in to hear every detail.

After another round of coffee, Caris smiled warmly at me. "Tell me about yourself."

I described my career and the choices I made that lead me there. I told her about Malcolm and showed a picture of our wedding day, then related stories about high school and university. I described my parents and shared anecdotes from my childhood, all the while conscious of the deep divide between my early life and hers.

Caris nodded thoughtfully. "Do you and your husband have children?"

I shook my head. "Do you?" Belatedly, I realized this question might not be as innocent as I had intended, given what I knew of her background. I wished I could take back the question.

Caris hunched her shoulders and seemed to shrink, as if some of her confidence had drained away. She might have been distracted by our sharing, but my question reminded her of why we were meeting. "I had a son once." Her tone made it clear that this, too, was a painful subject. She looked sideways out the window. "I suppose you have as many questions as I do."

Curiosity ate at me, but I couldn't ask the one question I was dying to know. Instead, I asked, "Would you like to hear my part in this story?"

She nodded.

I flipped to the beginning page of my open notebook and began with the newspaper clipping that was folded and tucked inside the notebook's pages. She smoothed out the article and studied it for several minutes, her eyes filling with sorrow. Then she reached into her handbag, opened a black leather wallet, and pulled out a newspaper clipping of her own. This one was printed from an internet site and had the same rudimentary sketch.

"I'm surprised a cold case story from Canada reached Los Angeles," I said.

"I didn't entirely cut ties with Vancouver when I left, though, for the sake of my recovery, I probably should have. I still check the news every so often to see what's going on, what's new, what's changed. Who might have died...." her voice trailed off.

I held my breath, sensing she was weighing what to say next.

"I should have called the hotline sooner, but I didn't want to believe that the sketch was of my sister. Then I didn't want to revisit the past. It's all over now and best forgotten." With a sigh, she added, "We all wish we could go back and change things. So many things. And on some level, I'm sure I have some fault in my sister's death."

"I don't see how," I said.

She shook her head as if to imply there were some things I simply wouldn't understand.

At her urging, I explained the journey that Malcolm and I had taken from Tome to 100 Mile House to Prince George to Lachlan. I told her of my DNA test, Marcia Garvey's classmates, and Aunt Eleanor's contribution to the puzzle. "Until a few months ago, I didn't know of Ellen's existence and believed that Marcia Garvey was both my mother and Jane Doe." While I spoke, I watched Caris's face, hoping to see some indication of whether my assumptions had been correct.

Her face remained impassive.

I explained that Aunt Eleanor submitted a DNA test that proved one of her nieces was Jane Doe.

"Eleanor? The other person Inspector Chilton mentioned?"

"Yes. Eleanor Reinhardt. Your father's sister."

Again, her face betrayed nothing.

At this point, I wanted to ask if Caris would tell me which girl was Jane Doe, but I sensed this wasn't the moment to ask.

Silence settled before she finally asked, "What did you discover in Lachlan?"

"Most of it was rumor that we haven't been able to substantiate. We know that Allan and Renee married young, had two daughters, separated, and later divorced. Allan died in 1974. We also know that Renee remarried a local man, and they had more children. In 1976, Marcia went to live with friends in 100 Mile House, but we haven't been able to find Ellen's story—when she left, and so on—and we don't know how many of the rumors were true."

"I'm sure they all were," Caris said quietly. "And much more." She remained silent for several minutes, her eyes glazed. Then she blinked and glanced around as if to reassure herself that she sat in a coffee house and not in the shack thirty years ago.

When she asked how Renee and Gordon died, I explained the murder-suicide supposition.

Caris showed no surprise. "I always wondered." I couldn't fault the vehemence in her voice when she added, "It was no less than they deserved."

I knew I couldn't understand. "I'm so sorry," I said.

"1980."

"Sorry?"

"Ellen ran away late in 1980 and came to Vancouver looking for Marcia, who came to the city in 1977. Ellen slept in hostels for weeks and walked the streets during the day, searching. She didn't have much money or many options for earning any, you see, and as for finding Marcia...Vancouver was a large city, even in the '80s."

It struck me that Caris spoke of the girls in third person, as if to distance herself from their past.

She looked out the window. "I've never minded the rain."

I followed her gaze. The rain had let up, though the sky remained gray as if threatening to start again.

"Can we walk? It's not far to Stanley Park."

I never minded the rain either, and it was warm for late November. Coffees in hand, we vacated our table.

We walked down Davie Street to Beach Avenue in silence. Beach opened onto the seawall that surrounded the park. We left the clamor of the city behind.

Few pedestrians strolled the seawall. As we walked, I gazed across Burrard Inlet into North Vancouver. I located the neighborhood where I grew up, where my parents lived still.

Caris seemed to be gathering her courage. As eager as I was to hear her story, I understood that she couldn't face me and tell her story within the confines of the coffee shop, where we might be overheard, or she might feel trapped. By walking, she didn't have to stare at the likeness of her dead sister. She was protecting herself, just as she did by speaking in third person about the girl she had once been.

I stared at the wash scraping against the seawall and waited.

"Sharing my story is the least I can do for the sister I lost and the niece I never knew I had. It's time for you to know these things." Her jaw clenched. "Are you sure you *want* to know?"

"I don't know," I answered honestly. "I've imagined so many things. It scares me to know the backstory of where I came from, and there are some things I wish I could unlearn. Or that hadn't happened. But ignoring my roots is disrespectful to my mother. You know?"

Another moment passed before she sighed. "It's tough being back in the city. I thought enough time had passed."

I understood the double meaning in her words. "Is this the first time you've been back to Vancouver?"

Caris shook her head. "I've returned several times, but I've always been careful to avoid the old places. When I left, I was determined to leave everything behind. I changed my name, invented a new biography, and changed everything about me that I didn't like. I chose 'Caris' because it means 'grace' in Greek. And I chose 'Jones' because it was common. I could blend into a crowd of Joneses and disappear. I refused to think about who I used to be." Her deeply melodic voice carried a defensive undercurrent, as if she felt the need to justify her choices.

"I will listen to whatever you feel comfortable sharing." It took all my will to temper my thirst for knowledge.

"I'll tell you everything I know to be true. There are things I myself don't know. I have guessed, and I've heard rumors. But I don't have the answers to some things, and I don't think I ever will." She stopped and pointed to a portion of the city still visible. "You can't quite see Downtown Eastside from here. Have you ever been there?"

I nodded. I had driven through that neighborhood, but never at night.

"The poorest postal code in Canada. That's what they call it. That's where my sister and I shared a flat. We lived together for two years. She tried to save me. She was the better girl, by far. I responded by trying to destroy myself and everyone around me." She tipped her head back and closed her eyes. "It shouldn't have been her. She should have lived. She was strong enough to make it, and she would have made the world a better place. If it had to be one of us, it should have been me."

I had never known the fear and desperation and despair that this woman had, and I prayed I never would.

Rain started to fall.

After a pause, Caris lowered her head and looked at me, tears streaming down her cheeks. "My name, before I left, was Marcia. Ellen was my sister."

Chapter Twenty

Ellen Garvey was my mother. That knowledge left me entirely bereft. I thought I might feel peace, or a sense of closure, but suddenly the truth was real and tangible and I could only mourn for the girl my mother had been.

Caris's face remained passive even as her tears mingled with the rain collecting on the collar of her coat. I wanted to reach out and touch her in order to eliminate the emptiness I felt.

She began walking again. I fell in line half a step behind her, unable to look anywhere but at the ground as she began talking.

"Ellen told me that she didn't know for sure where I'd gone, but she had a scrap of envelope from a letter one of my girlfriends had sent me. It bore a return address in 100 Mile House, and that address was her sole connection to me and her only hope of finding me.

"In Prince George, she found a truck driver who gave her a lift south. She told me she was sick for most of the trip and the truck driver kicked her out on the side of the road just outside a small town. I think she said there was a bad snowstorm and she had to go to the church in town before finding someone else to hitch with. She got to 100 Mile the next day and found Shelly's parents' house.

"I guess Shelly was already married, but her parents recognized Ellen as my sister and insisted she stay with them for the night. They're the ones who told her I'd come to Vancouver. They gave her money for a bus ticket and drove her to the station after breakfast the next morning."

Around us, the wind whipped up suddenly. I shivered and stuffed my right hand deep in my pocket. My left was wrapped around the cardboard of the cup, the lukewarm coffee failing to protect my hand from the cold.

Caris seemed not to notice the wind and gave no indication that she was affected by the cold. "Ellen spent her first night in Vancouver on the cold, wet streets, not knowing where to go. After that, she stayed in hostels and shelters while looking for me. Finally, in late January, she found someone at a shelter on the Downtown Eastside who recognized my name and directed her to the flat I kept on the fifth floor of a crumbling ex-hotel. The rent was a few dollars a month, a single room with a toilet in one corner and a leaky shower that worked some of the time, and a microwave on a shelf, no kitchen, and a dirty mattress on the floor. But it's where she and I lived.

"She was determined to help me get clean. But I had a stronger influence on her than she had on me, and it wasn't long before she fell into my lifestyle. This went on for a long time. Two years we lived in that flat, getting high and turning tricks and getting high again." Caris glanced at me suddenly as if remembering a forgotten detail. "Ellen mentioned you."

I fought an urge to cry. I couldn't speak but simply looked at her, hoping she would elaborate.

"We got high one night. Ellen was in a real bad way. Broke down hysterically and said she'd lost a baby. I was too high to really take care of her the way she needed. I assumed she'd miscarried, or the baby had been taken away by the Ministry." Caris shook her head. "I remember thinking she would get over it." She looked at me. "I guess now I know the truth. It was the only time she talked about it. When I asked her about it—you—later, she pretended not to know what I was talking about."

I whispered, "When did she leave?"

Caris didn't hesitate. "1983. I'll never forget. When I moved here, my boyfriend came with me. Kenny. Sweet boy. But he got taken to prison for several years and left me alone. He finally came home, and for awhile it actually felt like a family for me. He'd cleaned up and wanted the same for me. Just like Ellen. And just like Ellen, I sucked him back into the life. He died from an overdose three weeks after he came home, and I intended to die, too. I took a huge hit and lay down next to his body and didn't care if I woke up. But I did, and Ellen was sitting with me and taking care of me and crying because she finally realized that she'd never be able to save me." This was all stated matter-of-factly.

Caris drew a short breath and shifted her gaze to the clouds. "That must have been right around the time we heard about Gordon and Renee. They were dead. Ellen found out. I think through a newspaper, or maybe she still had contact with someone back home. I don't know and I didn't really care. I was just glad they were gone. I finally felt free from something in my past.

"Ellen did, too," she said thoughtfully. "It was like she woke up suddenly. She was determined, almost angry at the world, and she started to pull away from me. I think some part of Ellen believed the bonds of sisterhood couldn't withstand the reminders of our past. When she looked at me, she saw only the young girl I had once been, and it was the same for me when I looked at her. We were reminders to each other of a past we wanted to forget.

"She told me she was leaving. I woke up late one afternoon and she already had her shoes on. She was simply sitting, waiting for me to wake up. Said she found someone who would take her north to 150 Mile House, and they were leaving that night. She needed a fresh start. She was going to Lachlan to burn down those damn houses, to get rid of the demons. Then she wanted to see if she could find out what happened to her baby." Caris took a deep breath. "She told me she loved me but hoped I would understand that she needed to not see me for awhile. And I did understand. I was too busy trying to slowly kill myself to care that she was leaving. I gave her a half-hearted hug and let her walk out of the flat. I never saw her again." Her voice broke. She took a moment to compose herself, then looked at me and whispered, "Now I know why."

"I'm sorry," I said, my voice barely more than a whisper. "I can't imagine."

"I think part of me has always known she was gone. Somehow, I just felt it, that I was the only one left. But I never imagined the truth. I was angry at Ellen for a long time, for not continuing to try to save me. But she had tried again and again, when it wasn't her responsibility to save me. I loved her and hated her, because she was so much stronger than I was, strong enough to walk away. As far as I knew, she got clean and started over, and that was what I wanted for myself. So I told myself that she was living happily ever after somewhere. I wanted the best things possible for her to make myself feel better about being so selfish."

Her sentiment echoed what her own friends had hoped for her, but I didn't say this.

"I only knew for sure when I saw the police sketch. It was such a shock. It's one thing to guess, but it's another thing to be presented with the truth. So many regrets. So many things I wish I had done differently." She choked on a sob. "Then I got to thinking about the little moments when we were young and happy, even for a brief time. The squabbles we'd have over toys or clothes. She used to put on my clothes, you see, and wear her hair the same way I did, and she would pretend to be me. She hung on my every word and followed me around. I taught her how to dance, how to smoke, how to drink. I was her hero. And when she followed me to Vancouver, somehow, she still believed the best about me and wanted to save me. And I hated that she gradually came to see the truth. I hated that I was no longer her hero, and rather than face that shame and get clean, I dragged her down to my level. I taught her how to shoot up and light up and pick up johns and how to feel good. And that's why it's my fault."

"But she made her own choices," I said quietly. "She was hurting, too, and she turned to drugs because she needed to."

Caris pressed her lips together. Whether she agreed with me or not, these were things she needed to decide for herself, that she needed to reconcile.

The squish of our boots on wet pavement filled the silence.

"She was trying to find me," I murmured, still in awe.

"That's what she said. Said she regretted losing you and wanted you back. She was going to destroy the houses we grew up in, then find her baby and start a new life."

If only she had known that I lived mere kilometers away, across Vancouver's Second Narrows Bridge.

Now I knew why Ellen returned north. The details about the night I was born were still unclear, but I now had a better guess. Ellen was eight months pregnant when she left Lachlan, though I had no knowledge whether she had been aware of her condition. If she had, her bravery in starting out was so much more commendable, not only because of the long journey and the uncertainty of what lay at the end, but because she had refused to bring a child into the household where she'd been abused. But if she hadn't known she was pregnant, she must not have known what was causing her sickness during that long trip. I didn't know whether anyone had been there to help her deliver me or if she had been alone, but somehow, I arrived safely, though prematurely. She wrapped me in her t shirt and coat, likely the only warmth she had, and continued into the town. Then that evening, she left me at the church and continued her search for Marcia.

Whether she had known about her pregnancy or not, she would have been terrified when she went into labor. Had she intended to come back for me after finding her sister in 100 Mile House?

"Do you have any pictures of Ellen?" I asked. "I only have one. She was a baby and you were three. You wore a cute little dress and had your hair in pigtails."

Caris shook her head.

"Not even school pictures?" Belatedly, I remembered that Renee didn't let her children go to school.

Caris shook her head.

"Do you remember when Ellen's birthday was?"

This question, too, was met with a shake of her head.

"Did Ellen have a middle name?" I asked.

Caris shifted her gaze as if deep in thought. "I'm sure she did. But I can't remember."

"Do you have any idea who Ellen might have dated after you left? Who might have been my father?"

She recoiled as if I'd struck her. "I have a guess," she said, jaw clenched. "But no. And don't go looking into things you really don't want to know."

I shuddered at the implication of her words, and we lapsed into silence again. I was conflicted, feeling that this would be my only opportunity to get answers to my questions, and yet wondering which topics were safe to ask about.

I broke our silence by asking if Caris could tell me more about Ellen.

A petulant look crossed her face, as if she resented sharing those memories. Her voice went flat as she said, "She kept her hair long. Had a bit of a gap between her front teeth, but not too bad. She hated her dimples. When we could get away with it, she loved dancing and listening to Jimi Hendrix and the Rolling Stones." Her voice softened, "Ellen didn't seem to remember our real father. She didn't know any life but the one we had after he left. She was a sweet girl. Always cheerful and optimistic. She didn't seem to care that our mother taught our half-siblings to hate us. It was always she and I against the world, against Gordon and Renee, and the kids who were as nasty as them." Her features grew stony. "As we got older, Ellen seemed to suffocate. I lashed out at Gordon and Renee and the other kids and refused to be cowed, but Ellen withdrew into herself, became a ghost of the girl she had been."

Not for the first time, I felt heartbreak for the plight of the sisters and rage at the adults who had done this to them. "They had no right," I whispered.

"No, they didn't." Caris seemed to feel empowered by speaking this sentence, as if charging her mother and stepfather with their crimes. "We were controlled, manipulated, neglected, used, and abused. He used his twisted perversion of religion to justify everything he did, and she was happy to let him do so because she resented us and hated our father. They were already emotionally unstable, but he was always drunk and she was always abusing prescription pills. Ironically"—a bark of humorless laughter escaped her—"Renee had bi-polar disorder, and she was in denial. The only prescribed meds she didn't abuse were the ones that would have regulated her moods. I don't know if you can imagine what that was like."

I was stunned. The truth ran so much deeper than I had realized, and the surface knowledge had horrified me enough.

Caris shook her head, her lips twisted in a parody of a smile. "You wanted to know."

"It's hard to hear, but thank you for telling me. I'm so sorry," I said for what felt like the hundredth time. What else could I say?

Caris shrugged. "Years of therapy have helped me come to grips with those years. I was only a child. I had no control over what those people did."

"What happened to you after Ellen left?" I asked.

Her small laugh surprised me. "Part of my job as a counsellor and motivational speaker is to tell my story to recovering addicts. I suppose I can tell it to you.

"I ran away from home for the first time when I was eleven years old. That was also the first time I hitchhiked from Prince George to 150 Mile House, with an older man who promised to let me have some fun. He took me to a dance club where he told me to put my hair up so they would think I was older. He bought me drinks in between dances. Straight shots. I liked the attention he gave me, and I wanted him to be impressed. He offered me a cigarette and laughed when I coughed and choked on the smoke. He told me he'd give me something even better if I went out to his truck with him. So all in one day, not only did I run away and hitchhike for the first time, but I had my first drink, got drunk for the first time, had my first cigarette, had my first hit of heroin, and had my first sexual encounter in the back of a truck. I don't remember most of it, or when I blacked out. But I woke up the next morning in the vestibule of a dilapidated apartment building in 150 Mile House. With nowhere to go and nothing to eat, I had no choice but to go back to Lachlan.

"That was the first man I went home with, but not the last. Within weeks, I ran away again, to the same dance hall in 150 Mile House, because I had loved the drug he'd given me and hoped I'd be able to find more. Back then, I didn't even know what it was called. And that became my life. Every time I ran, I was determined I would never go back. If I could get a ride south, I'd go to the dance hall in 150 Mile, but if I couldn't, I knew the haunts in Prince George. It never took long for someone to buy me a drink, or for me to agree to go with them when they wanted to leave. I didn't know at the time that they were taking advantage of me. I thought their behavior was normal. I thought I was in control. I took the drugs the men gave me because I wanted to forget. When I didn't have any men who would give me drugs, I started stealing or trading sex to get it. After years of mental and physical abuse at home, I convinced myself that by deciding who I had sex with, I was taking control of my body.

"But when I came down from the high, with nowhere else to go, I was forced to go back to Lachlan. As punishment for running away, I was hit and slapped and starved and locked in the woodshed out back, even in the dead of winter. Only Gordon had the key to the woodshed, and only he was allowed to let me out when he deemed I'd been punished enough. But he preferred keeping me in the woodshed. The first time he molested me, I was seven years old. He began raping me when I was twelve. He was disappointed that I wasn't a virgin and beat me horribly for this sin. It went on this way for another three years before I left for the final time. I went to live with a girlfriend, far away from Lachlan, in a warm home where I was allowed to eat whenever I was hungry and sleep in a bed with warm blankets.

"I didn't trust the safety I felt and wondered when something was going to be expected from me. I never let myself be alone in the room with her father because I'd only known one thing of all the men in my life. But she and her parents were good to me. They coaxed my walls down simply by treating me with respect. They enrolled me in school and tutored me in the evenings. I made friends, had normal experiences, dated boys my own age. And I was free, for a short time. I thought I had left the horrors of Lachlan behind, but they were never far away, and I could never completely escape from the woodshed. I hadn't run far enough.

"I ran to Vancouver and fell immediately into the hippie lifestyle. I lost years of my life to LSD and weed and free love, and I told myself I was free, all the while trapped by the memories I couldn't run away from. I was messed up for a long time. I did whatever was necessary to secure that high, so I would stop feeling and stop remembering. Nothing mattered but my next fix. I was arrested countless times, and the offences grew more and more serious. I landed on the streets. I hit rock bottom, got clean, and relapsed. Got clean and relapsed again. I lost friends and boyfriends and people I cared about who cared about me, who couldn't handle watching what I was doing to myself."

She took a deep breath. "Even Ellen walking away in 1983 wasn't enough to get me to clean up for good. It took…." She paused. "It took my son. I had him, then I lost him. Then I cleaned up and was allowed to be part of his life. And then I lost him again and I tried to kill myself. That was in 1992," Caris choked on her words, but steadfastly continued. "Three months after Ellen walked out, I left Vancouver for the final time. I drifted for months before landing in Los Angeles.

"Aaron was born in 1985. I gave him Kenny's last name, though he wasn't Kenny's son. Kenny was my first and only love, and I wanted Aaron to be connected with him somehow. It doesn't make sense, but that fictitious connection comforted me. From the moment I discovered I was pregnant, I was determined to be a good mother. It wasn't the first time I had been pregnant, but I had always miscarried or aborted my children. Aaron was different. I wanted this one, for no other reason than I wanted someone I could love and who would love me. I finally had something more important than my addiction. The name I chose for my baby boy meant 'strength.' He was my new beginning, my new purpose, my reason for being strong.

"But I screwed up. Seven months after Aaron was born, I relapsed, and my boy was taken by the authorities and placed with a foster family. I wanted to die without him. But the desire to get him back was enough for me to complete court-mandated rehab and get clean. I'll never forget the day the judge told me I could see him again. Judge Gerard Bauden. I remember his name and his face. He treated me with kindness and let me be with my boy again. Our visits were limited and always supervised by a social worker, but this time I stayed clean. Eventually, I was allowed to visit with him unsupervised, and then for longer hours, and then for whole days, and then overnight. He was the sweetest boy. He loved me and was always happy to see me. I went to his soccer games and school plays, and when he learned how to play the recorder in kindergarten, I went to every one of his recitals."

"I was weeks away from getting full custody of my boy. I had a full-time job as a cashier at a grocery store and went to twelve-step meetings three times a week. I was two thousand, three hundred and sixteen days clean and sober. During that visit, we went to the beach. He held my hand and we walked barefoot together. The tide was out. We stepped on seaweed and found pretty shells and smooth rocks and little crabs scampering to hide in the shallows. Aaron mimicked the seagulls overhead and laughed when he saw one of them poop. And then we drove back to my apartment, and stopped for chicken nuggets and French fries and chocolate milk. It was a Sunday night. He'd been with me the whole weekend, and because it was a school night, his foster mother picked him up early that evening. He hugged me tightly and kissed my cheek and told me he loved me and would miss me and couldn't wait until Tuesday, because that was his soccer game, and he would see me then, and he asked me to bring him more chocolate milk."

Tears streamed down her face. "I was already in bed that night when his foster father called. Tim was his name, Tim Parnian and his wife Lisa. They had two older children, but they took such good care of my boy. They never judged me or kept him from me. They let me be a part of his life and made sure he knew who his mother was. And they made sure he knew how much I loved him. I'll never forget what Tim said. 'There was an accident, Caris. You need to come.'"

Caris snivelled and swiped her left sleeve across her face. "The accident happened at a four-way stop. Lisa pulled into the intersection, and a truck blew through the stop sign and right into them. A 1987 Dodge ram, with a huge grill on the front. In their little car, they didn't have a prayer. It was just the two of them, Lisa and Aaron. He was sitting in the seat behind her.

"I didn't get to say goodbye. I didn't get there in time. Tim was waiting for me, and he held me while I screamed and cried and cursed the doctors for not saving my boy. The driver of the truck walked away with a broken leg, but my boy was gone, and Tim's wife was fighting for her life. I wanted to kill that man. They had to sedate me. They couldn't even let me see Aaron one last time. I wanted to touch his hand, stroke his hair, kiss his face, but they didn't let me.

"I didn't go to his funeral. I couldn't. Tim did, and his older two children. But I couldn't. Instead, I found a friend who had a stash and bought a lethal amount of heroin, determined to end it and never wake up.

"But I didn't take the heroin. Even in the midst of my grief, I was so proud that I'd managed to stay clean for six years that I didn't want to die a druggie." She stretched out an arm and began rolling up the sleeve. The skin on her wrist bore a long, white scar. "This was easier, and I thought it would take less time. I sat in the bathtub in my apartment, slit both wrists, clutched the seashells Aaron and I found on that last afternoon, and waited to die.

"But Tim saved me. He was worried that I hadn't gone to Aaron's funeral, and while his wife lay unconscious and dying in the hospital, he came to my home and found me and kept me breathing until the paramedics arrived. Somehow, I kept going. I made it though that first twenty-four hours. Before I knew it, a week had gone by, and then two, and then a month, and I found the will to keep going. I still don't understand how. Slowly, I put my life back together. And I never took another hit. I've been sober since 1986. Twenty-four years."

She fell silent.

"Congratulations," I said at last, in barely more than a whisper.

She nodded.

I swiped at my own silent tears. Caris kindly refrained from commenting.

I didn't trust myself to speak. I didn't know what I could possibly say.

We walked in silence for several minutes. When I felt I had regained control of my emotions, I took a deep breath. "Thank you. It can't be easy to be so vulnerable."

"Therapy works wonders," she said, her voice listless. She stared at the north shore, across the Burrard Inlet. Then she turned her face to me and nodded once, curtly, as if to reassure me that she was all right after having shared her story.

"Is it all right for me to ask about your father, Allan?"

She shrugged. "I barely remember my father. He left when I was young and I never saw him again. I heard he died, but it didn't make a huge difference to me, because by then, Renee'd remarried and I was consumed with survival."

"I don't suppose you remember Allan's sister, Eleanor? Your aunt?" I held my breath.

Caris shook her head. "I don't think I ever met her. Renee never told us anything about our father or his family, except to say they didn't want us."

I felt it would be cruel to mention that Eleanor lived in 100 Mile House. If the teenaged Marcia had gone to live with Aunt Eleanor instead of Shelly, Marcia's and Ellen's lives might have turned out very differently. "Eleanor met you a few times when you were very little. She remembers you and wants to meet you, if you are willing." I hoped this might coax her to smile, but she was already shaking her head.

"It's better they remember me as I was. Better they believe Marcia Garvey is dead. Because she is." She sighed. "You have to understand, there are some things I simply don't remember. Maybe it's because I really don't want to, and I tried for years to forget. It's also probably all the drugs. It took years of therapy to work through everything that was done to me by others and by my own hand."

"Is there anything I can do?" I'm not sure why I offered, but I wanted to let her know that I considered her family and wanted to support her in any way I might.

"No." The speed of her reply closed off the past and shut down the possibility of a future.

We approached the end of the seawall, having circled around to the rowing club and marina just off West Georgia. The city skyline was barely visible through the dense fog that had settled in. In a few moments, we would cross the bridge and return to the lives we had left behind.

I suspected that as soon as we did, Caris would be swept away, and I would never see her again.

We waited at a stop light for the signal to change.

Caris said, "I'm returning to my hotel now. I'm quite tired."

She was slipping away. I knew we had no place in each other's lives after today. I was a painful reminder of her sister, of their shared childhood, and shared traumas. Still, I asked, "Will I ever see you again?"

Caris looked puzzled. "Why would you want to?"

"Because…we're family."

"Maybe," she said.

"I would love to keep in touch," I said, trying to hide my desperate desire to keep her from slipping away. "Just to hear how you're doing, or to let me know when you're in town."

She gave a fleeting smile and looked away.

"My husband and I intend to have a proper service and burial for Ellen now that we know her name. Would you like me to let you know when her funeral is, in case you want to come?"

Caris firmly shook her head. "I won't come. Ellen will understand."

The light turned green and the crowd around us surged past.

Caris looked at me for a long moment before she nodded and said, "Goodbye."

I watched my aunt as long as I could. She never turned around, and part of me was glad that she didn't. I wasn't sure I could handle the emotions I might see on her face.

Then she rounded a corner and was gone.

I stayed rooted in place, barely noticing the jostling of pedestrians gathering around me, waiting for the signal to cross. I didn't see the cars in front of me or hear the muted bustle of the city.

How long I stood there in the rain, I couldn't be sure. It was growing dark when I finally walked back to my car. I sat behind the wheel in my sopping raincoat and listened to the rain drum on the roof.

Ellen Garvey, my mother, was born in 1963. She grew up in a horrifying household and ran away from home in 1980, when she was eight months pregnant. She gave birth to me on the outskirts of the town of Tome and left me at the Parish before continuing to 100 Mile House and then eventually to Vancouver. She found her sister, and the girls lived together for two years, united in grief and despair. Ellen never forgot the baby she left behind; and thoughts of the child consumed her. Her daughter became her motivation to clean up and walk away in 1983, after learning of the deaths of her parents and accepting the unlikelihood of her sister's recovery.

Ellen returned north and destroyed the homes of her past before intending to return to Tome to find her daughter.

I found myself admiring her strength, her determination, and her tenacity, and wondered whether she ever made it back to Tome, or if she died before arriving. Had her last thoughts been of her daughter?

I didn't want to know the answer to that question. I'd come as far as I wanted to come.

I had accomplished what I had set out to do. I had given Jane Doe a name and an identity. I would make sure she would be remembered. Maybe this was as far as I would come, as much as I was meant to know. Maybe this was where the story of the past ended and the story of my future began.

I turned the key in the ignition, turned on the lights and windshield wipers, and began the long drive home.

<h1 style="text-align:center">Epilogue</h1>

Shortly after we rang in the 2011 New Year, Aunt Eleanor and I collaborated to order Ellen Garvey's gravestone. We intended to claim her remains from the medical examiner's office and hold a service in her memory.

The gravestone was delivered to Eleanor's home in late February, slightly more than a year after my journey with Jane Doe had begun. That same week, in the early evening hours on Wednesday, Doug called and wished me a belated happy New Year and asked about my holidays. "Do you have time to talk for a while?" he asked.

"Of course," I said, curiosity rising.

"Great. I'd like to begin by telling you that this is all strictly confidential."

I understood the protocol of his profession. "Of course." I crossed to the nearest kitchen chair and sat down.

"Do you still subscribe to newspapers from the Interior and up north?"

"I do, though I haven't given any of them more than a cursory glance in months." I glanced at the recycling bin in the hallway. My habit had been to glance at the headlines, perhaps scan the first page of each newspaper, then place the paper in the bin. I had reasoned that any important information would be front-page news, and that Doug would have informed me first before any significant development went to the media.

"I ask because there was a piece in the Prince George newspaper three or four weeks ago about an attempted bank robbery. I was wondering if you had seen it."

"I did not, I'm afraid."

"I'll fill you in, then explain it's significance. The robbery was brought to our attention earlier this week. Two brothers, Jim and Derek Elliott, stormed the branch office shortly after it opened, when they thought the tellers would have the most cash on hand and few clients present. The bank manager confronted them and assaulted Derek, breaking his nose, before Derek shot him. Then both brothers panicked and ran, leaving us lovely security footage."

"The manager is all right," Doug assured me. "Derek merely clipped him. Turns out that Jim had several prior arrests and convictions, and the bank manager was able to pick him out of a photo lineup. He was adamant that the second robber, the one he'd assaulted and been shot by, looked enough like the man in the lineup that they had to be related. This identification was enough to arrest both brothers and obtain a warrant for their DNA samples."

I listened, astounded by the tale, and wondered what in the world a bank robbery could possibly have to do with me. Clearly, the brothers were connected to Ellen, Eleanor, or me, and I waited for Doug to arrive at the point.

He chuckled. "They both insisted that it was a case of mistaken identity, and they couldn't have robbed the bank because they were trying to steal a truck on the other side of town at the exact same time. Of course, they intended this to be convincing, because who in their right mind would confess to a crime to establish an alibi? But Derek couldn't hide his broken nose and gave a weak explanation for the injury. His DNA sample was matched to the blood he'd left at the crime scene, and his obvious injuries corresponded with the statement of the wounded bank manager. Their story quickly unravelled, and they hastily pointed a finger at the other."

Eager as I was to reach the explanation of the significance, I had to satisfy my curiosity. "How does that work? What will happen to them now?"

"Regardless of which brother actually pulled the trigger," Doug explained, "Canadian law decrees that they're equally culpable in the shooting because it occurred during the commission of a crime. We don't have confessions, but in light of the evidence, I think it's likely they'll plead guilty in exchange for lesser sentences.

"Which brings us up to a few days ago."

I sat straighter, my muscles tensing.

"Derek and Jim Elliott's DNA samples also tested positive for a second DNA match in the RCMP database. A partial match."

"To Ellen Garvey?"

"No. To her killer."

His words struck like a physical blow. I braced my free hand on the tabletop to steady myself. I took several deep breaths.

"Nora? Are you all right?"

"Yes," I said, breathless and light-headed. After another deep breath, I cleared my throat and croaked, "Do you know who—?" I couldn't finish the sentence.

"Not yet. A partial match indicates someone in the same genetic line. The brothers were born in the 1990s, so we're looking a generation back. We were granted a court order to obtain DNA samples from the male relatives of the Elliott brothers. You can rest assured that we'll be thorough and exhaustive in our search. That process will begin in the coming days."

"How soon do you think we'll know?"

"Weeks."

ONCE AGAIN, I WAS AWAITING THE RESULTS OF A DNA TEST. Once again, I feverishly searched the internet, though this time the topic of my search was the attempted bank robbery in Prince George in January, 2011, and the focus of my social media perusal was anyone with the surname "Elliott."

In the meantime, I spent my free time finalizing the details for Ellen Garvey's memorial service, working closely with Aunt Eleanor. We chose the last Saturday in April, the 30th. I would begin semester break on April 16th, and be free to spend as much time in the Interior as I wanted. Uncle George and Aunt Eleanor had been gracious in delaying their trip to Nova Scotia, a yearly tradition that typically began in March, so they could attend their niece's funeral.

Once we confirmed the final details, I wrote a letter to Caris Jones in care of her non-profit organization. I gave her the details of her sister's memorial service and reiterated my willingness to have her be a part of my life. I resolved that this would be my only attempt to contact her. I would respect her wishes and maintain my distance, and leave it up to her to reach out if she so chose.

After my conversation with Caris in Stanley Park almost four months prior, I told her story only to Malcolm. I desperately wanted to reveal the truth to Aunt Eleanor, but I accepted that it wasn't my story to tell. Instead, I let Inspector Chilton tell Eleanor that they knew Jane Doe was Ellen Garvey instead of her sister Marcia, though how we were certain would never come to light.

On a Saturday morning at the end of March, not quite a year after Doug had called to tell me the results of my DNA test, he called again.

"We have his name," Doug said.

I stepped into the living room where Malcolm was playing a video game. He looked up and immediately paused and muted the TV as I sunk onto the couch next to him.

"We arrested Arnold "Dimes" Elliott early this morning for the sexual assault and murder of Ellen Garvey."

Chills traveled through me. A roar in my ears threatened to drown out his voice.

"The report will be released to the media later today. I wanted you to hear it from me."

I reached for Malcolm's hand and gripped tightly. Then I lowered the phone and pressed the speaker button so Malcolm could hear.

Malcolm leaned forward. "Hi Doug, I'm here too."

"Hi Malcolm. Nora, are you there?"

I was too overwhelmed to reply and glanced at Malcolm to telegraph my response.

He answered, "She is, just taking it all in. Are you able to tell us about the arrest? Or what he had to say?" Belatedly, he glanced at me.

I nodded to indicate that this was what I wanted.

Doug hesitated. "I can tell you the basic gist of what he said about that night. I also caution you that criminals attempt to mitigate their responsibility, so his version of events cannot be taken at face-value."

Doug took an audible breath. "He was a long-haul trucker across Canada from the late sixties to the late nineties. His nickname came from his habit of shooting craps for dimes in the late sixties, and he adopted that nickname as a sort of 'calling card.' After having 'liaisons' with various female hitchhikers, he would drop them off at a payphone with a single dime to make a call, as 'payment for services rendered.'" Doug paused, and then said flatly, "Those were his words, not mine."

I swallowed the revulsion churning in my stomach and focused on a speck of lint on the carpet, wanting to hear more but afraid of what would come. Even clenching the warmth of Malcolm's hand, my fingers were cold.

"At first, he denied picking up Ellen Garvey. Then he admitted to picking her up but denied having sex with her. Then he admitted to having sex with her but insisted it had been consensual, that it had been her idea, and that she hadn't done anything she didn't want to do.

"He also claimed she was alive when she left his truck, and that someone else must have murdered her. I confronted him with the witness statement placing him in 150 Mile House. He insisted that someone else must have picked her up when he dropped her off, but he gave conflicting answers when I asked where he'd left her. Eventually, he provided more details about their encounter, details I will spare you. Suffice to say that, either during or shortly after their sexual encounter, he choked Ellen until she lost consciousness, and then panicked when he saw she wasn't breathing. When he realized she was dead, he stated that he drove for 'quite some time,' searching for a turn-off road where he might leave her body. Afterward, he drove through the night to Vancouver and picked up an east-bound shipping run. Less than four days after killing Ellen Garvey, he was in Winnipeg. Based on what we can confirm from his employment records, he began this run on May 4th. Which means that Ellen Garvey was killed on or about May 3, 1983." Doug fell silent.

I lifted my gaze from the carpet to meet Malcolm's concerned gaze. I nodded curtly.

"So he confessed," I said hollowly. "He confessed to killing my mother."

"He confessed," Doug confirmed.

My shoulders slumped. When I had imagined being able to name Ellen Garvey's killer, I had imagined feeling triumph or satisfaction or vindication. Instead, I felt numb.

"What happens now?" I mumbled.

"He's been arrested and formally charged. He will appear before a justice on Monday morning to arrange any terms of bail. Then, at some point in the future, a trial date will be set." Doug hesitated. "Nora, the charge of sexual assault will likely be dropped. I'm sorry. We just don't have enough evidence to prove that the encounter was not consensual. The Crown prosecutor assigned to this case will likely look over the particulars and determine that, in the absence of this proof, they will not be successful on this charge."

"I-I understand," I said faintly.

"I also want to caution you that unless he pleads guilty, a trial is still several years away. Even if he does plead guilty, his sentencing hearing likely won't be until early next year, at the earliest. He is in his seventies and in poor health."

Malcolm frowned. "What are you saying?"

"I just want you to be aware that the office of the Crown *is* moving forward with the prosecution, as murder does not have a statue of limitation. However, the trial will be abated if the suspect dies before a ruling is issued, because at that point, the question of his guilt, along with the need to protect the public from his future actions, and the need to punish him for his crime, become moot issues."

"I understand," I murmured. I knew Doug was making sure I was aware of what could happen moving forward. Regardless, I had privately resolved that I would attend every court session, trial day, and sentencing hearing. I owed it to Ellen Garvey. She had no other family present.

"I think I need some time," I said finally. "Doug, thank you. Truly. For everything you've done."

Later that day, I opened my laptop and clicked on the icon for the internet browser. I typed in the name of the publication in 100 Mile House and found what I was looking for as soon as the webpage loaded.

A banner declared, "Arrest Made in Decades-old Homicide of Victim Found in Provincial Park."

For me, this portion of my story ended as it had begun, with the title of a newspaper article.

ON APRIL 30, 2011, ONE YEAR, TWO MONTHS, AND NINETEEN days after I saw the police sketch of Jane Doe in the newspaper, and almost exactly twenty-eight years to the day of her death, Aunt Eleanor and I laid Ellen Garvey to rest. Her gravestone bore all the details that were available to us:

ELLEN GARVEY
    1963-May 3, 1983
    "Come to me, all you who are weary and burdened, and I will give you rest."

THE BIBLE VERSE HAD BEEN AUNT ELEANOR'S IDEA. I DIDN'T know whether Ellen Garvey had practiced any type of spirituality during her short life—she had every reason to believe that life was empty, futile, and desolate—but the line comforted Eleanor.

I had initially envisioned a small graveside ceremony attended by the surviving remnants of our family and presided over by Father Clement. Father Clement agreed to perform the memorial service, but he and Una Braithwaite insisted that a proper mass be held and town residents invited. As much as I would have preferred a private ceremony, this town had adopted me as a child and maintained my memory for thirty years. Now, the congregation would adopt Ellen Garvey as one of their own and mourn her alongside us.

Mom and Dad rode to Tome with Malcolm and me. The day of the ceremony, I led them into the sanctuary to show them the candle, plaque, and guest book dedicated to Baby Judea. Mom's breath caught. Dad cleared his throat several times, and as we turned the pages and read thirty years' worth of best wishes and kindest regards, his hand found mine and squeezed.

Uncle George and Aunt Eleanor joined us in the sanctuary, along with Doc Tiny, who had made the trip down from 150 Mile House with his wife, Beth. John and Una Braithwaite, Doug Chilton, Michael Plummer, and his daughter Emily came, as well. The thirteen of us sat together in the first two pews.

It was an emotional day for all involved. I kept my head bowed, my hand in my husband's, aware that my mother and Aunt Eleanor glanced at me periodically to ensure I was holding up.

Father Clement identified Malcolm and me as those who had searched diligently to ensure the girl was buried with her name known. He also recognized Doug Chilton for his efforts in spearheading the search and solving Ellen Garvey's murder.

Caris Jones was not present. I may never know whether she received the letter I sent her.

Ellen's cremated remains rested in an elegant, deep mahogany urn on the raised podium in the center of the dais, surrounded by flowers. I hated that we didn't have a photograph of her as a young woman.

Father Clement, in full regalia, stood to the side and spoke from the heart about redemption and eternal peace and family bonds. I squeezed Malcolm's hand. He wrapped an arm around me, pulled me close, drew my head to his shoulder, and rested his head on mine.

Father Clement closed this portion of the service with a brief prayer, and at his signal, we rose to honor the passing of Ellen Garvey's remains. Row by row we entered the aisle and followed Father Clement to the parking lot where the gathered congregation piled into a dozen or so cars to proceed to the cemetery.

Eleanor and I had selected a cemetery plot underneath a weeping willow tree. The beautiful site rested near the gravesites of Thomas Chance and Bernard Beardsley. The deceased men, having watched over Baby Judea, perhaps would watch over Baby Judea's mother in death. Though sentimental, it was comforting to think that Ellen was no longer alone and abandoned.

After an elegant prayer, Father Clement signaled to the cemetery caretakers, and the men shoveled dirt over the mahogany urn. The gravestone would be positioned after the soil had been given a chance to settle.

The gathered flock were invited to return to the Parish to partake of refreshments. I lingered beside the grave and waited for the mourners to disperse, unwilling to leave yet. I thanked Doc Tiny, Doug, Michael, John, and Una for being there and promised to join them back at the church. Uncle George and Aunt Eleanor looked exhausted. It had been an emotionally overwhelming day. I urged them to rest in the sanctuary.

My parents returned to the parish with Father Clement.

Malcolm and I finally stood alone, hand in hand, and gazed at the freshly turned soil.

In a few days, spring would give way to the brilliant heat of summer, and in little over a week, a new semester would begin, but I was stuck in the past. As I stared down at Ellen's resting place, love for my parents, wonder at having found George and Eleanor, and gratitude to my husband overwhelmed me.

Malcolm raised my hand to his lips. "You should be so proud."

"Should I? I'm torn, and I feel guilty for being conflicted. I wish I hadn't learned any of this. But I'm ashamed of feeling that way, because to ignore what Ellen went through is to disrespect her memory. Everyone else forgot about her or didn't care what happened to her. I need to care, but it's hard to carry that burden."

"I'll help you carry it. I'm big and strong." Malcolm winked and smiled.

"I want to walk away and leave this, but I don't know if I can."

"The best way to honor Ellen's memory is to create the best future possible for yourself. You've already come so far and worked so hard. That's a tribute to Ellen, and to your adopted parents. You can't let this be the end of your story. I know it's easier said than done, but we still have our future."

I kept my gaze on the ground. "Babe?"

"Hmm?"

"I know we've been lukewarm about the idea of having kids, but I've been thinking...."

"Baby fever?"

I chuckled. "No. God, no. I'm very hesitant to pass on the genes from my biological family. I don't know much about my ancestry, but what I do know scares me."

"So...."

I sheepishly faced him. Never had I been so grateful that such a wonderful man had chosen me to share his life.

I took a deep breath. "Not right away, of course. Not tomorrow or next week or next month even. But maybe, in the future, let's talk about how we feel about adopting a child. Okay?"

FOR ALL THE PARENTS WHO ADOPTED ME, AND FOR THE FAMILY I DIDN'T KNOW I had.

Endnote

In late 2011, Arnold "Dimes"' Elliott was ordered to stand trial on a charge of manslaughter stemming from the May 3, 1983, murder of Ellen Garvey. In spite of his advanced age and deteriorating health, he'd been denied bail due to the heinous nature of his crimes. He was remanded to custody to await trial.

Seven weeks before his trial date, Arnold Elliott died of liver disease.

Sneak peek at The Hollywood Wife

GEMMA EVANS

The Hollywood Wife Blurb

Sixteen-year-old Rosalie has had a crush on celebrity, A-list actor Sam Urban for as long as she can remember. So, when Sam visits the diner where Rosalie works as a waitress and sits at one of her tables, she can hardly believe her luck and barely remembers how to take his order. Even more unbelievable is the interest he takes in her.During a whirlwind courtship, Rosalie's life becomes a Hollywood movie, full of glitz and glamor, with her as the leading lady. But Sam soon makes it clear that Rosalie's role as his wife is a lifetime commitment, and the only way she'll leave him is in a body bag. All too soon, Rosalie needs more than acting skills to save her life and escape Sam's iron-fisted control. But her greatest fear is that she's waited too long to make her break for freedom.

Trigger Warning: This book contains episodes of domestic violence.

Prologue

In 1990, I landed in West Hollywood, California, a fresh-faced sixteen-year-old on my own. As I look back at that year, I wonder whether I truly had free choice in the decisions I made. Most importantly, I wonder whether I could have said *no* instead of *yes* to the offer that changed the course of my life. If I'd said no, would I have escaped without the scars that mar my face and soul? Or was I already too emotionally scarred to have resisted the lure of wealth, glamor, and adoration? At the time, having no other role model for marriage and relationships than my parents, I think I feared that my mother's fate would become mine. That fear fueled my determination to do everything within my power to avoid replicating her life.

I was sixteen and largely powerless, so when a dream too good to be true strolled into the diner where I worked, I may have been running from my past as much as I was running into his arms. L.A. was as much a destination as it was its own living, breathing life-force. Hollywood has always been the producer of mainstream culture, but Los Angeles was where the culture was being lived. California was the land of opportunity, and I don't think my story could have unfolded anywhere else. After all, being a Hollywood wife can happen only in the city where dreams are made and sold.

Chapter One

When I arrived in Hollywood as an innocent sixteen-year-old, the city spoke of possibility and hope. I didn't come with the idea of fame and fortune, of being an actress. I came to live with my older brother Joey while our parents went through a very bitter, nasty divorce.

Our father was a long-time alcoholic, and our mother was a manipulative and overbearing woman. Mom was never satisfied with anything. She could have lived in a house made of gold and she would still find something to complain about.

That included her children. For the most part, Joey could do nothing wrong, and I couldn't do anything right. I had never been the kind of daughter she wanted. I wasn't a girly girl or skinny. I didn't learn how to do makeup until I was in my late teens. Jeans and tee shirts were my signature outfits, and it drove her crazy that I wasn't her perfect little doll. Neither one of my parents really cared about us; they just cared about hurting each other and had perfected that hurt to an art.

Joey had moved to West Hollywood the year before and Indiana was horrible without him. With Joey gone, my parents' screaming matches escalated into Mom having fits of rage. She threw plates and anything else she could reach. Dad screamed and cussed within inches of her face. What followed was a house filled with tension while they glared at each other through stony silence. The temptation to mouth off would overwhelm one of them, usually my mother, and the hell would start all over again. Anytime I left the house, I never knew what fresh hell I would return to.

When Joey lived there, we could endure the destruction of our family together. Once he moved out, our parents descended into a new kind of hell. I knew I had to find a way out, too.

In 1989, as soon as I turned sixteen, my mom gave me permission to drop out of school. I was ecstatic. I hated school. Classmates bullied me for my weight and for my parents' lack of money. Soon after I dropped out of school, my parents started the divorce process, and Joey invited me to come to Hollywood while they figured things out. I jumped on the next available plane.

Joey worked the graveyard shift at a local factory, and I got a job waiting tables at an all-night diner close to our West Hollywood apartment. Back then, West Hollywood was reasonably priced. Most of the housing was rent controlled, but even with that, Joey still had a hard time paying the rent and bills.

By the end of my first month working at the diner, I'd learned that Monday nights were slow nights. Donna, the older, second-shift waitress, took me under her wing, taught me the ropes, and looked out for me. She and I were the only two working the floor that Monday night.

Donna joined me at the beverage station. "You've got one at table ten," she said.

I rolled another set of silverware and sighed. The last thing I wanted a ten minutes before my shift ended was another table.

I got my notepad and walked over to the table. "Hi there, my name's Rosalie. Can I start you off with something to drink?"

"Just coffee, please," the man said in a voice that could melt sin on a winter's day.

I froze. I knew that voice. I looked down at him. Yes, the dark-haired man sitting in a booth in my section was my all-time favorite actor Samuel Urban. His perfect golden California tan made his skin glisten and stand out against his white button-up shirt. Beads of sweat formed on my forehead. Sam was one of the biggest stars at the time, and I had seen everything he ever made. I was a fangirl long before the phrase was coined.

Heart pounding in my ears, I hurried back to the beverage station. I couldn't believe I was actually waiting on Sam Urban. My heart sank a little as I risked a glance his way. There was my biggest, most lustful celebrity crush sitting in my section, and he hadn't even looked at me.

Was he supposed to? I mean, he was a big-name actor. Was he supposed to notice the waitress taking his order? *Get real*, I told myself. I returned to his table and turned the downturned coffee cup upright and poured his coffee, almost spilling the boiling liquid. I winced inwardly when I realized I had forgotten to ask if he needed cream and sugar.

Idiot, I inwardly cursed, then managed in a calm voice, "Here you go, Mr. Urban. I'm sorry, I forgot to ask if you needed cream or sugar."

"No, thank you, just black for me. And it's just Sam."

I almost fainted when his dark chocolate eyes lifted to meet mine. He had a smile that crossed somewhere between a mischievous child and something reserved only for the bedroom. It took all I had to remember how to speak.

"Have you decided on what you'd like?" I asked.

"Rosalie!" Nick, the owner and my boss, yelled from the open kitchen.

I ignored him.

"I may have." Sam ran his tongue across his bottom lip.

Cue swoon.

"Rosalie, now!" Nick bellowed.

I shot him a nasty look and turned back to Sam.

"You go ahead," he said. "I'll be here."

As hard as I tried not to, I giggled and told him I'd be right back. I stomped off toward Nick, making sure to glare at him all the way to the kitchen window.

"What?" I demanded.

"It's ten. Get off my clock," Nick said.

"Oh, come on. For one, I'm not in school so the ten o'clock thing shouldn't even apply to me, and two, I still have a customer."

"Nothing doing. Donna can take over your table that hasn't even put an order in yet. Besides, I promised your brother I would have you on your way home no later than ten. Now, off my clock."

"Fine," I whined.

What complete and utter bullshit. The one time I got to meet my celebrity crush and actually speak to him, and Nick had to ruin it all because he wanted to be a jerk.

Defeated, I walked back to Sam's table. "I'm sorry, Mr. Urban—"

"Sam."

I giggled again. "I'm sorry, Sam, my boss is an ass. Donna will be taking care of you this evening. I'm a huge fan, and it was amazing to get to meet you."

"I'm so sorry to hear that," he said. "I was really looking forward to your serving me."

My face must have gone about ten shades of red. I could only smile like an idiot. "I was, too. I hope you have a nice evening."

Sam stood as I started to turn. "Could I talk you into joining me?"

I'm sorry, did this A-list actor just ask me to join him?

"That is, if you don't have other plans," he said. "I'd very much enjoy the company."

I fought for all I was worth not to hyperventilate. "I would love to. Give me a minute to grab my things and get out of my apron."

Sam flashed a smile. "Absolutely. I'll be right here."

I pinched myself all the way to the break room, where I grabbed my purse. This kind of thing didn't happen to girls like me. I had been heavyset my whole life and lacked self-confidence because of my weight.

What in the hell could he possibly see in my fat ass? He was probably just being nice to a fan. More than likely, he wouldn't even be sitting there when I got back. But he was.

Sam's face lit up when I reached his booth. He stood up as I slid into the booth opposite him. This was really happening.

Once I sat down, I didn't know what to do with myself or what to say, so I reached into my purse and pulled out my cigarettes. My hands shook as I tried and failed to light one. Sam put a steadying hand over mine and flicked his lighter for me.

"Thank you," I murmured.

"You're welcome."

He watched me for a moment, a small smile playing on his lips. "You're not from around here, are you?" he asked. "Your accent gives you away. Let me guess. Illinois?"

That was the first time I had ever heard of an Illinois accent. "Indiana, actually."

"Indianapolis?"

"Terre Haute."

"Ah! Home to Indiana State University," Sam said.

I took a draw on my cigarette and turned my head slightly to blow out the smoke, then said, "I'm impressed. Very few people know where it's at."

Sam shrugged and smiled. My heart hadn't slowed since I realized who he was, and the way his smile played across his lips didn't help. I still didn't know what to say or do with myself.

From the fan magazines I read, I knew Sam was twenty-eight. I tried to keep that fact pushed far away in the back of my mind. Because I was sixteen, I didn't think we'd still be sitting there having a conversation if he knew my age. I was going to enjoy however long this ride lasted.

The way he looked at me made me squirm. I didn't know what to say, where to put my hands, or how to breathe correctly. Small talk wasn't an art I had mastered, but I tried anyway because if I didn't, the silence would drive me nuts.

"I really enjoyed your last movie," I offered. "*A Lover's Scent* was new territory for you."

Sam sat up a little straighter, clearly pleased. "Thank you. And you're right." He winked. "Definitely new territory for me. You're observant."

My cheeks burned. I bit my lower lip and looked down at the table. "I've seen everything you've made probably ten times over."

"Stalker," Sam teased.

I barked a nervous laugh. "Hey! Whose diner did you wander into tonight?"

"A very fortunate last-minute change in plans." Sam ran his tongue over his bottom lip again.

I tried and failed to suppress a shiver.

The light caught his eyes and made them dark pools of honey. "This is a pretty regular spot for me, but this is the first time I've seen you," he said.

"I normally work the lunch and early dinner shift."

"I see. The real question is what is such a pretty thing like you doing here?"

I laughed and raised an eyebrow. "I'm not exactly the actress type, now, am I? I moved out here to be closer to my brother."

Sam nodded. "Any other family out here?"

I stiffened. "No. Our parents are in Indiana."

"That must be hard."

"Not really," I muttered.

Donna brought me a fresh coffee and topped off Sam's cup. The interruption gave me a minute to catch my breath. Sam cocked his head to the side, and his stare bored into me as I caught his gaze. He'd picked up on my shift in body language, almost like he was studying me. The dissent into family matters made me uncomfortable.

"Sore subject, I gather?" He passed the creamer and sugar caddy.

I gave him the briefest of smiles. "We have a difficult relationship with our parents."

He grunted a laugh. "I get that. My mom's a little on the nutty side and Dad, well, Dad was always more of a friend than anything."

"My dad's an alcoholic and my mom just pushes him to drink even more." I concentrated on flavoring my coffee so I didn't have to look at him.

"Did you want some coffee with your cream and sugar?" he joked.

"Better than that black abyss of bitterness you're drinking."

"Hey now," he laughed. "That's my soul you're talking about. But maybe some brighter days are ahead?"

I smiled without shifting my attention away this time.

Sam placed his hand on the table. His fingers didn't quite touch mine. A palpable, electric charge seemed to vibrate between us. Everything in me screamed to either move my hand or hold his. I wasn't brave enough to do either.

I leaned against the booth and sipped my coffee. "My brother's lived here a little over a year. When he got the courage to come out as homosexual, our dad made him leave. I knew for years that Joey was gay, we all did, really, but a gay son was just a little too much for our parents to handle."

Sam's expression softened. "I'm so sorry, that's horrible. I couldn't imagine doing something like that to my child. Your brother couldn't have picked a better spot to settle than West Hollywood."

I laughed. "That exactly what thought when I got here. I didn't realize how big and close the gay community was out here. Joey's made so many friends. For the first time, he has a real support group. Something he didn't have back in Indiana."

I sipped my coffee. Memory of my dad calling Joey a faggot as he kicked him out of the house played like a movie in my head.

Sam changed the subject.

We shared a lot of things in common. We both loved books and many of the same authors. We also liked a lot of the same movies. Sam's favorite, though, was the theater, something I had never experienced. Outside of the college's few drama department productions, a college town like Terre Haute didn't offer much in the way of sophistication.

"You've never seen a theater production?" Sam asked.

I shook my head.

"I'd love to take you some night. When are you off?" he asked.

Did I hear this man right? Had he said he wanted to take me out? My face flushed as I struggled for words. "That would be amazing, and tomorrow is my day off, actually." Luck seemed to keep running on my side.

"Can I ask you something?" Sam said.

"Sure."

"How old are you?"

My heart sank. Here came the handshake and the "It was nice to meet you." There went my fairy tale.

"Eighteen," I lied.

Sam roared with laughter. "Honey, I'm an actor. I read people. It's what I do." He slid his hand across the table and patted my hand. His steady gaze reassured me. "It's okay to tell me. I don't really care. I just want to know what I'm working with."

I stared at the table. "I turn seventeen in December."

He squeezed my hand ever so slightly and rubbed his thumb back and forth across the back of my hand. The sensation of his skin on mine brought my attention back to him. My pulse jumped and, again, all I could do was look at him.

"Can I walk you to your car?" Sam asked.

"I don't drive. I only live a couple of blocks over."

Sam's jaw dropped. "You walk? In this neighborhood? At night?"

I laughed. "Yeah, it's not a big deal. I walked everywhere back home." I didn't see walking as anything but safe. I had been catcalled more times in Indiana than I had been in California. West Hollywood really was one of the nicer areas. Sunset Strip was only a few blocks away, and while a person wouldn't want to be caught there after dark, the diner and my apartment weren't in a bad area.

"Sweetheart, you're not in Indiana anymore. I'll drive you."

I shook my head. "Really, my apartment isn't that far. I don't want to bother you."

"It's not a bother. I'd actually be very happy to take you, and I'm not taking no for an answer."

Sam stood and extended a hand. Being there in that moment with him felt so surreal. I put my hand in his. Warm fingers close around mine as I stood. I knew then and there this might not be a beginning, but this wasn't an ending either.

Sam left Donna a generous tip even though she hadn't charged us for the coffees, then led me to his car, the only nice one in the parking lot.

"A brand new black 1990 Ferrari," Sam said. "Isn't she beautiful?"

I nodded, impressed.

"I have an eye for beautiful things." Sam's eyes gleamed.

A few seconds passed before I realized he wasn't talking about the car. I had never considered myself beautiful. For as long as I could remember my mother had bereted me daily about my weight. The self-hate tends to dig deep and stay. Doing my best to push those old thoughts out of my head, I simply enjoyed the compliment.

Sam opened the passenger door, and I climbed in. He closed my door and circled the car to the driver's side. He got in behind the wheel and I was in heaven.

My normal fifteen-minute walk took less than five minutes by car, leaving me disappointed when we pulled up to my apartment building. Sam shut off the car and faced me. His chocolate brown eyes searched my face. I could have lost myself forever in their depths. A nervous shiver ran up my spine. I looked down at my hands. No one had ever looked at me that way. I couldn't remember ever being observed so intensely.

"I really enjoyed our time together," he said.

"Me, too." Slowly, I brought my eyes back to his. The same intense stare met my gaze. "Thank you so much, Sam. I'm such a huge fan, and tonight was an absolute dream come true."

He smiled, brushed a strand of hair out of my face, and stroked my cheek with his thumb. Then, ever so slowly, he leaned in and kissed me. I froze. Never having experienced more than a peck on the cheek, I had no clue how to respond. My arms felt like weights. My mind swam. Were my lips too close together? Was I too far away from him? Should I run my fingers through his hair?

Sam cupped my face and a wash of goosebumps prickled my arms. I shivered and let his lips lead the way. Every worrying thought drained away as instinct took over. My body on fire, I wrapped my arms around his neck. As a virgin, I didn't know the things that Sam was making my body feel even existed.

After a moment, he slowly pulled away. He kept one hand on my cheek, but I couldn't look at him. My face burned and tears stung my eyes. I studied my hands and picked at my cuticles.

"You've never been kissed like that, have you?" Sam asked softly.

I shook my head. "I've never been kissed, at all. I've never *anything* before."

He gently tilted my chin up until our eyes met. "Then I am honored to have that position. There are so many things I could teach you. I meant what I said at the diner, I really do want to see you again. How about tomorrow night?"

I released the breath I didn't know I'd been holding and flashed a smile. I floated in a dream. Did things like this really happen in real life? My body seemed to hum. I was scared, excited, and ecstatic all at the same time, and I didn't know how to process the thoughts and emotions running rampant through me.

"I would love that."

"Me, too."

He kissed me again, and I responded easier and quicker this time. Oh. My. God. I didn't want this to end. I didn't know anything could feel so amazing.

"I don't want to let you go," Sam said.

I giggled because I could have run away with him in that second without a single regret.

"But I probably better. Can I walk you to your door?" he asked.

I checked the time and realized that my brother had been at work for a while now, so no worries there. "Sure," I answered.

Sam exited the car, came around to my side, and opened my door. His hand rested on the small of my back as we walked to my apartment.

"Five fifteen, that's me," I said shyly.

"Pick you up at six tomorrow night?" he said.

I nodded.

Sam leaned in close and backed me against the door. He placed his arms on either side of me and kissed me again. "One last parting kiss," he whispered in my ear, then drew back. "See you tomorrow."

"Tomorrow," I repeated in a breathless voice I barely recognized as my own.

My hands trembled so much that it took three tries to get the key into the lock and open the door. Once inside, I closed the door and leaned against the wood. Holy hell! What in the world just happened?

My skin burned hot and cold at the same time. I didn't understand my body's reaction. Butterflies danced in my stomach, something I had only read about and had never experienced. I pinched myself to make sure I hadn't lost my mind and imagined the whole evening. Things like this just did not happen to girls like me.

I took a shower. When I got in bed, my mind raced, replaying the night's events over and over again. I figured sleep would elude me, but I was out in minutes.

Chapter Two

I woke to two of my favorite scents: coffee and bacon. That meant Joey was home. I jumped up, threw on clothes, and headed into the kitchen.

"She's alive." Joey flashed his trademark, goofy smile. Although he was five years older, he never teased in a mean way.

"Ugh," I grunted.

He poured coffee and handed me a cup as I lit a cigarette. I glanced at the clock on the stove, almost 12:30. I never slept in that late.

"So, you got in late, I heard."

I rolled my eyes. That old hag in 512 must've been peeking out her door. She spied on everyone all the time and told Joey every move I made.

"And with a guy?" Joey raised his eyebrows over his cup.

"Not just any guy, and no, he did not come in."

"Oh?"

"You wouldn't believe me if I told you." I smiled.

"Try me."

I shrugged. "Sam Urban."

"Sam Urban?" He set his cup down. "The actor Sam Urban? The one you're so nuts over?"

I nodded.

Joey laughed. "Bullshit."

"I told you that you wouldn't believe me. Stick around tonight, he'll be here around six. We're going to dinner."

Joey narrowed his eyes. "How old is he?"

I wasn't about to tell Joey that Sam was twelve years older than me. Cool big brother who let me move in at sixteen and pretty much do as I pleased or not, he was still my big brother and was going to act like one.

I shrugged. "Don't mom me, please."

"I don't like this."

"And?"

Joey sighed. "Can you just be careful? You know, don't get pregnant or wind up dead in a ditch somewhere. Mom would be seriously pissed at me."

I rolled my eyes and returned my attention to the coffee and cigarette. A knock at the door startled us both. Miraculously, we weren't late on rent, so neither of us had any idea who it could be. Joey answered the door. A delivery guy thrust a bouquet of bright yellow roses surrounded by delicate baby's breath into Joey's hands and asked him to sign.

My heart fluttered, and I fought to keep the grin off my face. I knew before Joey turned around the flowers were from Sam. Excitement flowed through me. I trembled, waiting for Joey to turn around. I had never been given flowers let alone had them delivered to me.

Joey read the card attached to the bouquet, then just stared at me. I could only smirk.

"Holy shit," he whispered, and handed me the card.

Beautiful flowers for my beautiful girl. Can't wait to see you tonight, Sam.

"You really did bring Sam Urban home last night?" he said.

"Told you so."

Joey gaped.

I laughed. Today was going to be a good day off.

As the day wore on, I grew more and more nervous. Seeing Sam was the only thing I could think about. I had no idea where he planned to take me, so I was unsure of what to wear or how to do my hair and makeup. The only thing dressy I owned was a classic little black dress that made me feel self-conscious. I hated the swell of my stomach and my flabby arms. I was almost in tears by the time Sam knocked on the door, right at six. There was no way I was something he wanted. Not when he was surrounded by some of the most beautiful women in the world.

I opened the door with a trembling hand. Sam, at six-foot-two, towered over my five-foot-two stature. His black hair was perfectly styled, not a single strand out of place.

"Hello, beautiful." He leaned in for a kiss, but Joey, standing in the kitchen, cleared his throat and stopped him short.

Sam's fingers intertwined with mine as I led him into the apartment. "Sam, this is my brother Joey. Joey this is—"

"Sam Urban. Wow, this is an absolute pleasure." Joey, obviously just as starstruck as I had been, stuck out his hand to shake Sam's.

"Nice to meet you." Sam gave Joey's hand a firm pump.

Introductions over, we all stood there in an awkward silence.

Sam finally cleared his throat. "We should really get going if we're going to make our reservations."

"Oh, of course," Joey said. "Don't let me make you guys late. I'm just so honored to meet you. You guys stay out as late as you want. Have a good time."

As Sam and I left the apartment, I caught Joey's eye and shot him a smug, triumphant smile as I closed the door behind me. As Sam and I started down the hallway, he said, "You look amazing."

I tried to meet his eyes but couldn't. "I don't really have anything nice. I hope this is okay."

"You look perfect. We'll take care of the things you don't have later. Tonight, you're all mine."

He sported a dark purple suit that looked amazing on him. Being the center of someone's attention was usually a bad thing in my limited experience, but I was just so happy to be with him. I marveled at the fact that his eyes never left me.

My mother used to tell me that unless I lost weight, put on makeup, and dressed like a girl, I no man would love me. But Sam was looking at me now the same way he'd looked at me last night, when my hair had been up in a ponytail, I'd worn no makeup, and had been dressed in that dreary server uniform.

Sam took me to a fancy looking Italian place called A'Mour. The restaurant was packed, but the low lights with bright red table linens and candles made for a very romantic atmosphere.

The *maître d'* escorted us to a small table in a back corner, and Sam held my chair for me. I was thankful there wasn't more than one fork at the table. Having grown up using chipped, mismatched dinnerware, I would never have successfully navigated a formal dinner. Sam took his seat and ordered a bottle of red wine and two glasses. My heart jumped, and I feared the waiter was going to card me, but he didn't.

Although I rarely got carded, I worried that tonight would be the night my luck ran out. Apparently, though, as long as I stayed with Sam, rules didn't apply.

Despite the full house, Sam's attention remained focused on me. He gave my hand a quick squeeze. Being there with him didn't feel real. My thoughts spun in my head so fast I couldn't keep up with them. The excitement of this little movie I seemed to be starring in was a wild ride.

My hands shook a little as I held the menu. The menu used traditional Italian spellings. This was definitely not an Americanized Italian restaurant. When the waiter returned to take our order, I shot Sam a helpless look, so he ordered for both of us. Self-consciously, I looked around the restaurant as we waited for the waiter to put our order in and return with our wine.

"Thank you," I whispered after the waiter left.

My face heated and, in my embarrassment, I looked anywhere but at Sam. That hard ball in my stomach knotted. What was I doing here? Did I really think this was something I could pull off?

"Hey," Sam said softly.

His tone brought my eyes to his.

"You're fine. I'm sure this isn't something you're used to."

I emitted a nervous laugh. "Not even close. Back home, going out to dinner meant going to the Ponderosa. Believe it or not, we do have a country club, but it isn't for people like me."

Sam's brows furrowed. "People like you?"

"Poor white trash, if you go by the kids in high school." I had stuck my foot in my mouth and couldn't pull it out. Tears threatened to blur my vision.

"Well, good thing I don't make judgments based on other people's opinions, huh?" He winked.

The knot in my stomach relaxed a little, and I returned Sam's smile. Determined, I pushed through my nervousness to keep the easy conversation going.

"What about you, Mr. Hollywood? Were fancy, gourmet restaurants common for you growing up?"

Sam sipped his wine and licked his lips. "Pretty much. Dad's a writer and has done fairly well. He's directed a few obscure independent films in the last couple of years. Mom's a painter. She paints these huge, abstract things that make zero sense to me, but she rakes in the money. When I was a kid, we spent summers in New York, and she'd have showings in a lot of the big galleries up there."

"Did you always want to be an actor?"

I couldn't take my eyes off the way the lights played on his face. The soft glow turned his eyes into shimmering pools of dark honey. His full lips turned up slightly at the corners, somewhere between a smirk and a smile that reduced me to a quivering mess.

"I kind of stumbled onto acting in school and was surprisingly good at it. Drama Club was my one and only reason for going to school most days," he said.

That I could understand. A handful of classes and teachers made my high school days bearable.

"I don't know exactly what your home life was like, but for a long time, the drama club and plays were my safe place," Sam said quietly. For a moment, he stared down at the table, then gave me a sad smile.

"My dad's an alcoholic," I said. "Home was nothing but hell and darkness. Especially after Joey admitted he was gay and they kicked him out."

Sam slowly nodded. "Dad took just about anything he could get his hands on, and Mom just wasn't there. She was a very emotionally unavailable mother. I really think she has mental issues. She used to hide when the doorbell rang. There's always been something not quite right with her, but they both insist that she's fine and doesn't need to see someone."

"Was your dad abusive? Mine was mainly just verbal stuff."

Sam shook his head. "No, not at all. My dad's never really been Dad. He was the friend, the cool guy who let me do whatever I wanted. That side came out even more when he was using. He's mostly stopped now. He smokes pot every now and then, but that's about it."

The waiter brought our food. The plates were thick and white with gold edging. The waiter set a plate of shrimp and pasta covered in a thick, creamy white sauce in front of me. I could make out a faint trail of steam as the scent of garlic wafted up to me. The dish looked too pretty to eat. I suppressed a laugh as I spread the red cloth napkin across my lap. This definitely wasn't the kind of meal I was used to.

"What about you?" Sam asked. "What is it you want, my little Rosalie?"

I froze, my fork mid-bite. Hearing Sam call me "my little Rosalie" sent a warm fuzzy sensation coursing through my body.

I realized he was waiting for an answer, and I said, "I don't know, honestly. The only aspiration I had growing up was getting the hell out of that house. I used to daydream about the day when I'd be free, when I wouldn't have to wonder what was waiting on the other side of my front door."

"Oh, honey," Sam whispered.

I couldn't stand the pity in his eyes. I looked at my plate to gather myself and brought my eyes back to him.

"Well." He cleared his throat. His jaw clenched as he dabbed the corners of his lips. "You're free now. You're safe, and you don't have to wonder about that ever again."

Losing myself in the deep velvet pools that were Sam's eyes, I swallowed the lump in my throat. He wrapped his fingers around mine and squeezed. Safe had a new meaning for me with Sam. *Safe* was something real and tangible that I could grab on to and trust.

All my life, I had been suspicious of people. I'd wonder whether they were genuine or if I was being fed whatever line of bullshit would get them what they wanted.

I decided I wasn't going to do that with Sam. He had a career, money, and fame. There was nothing I could offer him that he didn't already have, so what wasn't there to trust? I so badly wanted the love and attention he freely offered. I decided in that moment to throw out any doubts and just trust him.

We fell into a comfortable silence as we ate. Sitting in that dimly lit room with Sam, I didn't feel naïve. I felt like a grown up. Anything that had happened before that moment was a dream I couldn't quite remember.

The waiter refilled our wine and cleared the plates. Doing a quick calculation in my head, I realized this would be my third glass. I liked the pleasant fuzziness in my head. I was floating more than anything.

"Has acting and Hollywood been everything you thought it would be?" I asked.

"Yes and no. I really just wanted to have fun and make movies. I didn't think I'd actually be as big as I am. I think the success tends to go to my head sometimes."

"Really? I don't see that."

"That just proves how good I am," Sam laughed. "I'm kidding. I didn't realize there was so much actual work involved in making a movie. Between preproduction and postproduction, a movie can take well over a year to finish. My scenes usually take seven or eight months to finish just on their own. Eventually, I want to direct and produce. I want to have control over the stories I tell. Now, the theater? That's my heart and soul."

As Sam paid the bill my heart swelled. He was so exotic to me. The way he moved and carried himself. Charm oozed from him. I had no real experience to compare him to, but he wasn't anything like the guys back home. Sam held his arm out and I wrapped my hand in his. We left the restaurant and, although I didn't want the night to end, Sam took me home.

Sam held my hand all the way back to my place, a shy and quiet smile playing on his lips.

"It's a shame tonight has to end," he said, perhaps reading my thoughts as he shut off the car in front of my place. "There's something so different about you, Rosalie. Something I can't put my finger on, but I don't want to let you go. You're like fresh air after being under water. The idea of being the first man to show you things, do things for you...I can't explain the way I feel."

My heart began to pound. "But why in the world would you want someone like me? I'm not pretty, I'm fat. You could have any woman you wanted. Why would you want a fat, plain Jane?"

"Don't ever say those things about yourself again," Sam said, his voice sharp. "You are absolutely beautiful. I've wanted you from the moment I laid eyes on you. I want you now, if you'll have me."

"S-Sam..." I stuttered. "Of course. I do..."

"I know this is fast, Rosalie, and I know you're scared, but I promise you, I will love and take care of you. I'll show you. Will you at least let me show you how much you deserve to be loved?"

Tears welled in my eyes. I did not know what it was to be loved, but I did know that was the only thing I wanted. Someone to just simply love me. How could I say no?

"Okay," I whispered.

Sam pulled me close and kissed me. When he released me, he said, "What time do you work tomorrow?"

"Two in the afternoon until ten."

"I'll be here to pick you up for work. Would that be okay?"

"Sure."

Sam walked me to my door. He hugged me tight and whispered close to my ear, "I'm falling in love with you, Rosalie. I think the thought of someone loving you scares you, but I'm going to show you. That's if you're sure you want me to, because once you're mine, that's it, you're mine. There's no going back."

"I want to," I whispered.

He pulled back. "I'll see you tomorrow."

I went inside on shaky legs. The need that pounded through my body threatened to drown me. If Sam wanted me, then I'd let him have me.

For the next two weeks, Sam drove me to and from work. Most days, he'd sit at the diner during my shift, and we'd go out afterwards. That time together felt like a fairy tale. Sam talked about wanting to marry and have a family, giving his children all the things he never had.

Sam told me how, in his early years, his family moved constantly from one set to another while his dad took any role he was offered. Sam's early education had been with tutors instead of in a classroom.

By the time he reached high school, each of his parents were leading their own lives and doing their own thing without Sam or each other. He finally convinced them to allow him to attend school in L.A., giving them the freedom to do what they pleased without the added responsibility of his being around. They stopped long enough to enroll him and then returned to their own lives.

ONE FRIDAY NIGHT AFTER WORK, SAM TOOK ME BACK TO HIS house, a beautiful, two-story Country French-style home with a detached garage nestled in the Hollywood Hills, a far cry from my West Hollywood neighborhood. Everything from the décor to the furnishings took my breath away.

White oak hardwood floors gleamed throughout the open concept downstairs floor. The living room opened into a massive dining room and family area, and the kitchen looked like it belonged in a restaurant.

A huge sliding glass door in the dining room overlooked a large backyard and a fire pit. Off the living room was a massive staircase that ascended to a small landing, then more stairs that led to four upstairs bedrooms. I'd never seen a house so large or so glamorous.

In the living room, we sat on a white leather sofa in front of the fireplace.

"What do you think?" Sam asked.

"Gorgeous," I exclaimed. "I've been in nice houses before, but I don't think I've ever been in anything as fancy as this. Do you have like maids and a butler?"

He chuckled and shook his head. "I have a lawncare crew that comes once a week and twice a month a cleaning service comes in and washes the walls, and the baseboards and the floors. I'm not here enough to have them come in more than that."

"Fancy," I giggled again taking in the living room.

Feeling his eyes on me I turned back to meet his gaze. Sam stared, eyes intense. Something between hunger and passion burned in that look. In that moment, I could have stared at him forever.

"Rosalie, you understand I love you, don't you?" he asked.

"Yes, Sam. I love you, too." I'd not said that to him before. I had never said that to any man.

"I want you, Rosalie, and only you. I want you here with me. This is your home, now. Let me love you. Let me give you all the things you deserve."

Sam kissed me, and I tangled my hands in his hair. His kisses turned demanding. My head swam. He trailed kisses from my neck to just above the buttons on my blouse. Slowly, he undid each button, peeled off my shirt, and then unhooked my bra. My heart did a flip and embarrassment washed over me. I grabbed for my shirt on the couch beside him.

"Stop that," he whispered. "You are beautiful. I love your body. Please, Rosalie, let me show you I love you."

Sam's lips closed gently over one exposed nipple. Desire streaked through me. I froze. He could have asked for my soul and I would have agreed.

Sam laid me back on the couch and came down on top of me. His weight crushed me into the cushions and felt so right. He continued kissing and stroking me. Fear and wonder held me powerless in his spell. My breath came in short gasps, and my body trembled.

Sam stopped and drew back far enough to meet my gaze. "See, I told you I could show you things."

I moaned a small protest and tried to pull him close again.

"Not here," he whispered.

He stood, grasped my hand and pulled me to my feet. Then he led me upstairs to the bedroom. Gently, he laid me on the bed and unbuttoned my jeans, then pulled them off along with my panties. Panic flared, deeper this time. I clawed at the quilt in an effort to cover my body. Carefully but forcefully, Sam pinned my hands to my sides.

He kissed my stomach and slid his warm mouth down to my inner thighs. His mouth did things to me I didn't know were possible. My climax rolled over me unexpectedly and I cried out as wave after wave washed over me.

Sam covered my trembling body with his and settled between my legs. "I love you," he breathed.

I couldn't speak.

"Is this what you want?" he asked. "There's no going back after tonight. After tonight, you are mine. You are here with me. Is that what you want?"

"Yes."

He reached between my legs and fitted his penis into my opening. "I love you. This will hurt just a little at first, but then it'll be over. You're sure that you'll stay with me?" he asked.

"Yes," I panted.

Slowly, he eased into me then, in one hard thrust, drove deep. A sharp, bright pain stabbed then, as Sam began to move inside me, the discomfort gave way to a pleasant soreness. As Sam reached his climax, he whispered his love for me in my ear. I held on to him for dear life.

Afterward, we spooned, our hands intertwined. Sam held me close.

"You promise?" he asked.

"I swear."

He smiled against my neck. "Tomorrow starts your new life."

"With you?"

"With me. Forever."

My stomach fluttered. I wasn't exactly scared. Maybe apprehensive. Events were happening impossibly fast, but I didn't care. Someone wanted me, and come hell or high water, I was going to stay with him no matter the cost.

I feel asleep sore and happy with Sam's arms wrapped around me. For the first time ever, I felt safe, secure, and loved. I didn't have any idea what dawn would bring, and I didn't care. I had everything I wanted.

www.scarsalepublishing.com